# The Spanish Widow

## Helen Bland

Grosvenor House
Publishing Limited

This book is published by
Grosvenor House Publishing Ltd
Link House
140 The Broadway, Tolworth, Surrey, KT6 7HT.
www.grosvenorhousepublishing.co.uk

A CIP record for this book
is available from the British Library

ISBN 978-1-83975-488-3

# Acknowledgments

Grateful thanks to my sister Kay Evans for her candid proofreading and to my friend Susan Tringham, who radiates fun from every pore.

# Preface

Love, be it altruistic or motivated by hidden agendas, will come to us all in many guises throughout our lifetime. The most precious of all is unconditional love, a love that can never be denied or erased.

There is a saying that women derive happiness through the love they give and men through the love they receive. Is this still true today when equality in both race and gender identity are so prominent in our thoughts?

My genuine belief that Mars and Venus are indelibly embedded in the male and female psyche may be unpopular and would definitely be spurned with derision by my leading protagonist Inez Roxberg, whose lifelong crusade for female supremacy masks an inner fear that her only real value is her wealth.

# Dedication

For Madeleine, Clodagh and Liam

# By the same Author

*The Other Sister.* Volume one of *The Roxberg Trilogy.*

Art gallery curator Giselle Villande and her husband, Gaston, an antique dealer from Menton in the south of France, find themselves drawn into an insidious web of poisoning and murder motivated by financial greed and sexual jealousy.

Nebulous tendrils of evil draw them still further to Paris and Honfleur then finally to Giselle's isolated family home, Roxberg Gate on the wild and beautiful Northumbrian coast.

In this sexually charged labyrinthine conspiracy, a plot is conceived to undermine and ultimately destroy Giselle's family.

Available in paperback and ebook.

# Cast of Characters

Inez Roxberg – Widow of Henry – Mother of Giselle and Honoré (deceased).
A tall, vainglorious redhead with hypnotic turquoise eyes, an uncertain temper and an unquenchable zest for life.

Gaston Villande – Husband of Giselle.
A charismatic French antique dealer in his late thirties, with captivating soft brown eyes that conceal a humorous but unconventional force of character.

Giselle Villande – Wife of Gaston and manager of Café Villande.
A volatile, green-eyed willowy blonde in her early twenties, now pregnant with her first child.

Simone du Val – The love child of Inez's husband and his mistress.
Statuesque dark-haired with dark blue eyes, in her early twenties and capable of unspeakable acts of evil.

Iona Kerr – Chef/Manager at Café Villande
An exuberantly energetic no-nonsense Scot, with flaxen hair and blue eyes, she and her fiancé abandoned their home in the north of England for a new life on the French Rivera.

Flora Innes – Junior Cook/Trainee Manager at Café Villande

A coltish tender-hearted teenager with long, unruly light brown curls and soft hazel eyes. An orphan and close friend of Iona.

Guido Faconi – Venetian Painter
Stylishly sexy with piercing raven eyes, in his mid-forties, a scheming intellectual and merciless seducer of women.

Allesio Faconi – Skiing Instructor and younger brother to Guido.
A slightly built, dark-eyed thirty-eight-year-old, a reckless hedonist who lives his life on the edge.

Venerio Faconi – Cousin to Guido and Allesio.
Short and stocky in stature, this ill-mannered, dangerously corrupt Faconi henchmen, lives alone on a canal barge in a Venetian backwater.

Alex Forbes – A muscular forty-six-year-old ex-army chef.
A perennial optimist with fair hair, smoky blue eyes and an easy nonchalant charm that conceals a burning desire to be free of life's restraints and obligations.

Villefranche-sur-Mare
Winter – 2016

# Chapter One

As the crimson card slipped from my trembling fingers, a sudden gust of salt-laden air from an open window sent it floating to my feet. My gaze travelled beyond the dark swell of winter sea to the horizon, in the wind I heard the words of Henry's ghost warning me of what lay ahead.

Suddenly my legs weakened with shock and lost all strength and rigidity, the room spun as I lurched forward, both hands flew involuntarily to cover my face as waves of conflicting emotions devoured my breath. My eyes burned in recognition of Henry's distinctive handwriting as a red mist clouded my vision. A glancing blow from the marble fireplace rendered me unconscious, lifeless and bleeding. I lay motionless until the clock chimed an hour later.

Waking in winter twilight, a swollen wetness covered my face and neck, the nauseating stench of blood and sweat filled my nostrils, making me want to retch. An arrow of pain shot through me as I lifted my head from the icy granite hearth, distressed, angry and cursing in my native tongue, I attempted to roll my aching body over onto my knees in an effort to stand.

'Don't let me die, not here, not now,' my anguished words echoed eerily around the empty house, my cries for help went unheard and unanswered. Blood dripped from my chin onto the bare floorboards. I crawled to a sturdy lamp table desperately seeking support while attempting to stand and catch my breath, staunching my wound on the linen cloth covering the table.

The storm raged, letting in torrents of rain through the open window as it swung back and forth on its hinges, cracking several panes. Stiffening my resolve, I staggered over to close the window; in my path stood the clock with a pearl face glinting in the incessant strikes of forked lightning now piercing the sky with startling light.

'You can wait,' I murmured into the darkness as a crash of thunder broke overhead.

The bathroom mirror revealed the full extent of my injuries, rivulets of blood had begun to congeal on my face and neck, my cut forehead had begun to swell and bruise to neon proportions.

The first night in my new home had become a nightmare, a creeping dread stole over me as I lay drowsing in a foaming lavender-scented bath while allowing my superstitious mind to wonder if the thunderstorm was a warning, an ominous omen of bad luck.

Later that evening after a sparse supper of leftover chicken casserole and stale brioche, washed down with two large glasses of rouge for mortal fortification, I finally gathered enough courage to return to the sitting room where Henry's dubious gift stood serenely glinting in the moonlight.

The blood-soaked fireplace and stained floorboards turned my stomach, *that mess can wait till morning,* I decided turning my attention to the clock.

Henry's card lay face down on the floor, his message hidden from view, my irrational fears, now heightened by the quantity of alcohol I had consumed, seemed to feed my fertile imagination; perhaps by some macabre trick, his words had been replaced by his image, leering at me from beyond the grave.

On the window seat, I sat watching as a powerful full moon cast pools of light on my hand and on the card, which lay in my palm.

*Why the hesitation?* I thought, he cannot harm me now.

The card felt hot, burning my palm as his words had burned my eyes, one flick of my fingertips and there were his words, his lies, his never-ending lies. My face flooded in anger as I read and re-read the inscription on the card.

*To Inez, my one true love x*

I tore the card into tiny fragments and threw them into the fireplace, Henry's love had been captured and held by another woman, his false protestations of love were not for me, but for my wealth.

'Too late, Henry,' I shouted, kicking the lever and watching as the secret drawer opened to reveal its glorious treasure.

A well of unshed tears began stinging my eyes and drenching my robe, how I loathed that man for squandering my youth and for separating Honoré from Giselle and myself, for forcing us to move away to France, away from his constant demands for money, away from the pain of witnessing his utter devotion to our scheming housekeeper.

My simmering resentment dissipated as the twilight deepened into a velvet darkness, stars framed my view of the deserted harbour and beyond to the turbulent storm-driven waves crashing against the harbour wall. I lay on the window seat mesmerised, caught in a veil of enchantment, imagining myself as a mermaid, slipping languorously into the blue abyss, submerging my old life to begin again in another world.

Hearing melodious chimes, my reverie melted away, the clock with its pearl face reflecting in the moonlight stood mocking me for my weakness.

*Accept me, accept my treasure as your own.*

Why didn't he warn me? So typical of Henry, a man who spent his whole life disregarding the consequences of his actions. This is his triumph made real from beyond the grave, his thumbed nose at any authority other than his own.

Now I fully understood his almost obsessive attention to detail with regard to the packing crate and precise shipping instructions for the clock. I knew instinctively the jewels were stolen contraband, now Henry's criminal legacy had become my own.

Then my anger softened, perhaps the jewels were his way of repaying my years of financial generosity and stoic marital patience. Henry's precious gift began to convey so much more than mere monetary value, in my heart there was a need to find a deeper meaning, an affirmation of Henry's true feelings. Perhaps he did love me after all? Yet that insistent, small voice in my head contradicted me in saying. *He loved money more than you.* I drained the dregs of my wine in a final toast.

'To my Henry, a consummate deceiver,' I murmured into the darkness.

Sitting curled on the window seat, the jewels sparkling in my lap, I began to consider my next move, naturally an expert valuation would be out of the question, how could I admit to owning such a hoard without any documentary proof of ownership? Then other more alarming questions presented themselves.

Where and from whom did Henry purchase them, was he the legal owner and had he the right to bequeath them to me? The jewels had not been mentioned in his will and crucially, did anyone other than myself know of their existence? A trickle of apprehension crept up my spine as I returned the jewels to the clock base and watched as they disappeared silently into the secret compartment.

Sleep is not my friend tonight; vivid dreams toss my body and mind in wild imaginings of theft and imprisonment. My new home half empty of furniture, newly painted and refurbished to my exacting standard, held an air of sad neglect, a neglect that I promised to dispel at the first opportunity.

I will fill this house with artists, gourmets and musicians. I will teach children and adults to paint and appreciate art and sculpture in its many forms, bringing with them their own individual creativity. Their laughter and bright conversation will enliven these empty, forgotten rooms and I *will* make myself happy again.

At dawn, slipping from my warm bed feeling rested and optimistic about the day ahead, I paused momentarily at the sitting-room door on route to the kitchen, just as the clock began chiming.

*My dreams were real, you are still here, and I will find a way to silence your annoying chimes.*

Curling under a blanket in my favourite spot on the window seat, a steaming mug of citron tea warming my bruised hands and face, I watched a watery sun rise above the waves, then slept until the clock woke me chiming midday. The day had begun fresh and clear, but now the wintry sun had disappeared behind ominous clouds threatening to open at any moment and drench the shoppers hurrying along the harbour. The new day brought clarity of mind and solutions to my dilemmas, my earlier thoughts of casting the diamonds into the sea or posting them to a charity sounded ridiculous in the cold light of day.

*Let's face it,* reasoned my inner voice, *Henry could easily have disposed of the diamonds, but no, I prefer to believe he kept them for me, for us, for our future life together, a life terminated too soon by cruel circumstances. No, I will keep them safe, these emblems of trust and guilt, they are mine to cherish regardless of value.*

Hurrying to the clock, I knelt down and gently eased the brass lever with my finger, the secret drawer opened silently to reveal the diamonds sparkling in their lair, removing my wedding ring, I placed the white gold band amongst the diamonds. The drawer closed noiselessly into the base of the clock and with it, safely hidden from view, my hoard of unimaginable wealth.

# Chapter Two

The following morning while sitting outdoors at a harbourside café, drinking the first espresso of the day and absently making lists for Christmas, my phone rang, the screen registered unknown caller, intending to reject the call, my numbed fingers pressed the wrong button.

'Hello, Inez speaking, who is this?' My voice sounded terse and unfriendly.

A disarmingly accentuated Italian voice replied, 'Signora Roxberg, good morning, I am Guido Faconi, a close friend of your late husband. My apologies for contacting you so soon after your loss. I was saddened to hear of Henry's death, please accept my heartfelt condolences,' he said, sincerity deepening his voice.

My attention was drawn to the warmth in his tone, replacing my earlier reticence with avid curiosity.

'Henry was as a brother to me,' he continued his tone becoming more urgent. 'We were at school together and still have many shared business interests; I had dinner with him only last month,' he said convincingly.

'I am at your service, Signora Roxberg, perhaps when you are feeling more sociable, we can meet for lunch.' His request hung expectantly in the air.

'Yes of course,' I said falteringly not knowing how to respond.

'I will be in France on business next week, may I call on you?' asked Guido hopefully.

'Unfortunately, it's not convenient.' My voice sounded shrill and unfriendly.

'So sorry, must go, goodbye.' Pressing the end call button, I threw the phone into my handbag.

*Who is this man? Henry never mentioned him, and how did he obtain my mobile phone number?*

My usual habit of abstaining from alcohol before lunch was waved aside on this occasion as I felt in need of a stiffener and asked the waiter to bring more coffee and a single cognac to steady my nerves. Sitting alone and drinking before lunch. *This has to stop, go and seek some engaging society.*

Leaving the café, I decided to explore the local shops in an attempt to banish Guido Faconi from my thoughts. In every establishment along the narrow streets of this picturesque town, I was treated with reserved suspicion, another artist incomer bringing louche new ways of living, a threat no doubt to the local artistic community looking to preserve their territory. How I longed to be accepted for myself and not some wealthy chattel belonging to an undeserving husband or overly protective father.

As I wandered through the rain-soaked streets leading up from the harbour, my thoughts kept returning to Guido Faconi and to why he found it necessary to meet me so soon after Henry's funeral. Surely a lifelong friend and business partner would have had the decency to pay his respects in person, but then he had failed to attend.

*Yes, I will meet this persuasive Italian, on my terms and in my own time.* Then I willed myself to dismiss him from my thoughts. Arriving home with a small crab and various other grocery purchases, my thoughts turned to Giselle and Gaston; should I tell them about my secret diamond hoard? Perhaps not, at least not yet.

A surge of hunger gripped me as I set about extracting the aromatic crab meat from its unyielding shell and adding a little lemon oil and black pepper to warm noodles. As I sat at the kitchen table, eating my lunch and longing for an early spring, my attention wandered to the unkempt garden beyond the kitchen window, a view which afforded me no pleasure. I will replant next spring with scented flowers, herbs and perhaps a few vegetables.

Satiated and energised, my curiosity drew me to the pale-blue painted garden shed. To my surprise, hanging on sturdy hooks were seemingly new forks and spades all clean and gleaming with oil, including other miscellaneous equipment neatly stacked in wooden boxes ready for use. The fading light and late afternoon chill did nothing to deter my enthusiasm as I dug deep into the loamy soil of my new garden.

At five o'clock my energy levels began to dip, the sheer physical exertion of double-digging had begun to dilute the raw emotions of widowhood by replacing sadness and grief with a renewed sense of purpose and a burgeoning hope for the future.

The short winter days passed with alarming speed, busy with domestic tasks most days until mid-afternoon, the hours between three and five were reserved for reading or sketching in my favourite spot on the window seat, watching the dramatic changes of light intensity as the season moved forward; milky dawns and dramatic sunsets created their own short-lived pictures before fading into fathomless obscurity. On such days, my fingers itched to be on the shoreline with paint and brushes. Occasionally, Guido's seductive voice disturbed my thoughts like a hummingbird intoxicated by nectar.

*Go away; I'm not ready, not yet.*

On brighter days, sketchbook and crayons in hand, I began familiarising myself with the town, irresistibly drawn to the vibrant atmosphere and brightly painted buildings overlooking the busy harbour and seafront, revelling in my preferred subject matter of town and seascapes. Shopping daily in the local markets, making an effort to chat endlessly with neighbours and townspeople met on my daily walks among the crowded streets, filled me with indescribable joy.

During one lively dinner party at a local restaurant, my usual reticence deserted me under an avalanche of discreet questions from my fellow diners with regard to my past. Later that evening having regretted my candour, an inner voice reasoned that new friends were naturally inquisitive of a respectable widow with nothing to hide, well almost nothing, then a vision of my precious hoard came into view.

The following day I woke late, bleary eyed and slightly hungover. Groaning with pain, I turned away from the harsh midday light and reached for my phone to check the time and saw three missed calls from an unknown caller. Scrolling down to previous missed calls, I saw they were all identical; my heart quickened as panic seized me. *Guido Faconi is indeed a persistent stranger.*

Throwing a robe around my shoulders, I headed for the bathroom, thinking a shower would either enliven or completely exhaust me. Wrapping my wet, tangled hair and vetiver-scented body in a robe, I wafted downstairs to make an espresso. To my horror, lying face down on the hall floor was a crimson card, identical to the one found in the clock.

I stood for a moment transfixed, unbelieving of what my eyes were seeing. Is it credible that Henry is alive? Had his death been a dreadful mistake or some macabre trick used as a means of escape? His repeated mantra of *All things are possible, only death is insurmountable* rang in my ears as

I stepped forward to lift the card. There, written in bold black script, was an order from Guido Faconi.

*Call me. Felicitations, Guido.*

My rising panic evaporated like an early summer mist, leaving me seething with temper.

*How presumptuous and how dare he pursue me so openly.*

A sudden knock at the door took my breath and froze my blood. I stood motionless and listened as his shoes scraped the threshold in anticipation of entering my home. My phone began ringing so loudly I was sure he would hear, the screen displaying his number over and over.

After a seemingly endless wait, I heard his footsteps grow faint. Creeping silently downstairs into the basement kitchen, I sat in silence until my reserves of courage allowed me to check the window and door locks, not daring to look out for fear of being seen. Raw instinct told me to beware of this man, this self-appointed friend and associate of my late husband, who would in any event be an undesirable requesting recompense for an unpaid account, or some ridiculous imposter claiming to be a long lost relative. Even if he were neither, he had definitely become my enemy.

Feeling trapped and angry, I rang Gaston. In the past, my level-headed son-in-law when asked, would invariably offer sound advice and clever solutions to my problems. He answered my phone call immediately. 'You OK, Inez?'

'Not really, I have decided to spend a few days in Paris, may I call on you both?'

'You're angry; what's wrong?' He sounded concerned.

'It can wait until we meet, give Giselle my love.'

'Oh come on, Inez, you're upset and need to vent your wrath.'

'Yes, Gaston, I am angry and upset but it can wait until we meet.'

'As you wish, stubborn Mother.' A click and he was gone.

Feeling vaguely reassured at hearing Gaston's voice failed to alleviate my urgent need to escape from Guido's persistent phone calls.

Hearing chimes, I hurried to the sitting room, the clock with a pearl face stood glinting in its secluded alcove, kneeling down, I pressed the lever releasing my incredible diamonds from their lair underneath the clock.

'You're mine forever,' I whispered, pulling the lever to close the drawer.

# Chapter Three

The beautiful historic exterior of my new home completely belied its empty modernist interior, an interior that no longer reflected my taste.

*Everything needs to change.*

Later that evening with my packing complete and train tickets booked, I sat with my tablet idly searching for Parisian antique shops, markets and auctions in the hope of finding authentic items of furniture and lighting. On arrival in Paris, I took a taxi to my hotel in the opera district, leaving my bag at reception in order to begin shopping before darkness fell.

The streets were crowded with young elegantly dressed Christmas shoppers laughing and kissing, all intent on finding the perfect gift for their loved ones. Elaborate window displays and seductive assistants drew sophisticated lovers of perfume and toiletries through their doors. Frosted streetlights merged with distant stars, transforming the scene into a magical play in which we are the actors, but then I was alone in the most romantic city in the world.

After hours of intense browsing, I returned to the hotel empty handed feeling weary and wistful. The weather had turned to rain, water poured in torrents along brimming gutters, downpipes and drains. Hurriedly entering the foyer to escape a soaking, I almost collided with a dark-haired young man with hawkish features, presumably a doorman. To my surprise, he stepped in my path, bowed slightly, smiled and said, 'Good evening.'

Thinking nothing of it, I collected my bag from reception and went to my room, a comfortable large space with a balcony overlooking a small, enclosed courtyard where meals might be served on warm days, climbing greenery framed the window lending an atmosphere of secrecy and protection.

That evening, I decided to take advantage of room service in order to preserve what little energy I had left for more serious shopping trips planned over the following few days. Next day, after a long and reviving sleep, I was ready to shop like a trooper on a battlefield.

My Parisian adventure alternated between frenetic shopping expeditions and indolent reading in perfumed baths or lazing with a newspaper on the couch and generally immersing myself in the enchantment of the city.

There was no one to enquire as to my whereabouts, no one to criticise me cursing in my native Spanish tongue, total anonymity pleased me. In cafés and restaurants, I would sit and watch good French mothers teach their offspring exemplary table manners and the polite modes of speech required to enter the upper echelons of society after attending university. These affluent mothers appeared to lead happy and fulfilled lives, they ignore their husbands' occasional infidelity by taking *a sophisticated view*. Their traditional values and philosophies would be instilled in their offspring for the benefit of all French society.

What is the true meaning of happiness? Do we recognise it in ourselves or make compromises for the sake of others? Having asked the question of myself many times, I realised with a cold certainty that I did not know the answer.

One bitterly cold afternoon, I made my way to an atelier situated close to the hotel, an appointment had been arranged for two o clock to view drapery fabrics.

The proprietor, a petite lady of a certain age, dressed in olive green taffeta, eyed me speculatively through gold-rimmed half-moon spectacles.

'Good afternoon, Madame,' she said, scrutinising me over the top of her spectacles. 'First, may I ask if perhaps you carry an image of your home, we must consider your style preferences before we proceed.' Her grey eyes continued to discreetly appraise every aspect of my appearance.

'Yes, of course, I have photographs on my phone.'

'Ah,' said the matron turning her attention away from me.

'I see you favour the traditional style; a beautiful home deserves careful choices.' She gazed into my eyes with the intensity of a clairvoyant, then drew me into a room at the rear.

Bolts of silks, velvets, cottons and linen in a kaleidoscope of colours were displayed on deep shelves, and apothecary cupboards containing every conceivable design of tassel and trim, which were folded neatly and labelled according to their colour and type.

'Come, sit here, I have much to tell you,' she said, patting the cushion beside her. She took my hand in hers, an intoxicating scent of rose and patchouli wafted over me as she examined my palm. After a few minutes, her serious expression changed to one of outright alarm, she took up her fan fluttering it furiously in order to dispel what she had seen in my hand.

'May I offer you a hot drink or perhaps a glass of wine?' she said anxiously, the taffeta dress crackled with her every movement.

Intrigued by her strange manner, I accepted her offer of wine and rose-flavoured macaroons. She served the wine in exquisitely engraved crystal glasses, then turned to me abruptly.

'A man will enter your life, a beautiful fiend you will find hard to resist, but resist you must or risk compromising your safety. That is all I have to say on the matter. Now, Madame, to business,' she said firmly.

With calm, well-considered expertise, she began assembling a scintillating palette of fabrics and colours. Sitting in awe, I watched as the fabrics were coaxed into an elegant combination of styles suitable for an historic coastal house such as my own.

The dining room had an aspect to the north, so mustard and burgundy velvets trimmed with ostentatious tassels and cushions of a similar hue were recommended. For my bedroom, *the* most personal of rooms situated on the east side of the house to catch the ever-changing dawn light, Madame chose what could only be described as a vision of Parisienne decadence. Long, watered-silk bed canopies and drapes in shades of citrus and fern were chosen to diffuse the morning light, saving pale-blue checked linen for the sitting room, which faced south and had a panoramic view of the harbour and beyond to the sea. Prior to leaving the atelier, I asked the proprietor her name and how she sensed my fate.

'I am a mystic, a gift inherited from my Jewish grandmother, my name is Sara,' she replied, handing me her business card. With my shopping completed and instructions given regarding delivery, I kissed Sara lightly on her cheek and promised to stay in touch.

Light rain had begun falling as I stepped out onto the pavement, my vision almost completely obscured by my large umbrella. Turning in the direction of the hotel, I noticed the familiar figure of the young man who had greeted me so politely on my arrival at the hotel; he waved then walked briskly in the opposite direction.

*Was he watching me?*

Feeling quite unnerved and a little frightened, I scurried back to the hotel and locked the bedroom door. Fearful of meeting the disturbing young man again, I ordered room service and hid like a cowardly waif. That night my nightmares returned with a vengeance, devils, some with horned heads, some without, chased me along dark corridors, down into the depths of a tomb where I remained a captive until my death.

Next morning I woke clutching my rosary, memories of the terrifying dreams lingered on leaving me feeling nervous and unsettled. The weather was dry and unusually bright for the time of year, so I decided to take a walk along the Seine and find a romantic spot to eat brunch. Just then the phone rang, making me start with apprehension. Imagine my relief at seeing Giselle's number on the display.

'Mother, where are you? Not still in Paris surely, we are missing you so much, my pregnancy has been plagued with diabolical sickness,' she wailed.

'My darling, how dreadful, expect me tomorrow,' I replied without hesitation.

'How are your new staff settling in, are they adapting well to French life?' She was not in the least interested in my diverting the subject away from her concerns.

'Oh, yes, thankfully, they are all such good company, we are quite a family now, lots to confide when we meet, bon voyage and please hurry,' she said irritably.

Giselle's distress had robbed me of my appetite, so I kept walking, gathering rain clouds led me to take a detour back to the hotel. As I turned towards the Arc de Triomphe, a light drizzle began to weave its web over the city, leaving the pavements wet and shiny. A magical twilight had descended semi-shrouding the buildings in a soft-focus light; this is my favourite time, the transition from day into night is *the* most romantic time of all. Tucking my long hair inside my coat, I turned up the collar, tuned into my playlist and walked on.

Feeling reluctant to return to the hotel, I slipped into a tiny street bar to muse over the events of the past few months, while watching frenetic commuters head for the metro under the glow of Christmas lights.

The waiter brought my hot chocolate laced with a single cognac and left the bill on the table alongside the ubiquitous token book, that essential tool of female distraction when travelling alone.

Back at the hotel, I decided to dress up and dine in on my last evening in Paris. Arriving late, I found the dining room crowded with diners eagerly devouring their second course, a sharp-eyed waiter came over, seeing my despairing look at the debris cluttering every unoccupied table.

'Apologies, madam, we are very busy this evening, might I suggest you join the gentleman on table two? He has almost finished his meal and has offered to take his coffee into the lounge, I am certain he will not mind,' he said with a flourish while blatantly eying my breasts. Glancing in the direction of table two, I saw a dark-haired man sitting with his back to me.

'Very well, please go and ask his permission,' I replied without enthusiasm.

The waiter hurried over to table two, then hurried back his face wreathed in bonhomie.

'This way, please follow me, madam,' crowed the waiter effusively.

As I threaded a path through the tables towards the man sitting at table two, he stood up and turned to see my expression of appalled astonishment. It was too late to back away as everyone in the room had turned their eyes in our direction.

'Good evening, Signora Roxberg, so glad of the opportunity to formally introduce myself; I am Allesio Faconi the fiancé of Simone du Val, we are to be married during the Venice carnival and would be honoured if you would attend the ceremony,' he said with studied politeness.

*This beggars belief, an invitation to the wedding of my dead husband's love child. Is this man insane?*

'Presumably, you are Guido's brother; and furthermore, I demand to know why you are following me.' He had the grace to appear embarrassed.

'My brother has urgent matters to discuss with you, signora; your late husband has entrusted your safety to us both.'

Feeling my temper rise, I stepped closer.

'What nonsense; Henry only ever cared about my money, and I suspect the same can be said of you and your brother,' I retorted hotly.

Ignoring his disturbing news and vacuous pleasantries, I launched into a subject of vital importance and much closer to my heart.

'Then you will have met my daughter Honoré Roxberg before her death?' I replied utterly stunned by this unexpected turn of events.

'Sadly no, Simone and I met only last year, but I did have the pleasure of meeting your late husband,' he said, pulling out my chair. 'Please, Inez, may I call you Inez as we are soon to be related.'

*This charlatan is not only lying through his teeth, he has robbed me of my appetite, and I will not drink with him or sit at his table.*

'Why were you following me yesterday? You were, don't deny it.' He looked uncomfortable, like a boy caught watching porn films in his bedroom.

'As I have already said, your late husband asked my elder brother Guido and I to look after you,' he said, still holding the chair for me to take my place at his table.

I laughed in his face; his lies were becoming more incredulous by the minute.

'You are lying. No man except my father has ever looked after me,' I retorted sharply. 'Henry only wanted my money, and so do you *and* your scheming brother. So, you can tell him to stop stalking me or I will call the gendarmerie.'

With that, I turned on my heel and left the restaurant, my face flaming with anger.

Once again sleep is not my friend tonight, the noisy smokers in the courtyard below my window kept me pacing the room until after midnight. I remonstrated with myself for not taking an image of Allesio Faconi to show Gaston. Perhaps a little harmless online detective work might reveal something of interest about these secretive Faconi brothers. Reaching for my tablet, I entered their names into every social media platform and business portal and found nothing. No online presence! How odd, surely in this technological age, anyone with a business to promote would be mad not to have a website, unless they had something to hide.

As the hour passed midnight, I could no longer stand the raucous and sometimes lewd conversations of the smokers standing below my balcony. Leaning over, I called for them to either shut up or clear off. Their first response was unprintable, then remembering their manners they apologised and invited me to join them.

*If I had the balls for it!*

After a few minutes they took my unsubtle advice and melted into the night, just a few drops of lavender essence on my nightwear calmed me enough to sleep for six hours. Next morning while checking out, I casually asked if Signore

Faconi was in his room. The receptionist peered at her screen and advised me that Allesio had checked out late last evening and had not left a forwarding address.

After the unexpected pleasure of enjoying an airport breakfast, I boarded the internal flight to Nice and settled into my seat, my well-thumbed but never read token book lay on my lap like a decoy, thereby preventing any talkative fellow traveller from striking up boring conversations about the weather or the state of the economy, neither of which were of any interest to me whatsoever. Fortunately, the other seats in my row had not been taken, as my mood at such an early hour was anything but conversational.

As the plane lifted off the tarmac, I huddled into my cosy mustard coloured cashmere coat, worn over skinny tobacco jeans, long, supple tan boots and a cashmere jersey. Most of my female friends routinely packed masses of unnecessary items of clothing for weekend breaks, whereas my luggage consisted of just one lightweight bag on wheels containing the capsule wardrobe of a seasoned lone traveller. Thankfully, Giselle and I share the same size and taste in clothing and often borrow from each other.

My impatience to see Giselle severely compounded the frustration of not finding Guido or his brother on the internet, perhaps Gaston would be able to investigate further through his many contacts in the art world. Furthermore, I couldn't wait to tell him about my encounter with Allesio... and the diamonds.

# Chapter Four

As we landed in Nice, I hastily gathered my belongings and selfishly hurried to the exit door before the other passengers had stood up. The steward gave me officious look but still allowed me to disembark before anyone else after I had whispered the word *Emergency* in his ear.

After clearing customs control, I rushed into arrivals just as Gaston walked through the door; he came forward and gave me a suffocating hug, a huge grin radiating from his handsome face.

'Great to see you, Inez, hope you're going to entertain us all. Giselle is still complaining of morning sickness,' he said, raising his eyebrows.

'It must be catching because me and the staff have it too, that's because we're sick of hearing her moaning about it,' he said resignedly.

'You need to grow some sympathy, young man,' I replied with mock severity.

Gaston is the living embodiment of everything any red-blooded woman would ever want in a man; lucky Giselle, I thought, and not for the first time, as he lifted my bag and led me to the car.

Once seated, I braced myself for the journey ahead, at times I think Gaston hardly knows the difference between the accelerator and brake pedals, in fact anyone of a nervous disposition would be well advised not to travel anywhere with him at the wheel. Gaston drove off at his usual breakneck speed, while I held on to the door handle in an effort to gain traction against the sharp bends ahead.

'You could slow down and fill me in on the latest restaurant gossip, or better still let me drive,' I ventured cheekily.

'Bloody cheek, there's nothing wrong with my driving,' he replied sharply.

We drove on in injured silence for a few miles.

'How are your plans for Villefranche coming along?' Gaston asked conversationally breaking our pensive silence.

'Oh, well, it's a beautiful house, but there is still masses to do,' I replied.

'Then you won't take offence in my asking why you decided to pay us a visit so soon after that nightmare trip to Roxberg Gate, why the urgency? And don't give any lame excuses about missing Giselle, you're hiding something, it's written all over your lovely face.' Gaston's well-primed verbal guns need no ammunition where I am concerned, he can read my face like a road map.

'Come on, Inez, I would rather spare Giselle any unnecessary anxiety in her condition,' he said, coming to a halt.

He made it quite clear that we would not continue our journey until I relented and disclosed enough information to satisfy his curiosity.

'Do you remember Henry's parting gift to me?' I said coyly.

'Yes, some useless old clock in need of restoration, wouldn't give you five euros for it,' he replied.

'Trust me, Gaston, the clock needs no enhancements, it contained much more than a rusty pendulum and an inch of dust, in fact its contents gave me a shocking surprise.' My sly smile gave nothing away.

'OK, Inez, let me guess, a loaded firearm, or hand grenade.' He raised a quizzical eyebrow. 'Certainly nothing of value from your old miser of a husband,' he said with a chuckle.

'Gaston, it's getting late and I am looking forward to a large cognac and five minutes alone raiding Iona's fridge, so please let's discuss this in the morning. Giselle must hear my news first hand, now please drive on and divert me with your news.'

Immediately Gaston's expression changed to one of wicked humour as he launched into a detailed account of the advantages and disadvantages of employing untrained staff, some of whom were unable to speak in the French language. He said Iona had proved to be a popular manager from the outset, she had gradually introduced her own interpretations of classical French dishes. Initially this was met with derisory comments from the regular diners, undaunted by their reticence, she began organising charity fundraising soirées, offering only her new culinary creations to tempt their jaded palettes.

'Honestly, you should hear the way she carries on, she marches around the kitchen like an army general about to do battle, brandishing her cookware and swearing at the top of her voice, she has us in fits of laughter.'

He also added his appreciation of her direct manner and earthy candid humour, which has earned her a well-deserved reputation for fairness and reliability.

'I rather enjoy eavesdropping on her witty observations and lively repartee with the diners,' he said cheerfully.

He went on to explain that Iona treated everyone she met with a thinly veiled irreverence and got away without a snub from her victims.

'You speak very fondly of her,' I remarked.

'Yes, she has balls and style, my sort of woman; we are lucky to have her.'

'What news of her fiancé, has he found a job? I seem to remember him as rather a fluent French speaker.'

Gaston shot me a secretive smile.

'What a contrast in personalities, don't know what she sees in him if you ask me. Apparently, he is working with the French police, no idea in what capacity, he won't tell us or Iona what he's up to,' said Gaston shaking his head.

'Has he blossomed in our warm climate?' I enquired. 'My memory of him is of a tall and angular shaped man, with an otherworldly look one would expect to find in a dedicated academic.'

'He has a tan and has grown a beard, that is all. To be honest, he keeps to himself most of the time,' said Gaston thoughtfully.

'Tell me about Flora?' I asked.

Gaston's expression softened. Since moving to Menton, young Flora has emerged like a nymph triumphant from a chrysalis of sorrow, who compensated for her limited knowledge of the French language with kind gestures and disarming smiles.

'I regard her as a sort of daughter, paying for her French lessons and making sure she is safe. Iona keeps a watchful eye for any unwanted attention from male customers,' he said firmly.

'Flora and Giselle have become inseparable friends and confidantes. Flora is always ready to lend a sympathetic ear when Giselle's seemingly endless bouts of pregnancy sickness become too intolerable to bear, sleep has become Giselle's only refuge from her nausea.'

Gaston's growing concern was very real, it pained him to watch his vibrant young wife grow more listless with every passing day. Doctors had prescribed drugs, herbalists made soothing remedies, all in an effort to banish Giselle's debilitating sickness, however no pill or potion seemed to alleviate her symptoms. As we entered the private car park behind Café Villande, Gaston put his hand on my arm.

'Inez, you will find Giselle has altered in the past few months, pregnancy has changed her whole outlook on life, our joy as prospective parents has been systematically eroded by her constant sickness.' His look of concern was clear to see and my heart went out to him.

'Do what you can to divert her,' he said pleadingly.

We entered the apartment in sombre mood, gone was the shared laughter of our car journey together. Their vast apartment occupied the top two floors of the building, with Café Villande and Gaston's office situated on the ground floor.

Everywhere was in darkness except for a hall lamp, so we said goodnight. Gaston retired to his suite on the top floor and myself to the guest en suite, where I found a bottle of rouge, a large slice of cheese and vegetable tart liberally strewn with delicious black olives and two lemon madeleines.

A storm blew in from the west overnight, the wind beating a symphony in raindrops on the shutters, no ghosts of the past or future threats will spoil my sleep tonight.

Next morning I woke late, the storm had blown itself out leaving the sea becalmed, hearing soft waves lapping the shoreline reminded me of Villefranche.

Outside on the terrace, I could hear tables being placed ready for the breakfast covers to be laid. Iona, our early songbird was singing loudly, ready to greet the day and wring every ounce of joy from it.

'Come here, lovely lady,' she cried when I entered the kitchen. 'Let me give you a wee hug. Would ye like a kipper for ye breakfast, me dear.' Her accent had not mellowed since leaving her native Scotland. I asked how her French language classes were coming along.

'Oh, me dear, I won't be speaking that filthy language any time soon,' she retorted.

Still wearing my dressing gown, coffee in hand, I sat listening attentively while she recounted her first impressions of French life from a staff perspective.

'These French are too smarmy for my liking, but they pay our wages, and the weather is good for my old bones,' she confided.

As we talked, she worked tirelessly, deft as a juggler with magic fingertips, her organisational skills left me breathless, breakfasts were cooked then distributed to a full restaurant of hungry locals at breakneck speed by young Flora. Gaston had left a message on my phone, saying he had appointments and would return for dinner that evening. Giselle had still not appeared by 11 o'clock.

'I will knock on her door; she may feel like eating a fruit breakfast.'

'Leave the poor woman to rest, she's usually up by lunchtime, never eats much though,' said Iona absentmindedly. I wondered if Iona had been in touch with her family in Northumberland and more importantly, heard any news of Simone.

'Iona, have you any news from Northumberland?' I asked tentatively.

'You won't want to hear it,' she said briskly, eyeing me to gauge my reaction. 'Tell you all the same if you insist.' She crowed with laughter.

'Seriously, Iona, I need to know everything now, and in the future, do you understand?' She gave me a menacing look.

'Fine, I get the message, if it's that important to you.' She continued prepping vegetables for lunch, her chopping became louder and more forceful, her lips compressed in anger.

'Iona, what's wrong? Have I offended you?'

She turned to me waving her knife in mock attack. 'Don't ever say what I must or must not do ever again, do you hear me, lady?' She looked terrifying, like a Celtic female warrior defending her honour.

'Yes, yes, of course, please excuse my rudeness,' I said, slowly moving to the far end of the kitchen.

'I'll get dressed and give you a hand,' I said smoothly and rushed upstairs to shower.

After the lunchtime service had been served and cleared, Giselle appeared looking underfed and disconsolate.

'Mother, it's wonderful to see you,' she said, rushing over to kiss me. 'I am so glad you're here.' We hugged like old friends meeting after a long absence.

Her appearance did nothing to allay my worst fears, her once lively eyes appeared sunken and she looked thin and dehydrated. My disappointment at finding her in depleted health had not been exaggerated, but fussing over her would be of no help as she so dislikes being fussed over.

'Giselle, my darling, sit down, we need to talk.' Iona cleared her throat and gave me a stern look.

'Don't fuss her,' she said brusquely.

'We are looking after her welfare.'

This woman can read my thoughts, how do they all endure her well-meaning but overbearing manner. We sat at the kitchen table eating Iona's delicious artichoke soup and homemade parmesan bread stuffed with black olives, while Giselle gave vent to her many woes. Then Iona and Flora appeared; one holding a bottle of Chablis, the other an apple lattice tart and a whole camembert.

Filling our glasses, we toasted ourselves, then devoured our dessert while Iona read the official notes supplied unknowingly by her partner. Apparently the Northumberland police had become suspicious after hearing reports from the townspeople that Simone and a dark-haired man had employed various tradesmen to virtually ransack Roxberg Gate in search of the treasure she claimed her father had hidden there prior to his death.

The food in my throat began to swell and choke me, I excused myself seeking the sanctuary of the nearest lavatory in which to vomit. The shock of hearing Iona's words filled me with dread. *They know about the diamonds.* After washing my face, I returned to the kitchen, feeling quite unnerved.

'Who is this man, do we know him?' I said, finishing my wine and pouring another glass, my voice sounded brittle, quite unlike my usual dulcet tone.

'Some foreigner; he moved in just days after we left, they are being watched, evasion of death duties and all that I reckon,' said Iona dismissively.

Pushing the food away, too stunned to move, I made a mental note to never forget this woman's partner is a detective.

'Simone has had a difficult life, she deserves to find happiness,' said Flora, kind as ever.

*No, Simone has had an easy life, and she is not having my diamonds.*

In an attempt to change the subject, I began describing my new life in Villefranche; however, Giselle would have none of it until she had spoken her mind.

'Listen, all of you, Simone is a lying, deceitful piece of work. Gaston and I believe she pushed Honoré off that mountain in

Switzerland in order to steal her inheritance. No doubt her evil mother devised that ludicrous plan to impersonate Honoré, little wonder you were prevented from visiting her for five whole years, Mother,' said Giselle vehemently.

'Gaston and I want to reopen the case,' she stated boldly. 'We are both sceptical and are united in our opinion that Simone is a murderer like her mother. Let's face it, she had the opportunity, there were only three of them on that mountain when the avalanche struck, the ski instructor claimed he saw nothing but I have always believed he lied,' she said with conviction.

We all remained silent throughout Giselle's repeated tirades. At last when she had calmed, I tucked her into bed then went to rest in my room to muse on my own problems.

That evening when Gaston returned and the staff were busy with service, I suggested he and Giselle joined me for dinner at a more secluded restaurant of their choice.

'Yes, Inez, we are positively dripping with anticipation to hear about Henry's remarkable gift,' he said dryly rolling his eyes.

'What are you talking about, what gift, why am I always the last to know?' Giselle pouted.

'Darling, hush for now, we must avoid eavesdroppers, leave your questions until later.' Seeing my serious expression, she nodded in agreement.

Café Villande is busy with diners tonight, we all detected a slight air of resentment from Iona as we departed for the evening.

'Why can ye not dine here, isn't my food good enough for ye?' Iona called after us as we walked to the taxi.

Gaston turned and gave her a wink.

'Family stuff; get back to the kitchen, woman.' She roared with laughter.

'That's fine then, just this once.'

'Darlings, we cannot afford to upset the staff, I am no use at all around food as you know.' Giselle's mood had obviously improved since my arrival.

'They can manage, I pay them well to do just that,' said Gaston with an air of finality.

The pretty seaside town of Menton glittered with Christmas lights, each house in every street and alleyway was illuminated by candles or fairy lights. Lights hung from trees planted close to the sea front, reflecting their warming glow on the incoming tide.

*What will they say, will they insist I inform the police, will they accuse me of subterfuge and say the diamonds are not legally mine to keep?* I was taunted by my inner voice.

Any hope of delaying my news until the end of the meal was soon dashed, on Gaston's insistence to be told everything immediately.

'Right, Inez, let's hear about your fusty old clock to save me from indigestion.'

After taking two sips of wine, I took out my mobile phone and showed them a picture of the diamonds, they both sat for some time in stunned silence.

'Mother, are you telling us these incredible jewels were hidden in your clock?' Giselle gazed at the picture in utter disbelief.

'Yes, darling, they were hidden in a secret drawer concealed in the bottom of the casing along with a heartfelt note from your father.'

'Oh, no.' Giselle covered her face. 'Iona told us that Simone had torn the lodge apart looking for treasure, I wondered why you nearly fainted on hearing her news.' A look of deep concern clouded her beautiful face. 'My self-obsession has to cease right here; it's making us all so miserable, and my sickness will end when the baby comes,' she said reflectively.

'Now hearing this riveting news has renewed my sense of purpose.' A sly smile stole over her face, she looked at me through narrowed eyes. 'You have the treasure she is seeking, so now you have the power to discover what really happened on that mountain five years ago and, Mother, I insist you use your power wisely.'

'Hold on minute,' interjected Gaston. 'If Simone knows about the diamonds, the question is who else knows of their existence? They must be worth millions; seriously, Inez, you must be sensible, they need to be kept in a bank vault not a flimsy old clock,' said Gaston wagging his finger in my direction.

Giselle could barely take her eyes from the image.

'They are incredible, we must see them for ourselves,' she said to Gaston.

I ordered a lobster salad, knowing full well that a hot meal would grow cold under the weight and gravity of my other interesting news.

After the waitress had served our coffee and cognac – nothing for Giselle – I recounted my supposedly coincidental meetings with Allesio Faconi in Paris.

Of course, I should have mentioned his brother Guido's incessant phone calls and revealed the more salient points of my heated conversation with Allesio in the hotel dining room, but somewhere in the depths of my mind, instinct prevented me from doing so.

'Hmmm.' Gaston frowned. 'Inez, you need to proceed with extreme caution, there are unscrupulous bastards out there who would kill their whole family to get their hands on those gems.'

'Don't concern yourself, Gaston. The jewels are safely hidden; at some point decisions will be made but not yet, I want to enjoy them for a while.'

'That's nonsense, Mother, you need to rethink your home security or as Gaston said stash them in a bank vault, it's just plain irresponsible to keep them in a drawer, however secret,' said Giselle rudely.

'Please don't ruin our pleasant evening with your unwanted advice, Giselle. If your opinion is required, you will be the first to know, now shall we leave.'

'So sorry,' said Giselle, reduced to tears.

We walked home in silence, a silence that continued until after lunchtime the following day. As Iona had the afternoon and evening to herself, we decided to drive into Nice and immerse ourselves in Christmas shopping, then dine at one of the many chic restaurants near the market.

That evening after service had ended, we all lazed around the kitchen table sampling Iona's new cocktail creations. She mentioned in her usual offhand manner that she had received some rather interesting emails from friends living in the village of Roxberg. They had described in detail the handsome young man who had recently moved into Roxberg Gate shortly after our departure.

Seemingly, both he and Simone had been seen shopping and dining out in the village, causing much speculation and comment amongst the locals. Suddenly, Giselle, who had been listening intently to Iona's news, exploded in temper.

'First Simone has the temerity to deceive us her own family, then we hear she is flaunting her new lover around the district, scheming bitch. Iona, would you make some enquiries please, we must find out who he is,' she said with hauteur.

Hearing news of Simone's new man had so incensed Giselle that she had quite forgotten her nausea and regained some semblance of her former volatile self.

When the others had left the table to resume their allotted tasks, Giselle and I sought sanctuary in her bedroom to talk in private. She said her sickness had begun at the beginning of her pregnancy, in fact even before she had realised her condition.

'Mother, you must understand my career is everything to me. The gallery can only afford one curator of exhibitions, the director has borrowed a young man from our sister gallery in Nice for a short period, but how do I know he won't inveigle himself and steal my job,' she complained bitterly, looking down at her burgeoning bump.

'You have much to answer for,' she said, prodding her stomach.

'Naturally, Gaston's business often takes him abroad, leaving me here feeling lonely and unwanted, even waitressing in the café failed to alleviate my boredom, the aroma of food made me sick sick sick,' she exclaimed petulantly. Of course, it's fine for men, they don't have to suffer nine months of inconvenience or the resulting pain and discomfort of childbirth. Gaston has recommended brisk beach walks, which is his remedy for everything,' she said, a wistful look clouding her features. 'He was right though, not that he will ever hear it from me,' she giggled.

'Truth to tell these walks have become my only solace, the ultimate panacea for my restless mind, trust him to solve my misery.' She grinned.

She went to the window and gazed upwards to the silver moon pouring pearl drops of shimmering light over the dark waves beneath, reminding me of the clock with a pearl face waiting in the darkness for my return.

'Let's go out, we can take 'Thing'; Flora won't mind,' she said, heading for the door.

'Who is Thing?' I enquired.

'Maud's replacement, although Gaston has yet to accept him, he dislikes the thought of another male in the household stealing all the attention, I suppose.'

Off I went to the boot room to collect my outdoor coat and boots, and within 10 minutes we were striding across the beach, the salt air tore at our hair and stung our eyes, the exhilarating sensation of being at one with raw nature left us both feeling revitalised.

Scurrying at our feet was Flora's latest acquisition, a small sand coloured dog of indeterminate breed. We threw sticks into the darkness for him to retrieve, which he ignored with an air of disdain, preferring instead to follow close at our heels, his tongue lolling from his mouth, clearly revelling in our company.

I asked Giselle how they came by Flora's new pet, as he was not a puppy but a sturdy adult dog much like Gaston's temperamental bitch, Maud, who had died in tragic circumstances the previous year.

'Oh yes, funny little thing. I found him wandering alone on the beach, unkempt and rather smelly,' she replied, wrinkling her nose in disgust.

'Couldn't get rid of him, dusk was falling, and the tide was racing in, the pathetic animal might have drowned. I made several attempts to shoo him away, but he just wouldn't go,' she said, laughing at the memory.

'When Flora saw him it was all over, there was no way she would ever give him up. I rang the gendarmerie to ask if anyone had reported a missing dog, no one had so it was decided between us that in the short-term, Flora would be responsible for his care. After a bath and a meal, he seemed very pleased indeed to be under new management, so to speak,' she said fondling the animal. 'Gaston was away on business in Italy at the time, we all dreaded telling him as he still mourns the loss of little Maud, naturally it was left to me to recount the saga of the dog. After he arrived home, I suggested dinner at his favourite restaurant, and, after plying him with his preferred Chablis, I broke the news about 'Thing' then waited for the sky to fall on my head.' She laughed, her hands half covering her face.

'I won't pretend he hadn't guessed something was brewing, as I ate practically nothing and drank even less.' She paused, a thoughtful look in her eyes then continued. 'He took it rather well at first, so I fetched the animal after we arrived home thinking, as an animal lover, Gaston would warm to the pathetic little thing. Gosh, I was so wrong, only then did I realise the animal slightly resembled the tempestuous Maud! Gaston duly thanked me for my insensitivity then retired to bed, next day he told Flora to keep the animal out of his sight and more importantly out of his kitchen, since then he has shown no interest whatsoever in the animal.'

The day prior to our departure for Villefranche, Gaston and Giselle settled their differences with regard to the dog, she was forgiven, he apologised for overreacting and insisted on the animal being taken to a vet for a health check.

A pleasant air of anticipation gripped me at the thought of returning home and to my new life. I helped Giselle pack and filled Gaston's car with fuel, such was my sense of urgency to leave Menton.

'To think, Mother, anyone could have stolen the clock in transit and worse still you have left those diamonds in a half-empty house without a security alarm,' said Giselle, furiously throwing clothes for me to pack. 'Father was such a deep demon, but he did think of you in the end,' she said kindly.

My look laden with suspicion and doubt conveyed everything.

'No, my darling, he just wanted to hide his diamonds in the safest possible place, with me; undoubtedly, he would have returned at some point to retrieve them. Strange how fate decided otherwise, now we will never know the truth.'

*Perhaps one day the truth will be revealed, perhaps the real truth lies with Guido Faconi?*

The next morning as we prepared to depart for Villefranche, Flora appeared with Thing, as she spoke his eyes never left her face, the animal was besotted by her, she rushed over to Gaston with the dog in her arms.

'Please, please, Gaston, may I be allowed to keep him? I will look after him and pay for his food, please, please,' she implored, giving him a winning smile.

Gaston eyed the animal with mock horror, then reluctantly agreed.

'He can stay, as long as you promise to keep him out of the kitchen,' he said firmly.

'Thank you, you won't regret it, I won't let you down,' she gushed with relief.

To my annoyance, Gaston kept disappearing into the kitchen, issuing final instructions to Iona.

'Come along, do hurry, we must arrive before nightfall,' I chided.

The day had dawned bright and mild; in this part of France, no frost will leave its icy feathery fingers on the branches of the pine trees, nor freeze the swimming pools of the rich and famous inhabitants who spend their winters here. They are the fortunate ones, the people who live free from debt and violence in this most prosperous department of France.

The journey was fraught with delays and diversions, Giselle's nausea was evident throughout, on two occasions she asked Gaston to stop the car then ran to a hedge in which to deposit her bile.

As we drove on, my thoughts turned to Guido Faconi and our phone conversation; during the past few days he had left 18 missed calls on my mobile phone. If Gaston knew, he would definitely warn Guido not to contact me, then how would I discover more about his business with Henry.

Guido will keep ringing until we agree to meet, then surely Giselle will know that I have kept his existence a secret, she may think me secretive, or worse still foolish for withholding such vital information.

While sitting quietly in the rear seat lost in thought, my mind clouded with indecision as to the best course of action, the same questions kept repeating over and over in my head. The most intriguing of all would be to discover the exact nature of his business with Henry. Why now, after all these years, did he want to meet me? Finally, the need to share my concerns led me to confess all.

I told them everything, Guido's incessant phone calls and the lurid details of my encounter with Allesio in Paris.

'Mother, you are such a sly cat, why didn't you tell us earlier, we could have made enquiries about him, is your wi-fi working yet?'

'Yes of course, the modern day essential to life, more precious than food to some people,' I commented airily.

Sensing a change in atmosphere, I quickly changed the subject to more mundane matters. Gaston's jaw set firm, a muscle rippled in his cheek, I knew this look, he was angry with me.

'Inez, you have had nearly a whole week to tell us about this man, why wait until now?' he said, looking exasperated.

'I didn't tell you because I knew my news would receive an explosive reaction.' I sighed with resignation.

'And you were in danger of being caught out, let's discuss this later when I have had time think,' jeered Gaston, his jaw set firm once more.

Driving at pace had made Gaston's gear changes more erratic and uncomfortable to sit through, the sky had darkened matching his mood, and Giselle spent most of the journey berating him for driving too fast.

'If you continue at this pace, I will throw up all over you,' she promised, and she meant it.

I had eagerly anticipated a happy homecoming, now my pleasure was spoiled, and it was my fault. Giselle began vacuous chatting to break our uncomfortable silence.

'Quiet please, Giselle, I am trying to concentrate,' Gaston barked at her.

We spent the last 20 miles of the journey in an uneasy silence, arriving late, I directed Gaston to the parking area at the back of the house. Having recently mislaid the back-door key, we gathered our luggage and walked around to the front of the house.

'I really must remember to change the locks,' I remarked innocently.

'Yes, Mother, you must,' said Gaston and Giselle in unison. Once inside, Gaston caught my arm, his face bright with mischief, his affable mood restored.

'Inez, don't worry, I have a plan, and before you ask, no I will not be disclosing it to you or anyone,' he guffawed conspiratorially. Giselle and I exchanged long-suffering glances, this could only mean trouble as Gaston so loved a mystery to solve.

The house felt unfamiliar to me and quite creepy in the darkness and so cold, as I had forgotten to leave the heating on. My hurried departure had forced me to leave the house in a state of disarray, unpacked boxes were piled into corners awaiting my attention, a motley collection of lamps and light shades stood askew on the sideboard.

Downstairs in the kitchen, arguably my favourite room, were pale-blue painted cupboards and matching breakfast furniture all in perfect order, warmth radiated from the French blue range cooker, which was never switched off.

'Glad to see your priorities haven't changed,' commented Gaston.

'Are we dining in tonight?' he enquired, raising an eyebrow in my direction.

Flicking the thermostat to a volcanic setting, I showed him where the firewood was stored.

'Yes, we are, but first you must build a fire in the sitting room, please.' He ran upstairs and immediately set to work; while he was waiting for the fire to catch, he couldn't resist the temptation of running his fingers over the clock, half expecting my diamonds to emerge.

'Not now, Gaston. Let's have an early dinner before the big reveal and do stop snooping,' I chided.

'Spoilsport,' he retorted, laughing.

I sent Giselle off to find linen and duvets, they could make their own beds tonight as my priority would be cooking our dinner.

'Do you mind if we take a quick look around?' called Giselle over the top floor bannister.

'Go ahead, help yourself but do be careful, some rooms are without lights,' I warned.

From the kitchen, I could hear them scurrying around like excited children at a fairground, now my new home felt real and enjoyed. I transferred a homemade chicken Mireille from the freezer to the hot oven, then made a pot of hibiscus tea and settled down to read my post. After an hour, Gaston joined me, saying Giselle had fallen asleep.

'Come on, Inez, don't keep me in suspense, show me your Roxberg hoard,' he wheedled.

'Such impatience,' I said, running upstairs to the sitting room.

'Oh, if you insist, but first close the shutters, one never knows who may be watching.'

He sat holding his breath as I knelt at the base of the clock, my fingers searching for the brass lever holding the secret drawer tightly shut, the drawer slid open to reveal more treasure than Gaston would ever see in his whole lifetime. He sat in speechless awe, completely mesmerised, incredulous at the sight before him.

'Are they for real?' His voice sounded low and husky.

'Knowing Henry, I would imagine they are the genuine article,' I replied with conviction.

He looked at me, his face white with concern. 'I'd like to bet this is the treasure Simone was searching for at Roxberg Gate and if she knows, then who else has she told. Iona said the whole village knew she was searching for treasure, but no one mentioned diamonds.'

We spread them out on the rug and waited for Giselle to join us.

'They look and feel genuine,' said Gaston examining each individual stone in the lamplight, 'how can you have them authenticated without raising suspicion?' His voice was full of doubt.

Just then Giselle burst in. 'Why didn't you—' She stopped mid-sentence.

'Oh my word, how beautiful, how amazingly beautiful, are they really ours, if so can I choose one for myself?' she asked, staring fixedly at the diamonds.

'Giselle, please, this is serious the diamonds are not ours; they belong to Inez, and until she can prove their provenance and true ownership, which given Henry's track record may be impossible if they have been stolen, they must remain our secret.'

We ate dinner in a completive mood, Gaston was lost in his own thoughts while Giselle listlessly picked over her food, eating hardly a morsel.

'I have driving fatigue,' announced Gaston, exhaustion etched in his face, Giselle readily agreed.

'Mother and I would definitely testify to your lamentable driving skills, not to mention your bad case of the grumps.'

He didn't even try to argue or make a jokey rejoinder, they both looked so weary.

'Leave the dishes to me and go to bed,' I said, squeezing their hands.

With hardly a word, they kissed me goodnight then disappeared upstairs, and I was relieved to see them go. Gaston may have concocted some hair-raising solution to my problems, but then so had I.

Next morning at daybreak, I heard the stairs creak as Gaston slipped quietly out of the house, no doubt in search of a quiet spot to meditate in peace and stretch his muscles, a ritual he observed every day whatever the weather. Over the years he had become my longed-for son, we shared confidences he withheld from my daughter, often complaining to me of the unwelcome constrictions of duty and family responsibility, which appeared to weigh heavily upon him.

He had told me of his hedonistic bachelor days, days of complete freedom, seeds of which lay in a tiny crevice of his mind, tempting him to escape from life's pressures, now they are all but distant memories. This man, this son-in-law of mine, I would trust with my life.

An hour later, I looked out across the harbour just as Gaston came into view, walking purposefully under a milky dawn, a chink of light from my kitchen window drawing him like a moth to a flame.

'Coffee and pancakes,' he said, kissing the top of my head.

My wrist ached from the rhythmic beating of the batter; the pan glistened with hot cinnamon butter. We both looked upwards on hearing Giselle footsteps rushing to the bathroom.

'Poor girl. I remember only too well, but my sickness passed after the first two months,' I remarked sympathetically. The weather had turned clear and bright, so after breakfast we decided to explore the town. Giselle and Gaston wandered around hand in hand, looking in each and every shop, talking to their owners who were pleased to stop and talk, as the summer tourist season had passed, and Christmas was some weeks away.

'Mother, how did you find such a friendly town, it's so like Menton,' remarked Giselle happily. By late afternoon the streets and restaurants had begun to fill with people chatting, school children's laughter echoed in the alleyways of the narrow side streets; footsore and parched we turned for home, storm clouds had appeared from nowhere as skittish raindrops began to fall. Nearing the front door, I remembered my wool wrap was still in the car.

'Gaston, my wrap is still in the car, would you be a love and fetch it for me please?'

'Of course,' he shouted, running towards the rear alley where the car was parked.

'Any chance of a coffee and a cognac?' he called.

'Yes, sir, every chance,' I called back saluting him.

'I would kill for a cognac right now,' sighed Giselle.

Gaston had parked his car in my allotted space in the service road behind the house. Having retrieved my wrap, he retraced his steps, nearly colliding with a delivery man, who was holding a bouquet of flowers so large it completely concealed his head. Giselle who had followed in his wake, rushed forward to take the card tucked inside the blooms which read.

*To the elusive Signora Roxberg, felicitations, Guido Faconi.*

On seeing the bouquet in Gaston's hands, I knew instinctively who had sent them.

'Mother, you sly fox, I want to meet this man,' said Giselle her inquisitive eyes narrowing to slits.

Turning to hide my embarrassment, I noticed a man carrying a ladder and a vendor sign under his arm. We watched as he began fixing the sign to the wall of the house next door, announcing it was for sale. Without hesitation, I walked over to the sign, registered the number and rang the agent on my mobile phone.

After a few minutes of intense negotiation, I proceeded to make an offer so generous it rendered Gaston and Giselle speechless.

Clicking the end call button, a feeling of muted elation crept over me.

This house would become a school of art, it would represent a new beginning and a purpose close to my heart.

The prospect of a new project instilled so much excitement in me that I was left momentarily blinded by my own imagination.

'Mother, you have several messages left on your landline,' called Giselle from the hallway, would there ever be another day like this, so much activity, so much to look forward to.

'Shall we hear the messages?' Giselle called out.

We all stood in the hallway and listened; the blood drained from my face as we listened again to the message from Iona's fiancé. Trembling with shock, a cold creeping dread seeped into my body, my head spun as I groped for a chair.

The detective in charge of the enquiry into Henry's business activities, had been asked to warn me that Simone du Val had made a formal complaint against me. Simone had accused me of stealing a king's ransom in diamonds from their family home in England.

Gaston poured me a large cognac.

'Perhaps we should stay a few days longer. To be honest, Inez, I fear for your safety if the diamonds remain here,' he said seriously.

'Thank you, Gaston, for your concern,' acid dripped from my words. 'I am perfectly capable of looking after myself, furthermore your constant interference in my affairs is annoying and unnecessary,' I retorted angrily, warming to my theme. 'How dare they insinuate that I am guilty of wrongdoing, the clock and the diamonds were Henry's to give and he gave them to me, they are mine and no one, least of all Simone du Val, shall take them from me.'

Gaston and Giselle exchanged meaningful looks, then retreated to the sitting room, there they lay stretched out on a sofa, drinking their coffee while discussing the dramas unfolding before them. Looking around, Giselle recognised some of the furnishings from her mother's previous home at Honfleur.

'I feel quite at home here already and not so sick.' She rolled her eyes.

'You and your family, the drama never ends, I should have received a large dowry from your father just to take you on,' he smirked.

They rolled around helpless with laughter. Giselle was tired after their sightseeing expedition around the town, she pushed her husband towards the door, saying she needed an hour of peace and a nap before dinner. They came through the door and caught me sitting forlornly on the landing floor, eavesdropping on their conversation. Gaston came and sat on the top step of the stairs.

'Well, scary mother-in-law, has my curative cognac calmed your Latin temper?'

'Yes, thank you,' came my sullen response.

'Please accept my apologies, it was unforgivable of me to rant at you of all people. Simone's accusations have unsettled me and even worse the diamonds are no longer my secret.'

Gaston slapped his thighs and stood up. 'If I am not mistaken,' he said, sniffing the air, there is delicious aroma coming from the kitchen, shall we eat?'

'Charmer, let's have an aperitif and wait for Giselle.'

My kitchen rubbish needed emptying, so with a bag and torch in hand, I walked round to the back alley behind the row of terraced houses, to separate the items into recycling bins. Turning my head, I saw a man watching me from the end of the alley closest to the harbour, a bitterly cold sea breeze blew his scarf over his half-hidden face. I recognised him immediately as Allesio and stared long and hard in his direction, challenging him to approach me, he nodded and stepped back merging into crowds of late-night shoppers like a coward.

Suddenly my mind cleared, whatever the cost or injury to myself, this mystery must be solved by me and in my favour, never again would anyone be allowed to rule or intimidate me. Returning to the house, I felt a previously untapped well of strength build inside me. If Gaston knew we were being watched, he would intervene on my behalf, if my suspicions are founded both he and Giselle could be in danger. No, I must solve this alone.

'Inez, are you really going to buy the house next door?' said Gaston, who sat idling at the kitchen table awaiting my return.

'Yes, as you know the arts are my passion and are often neglected or underfunded. I will continue to teach painting but not sculpture as there is insufficient outdoor space here. The clarity of light and undulating landscape has inspired me to paint again,' I replied pleasantly in the hope of disguising my internal disquiet.

I divided the remnants of sauvignon blanc used in the Mireille into two glasses and handed one to Gaston. As we toasted ourselves, his steady gaze made me feel uncomfortable. How can I keep secrets from this man who reads my mind as easily as his own?

'You're up to something and you're not telling.' His unwavering gaze drew a flush to my face. 'Before we leave, I want to know all about Guido Faconi; according to my associates and the internet, the guy does not exist.'

'Gaston, please, no questions for now, let's talk later when Giselle is here.' *He is not giving up.*

He ignored my reply and asked where we had met.

'We have never met,' I replied firmly.

'Then how does he know you? He has your phone number, next he will be here in your house,' said Gaston his voice rising.

'He was a friend of Henry's, he rang a few weeks ago to offer his condolences; that is all.' A fleeting smile passed Gaston's lips.

'Any friend of Henry's could spell trouble,' said Gaston, lowering his tone.

'He is probably some genuinely harmless old chap, wanting to pay his respects to the widow of a lifelong friend,' I said nonchalantly.

'A wealthy widow,' corrected Gaston interrupting. 'If he was close to Henry, he will be aware of your circumstances.'

'Gaston, please stop worrying, I will let you know what transpires after we have met.'

'Shall I lay the table?' said Giselle appearing in the doorway, yawning from her nap. 'What is that divine smell? Even I feel hungry, let's eat, and who cares if it reappears later.'

Apparently, I have surpassed myself yet again.

'Mother, I swear you produce your finest dishes when in a foul temper,' said Giselle, devouring another mouthful of the silky sauce covering the chicken.

'Not so, darling, it was made in a happy mood before you and Gaston came to stay.'

'Oh, thanks, are you still cross with us for interfering?'

Gaston ate in silence, preferring instead to enjoy the meal rather than reignite my wrath.

'Mother, you will not leave this table without telling me who this Guido is and more importantly, what is he to you.'

'Ask Gaston later, he will explain.' My retort was unnecessarily sharp. 'I am more concerned about that disturbing answerphone message.'

'Oh, ignore Simone, she is unhinged like her mother,' said Giselle venomously.

After the meal had been cleared, we gathered in the sitting room. In a shaded alcove away from the light stood the exquisitely decorated long-case clock, its pearl face glinting in the lamplight. I had arranged for the installation of two strong chains to be attached from the wall to its base, ostensibly to provide stability by preventing it from falling forward. Giselle clasped her hands together as if in prayer.

'Would you mind if I open the drawer, come on, let's see your treasure again,' she said like an excited child on Christmas Eve.

'Go ahead if you can find the lever.'

She crawled around on all fours until she found her goal.

'Yes, here is the leaf-shaped lever, would the assembled company close their eyes,' she said grandly.

Myself and Gaston, with a bow of mock servility, duly obeyed her command. Giselle pressed the leaver, the base slid noiselessly towards her.

'You can open your eyes now,' she announced in fanfare.

We opened our eyes and once again gasped in awe at the quantity of brilliants before us. The refracted light from a tiffany lamp illuminated the stones, transforming them into a mesmeric dancing aurora of splintering light. We all knelt like parishioners in prayer in order to fully examine what was now comically referred to as the Roxberg Hoard. Gaston's face clouded.

'Inez, I must warn you again, people would commit murder for a fraction of what you have here; these jewels are worth millions, they represent a lifetime of well-considered purchases. Henry's insurance against lean times.'

Henry's final note lay in the draw, Giselle read the words out loud then wept for the father she had never known.

'He did love you, Giselle, no doubt he loved all of his children, but finally it was me he trusted with his precious jewels, they are his legacy to us and I will never relinquish them.' My voice quivered with emotion. 'On a more sombre note, I must tell you that my intentions are clear, everything I own will come to you, Giselle. The notaries have drawn up my will, and I intend you to hold a copy as evidence.'

'I don't know what to say, thank you sounds so lame and insufficient, please, Mother I beg of you, take the jewels to a bank for safekeeping.'

'I will keep them in the clock as Henry intended, my mind is made up, they will stay with me hidden in plain sight. No one would suspect a mere clock would house such treasure and who would have thought that even after death, Henry had triumphed.'

Before returning the clock to its niche, I pointed to the dedication engraved in silver and fixed to the inside of the case, it read: Adeline, my one true love.

'Henry replicated these loving words, dedicated from his father to his mother, on his message card to me.' Again, Giselle looked close to tears.

'So, this beautiful clock had belonged to my grandmother,' she said wistfully.

'Yes, the grandmother who drifted into insanity after having given birth to her first child.' The very thought sent a shiver through me, and I immediately regretted having mentioned it.

Placing a log on the dying embers, we settled back to drink our coffee.

'Let me tell you about my shopping trip to Paris.' My attempt to change the subject and lighten the atmosphere fell on deaf ears.

Gaston undeterred by this diversion, asked me to hear him out.

'Look here, Inez, we all agree you must take this business of Simone's complaint seriously, if she has just half of her mother's acumen, she will never give up on her quest to find the diamonds.'

'Gaston,' I said with exaggerated patience. 'Simone never saw the clock or knew of its existence, it was delivered to the house when she was upstairs out of sight, playing the wounded sister.'

'I wouldn't put it beyond her to have this house burgled, so please at least have an alarm fitted,' advised Giselle.

I looked at my daughter with a degree of resignation. 'Very well, anything for a peaceful life, now please can we change the subject and forget about the clock.'

Giselle, drowsy with food and warmth, fell asleep on Gaston's lap. Lifting her gently, he carried her upstairs to bed only to return a few minutes later as I was clearing the cups and preparing to retire for the night.

'We need to talk.' His serious expression told me another lecture was about to be delivered. He asked me, yet again, not to interrupt and hear him out, his subsequent lecture, regarding my flippant attitude to the diamonds in particular and life in general left me stinging with resentment.

'OK, Inez, I should have known that alcohol and arguments are bad news at this hour, just humour me and make sure to install that security alarm and CCTV, please.' He kissed my forehead then disappeared upstairs before I had time to retaliate.

The following two days were spent in blissful union, all disagreements were cast aside in the spirit of family unity. The security alarm had been ordered, so I was no longer considered an irresponsible adult.

We viewed the house next door together, and wholeheartedly agreed it had great potential as a small residential school. The vendor had gratefully accepted my offer, the deal was signed promptly in the French manner and a date given for completion of the contract.

'I will name the house Maison des Artistes; it will be painted azure blue to reflect the sea and sky. The entire upper floor will be converted into a large studio space, the remaining bedrooms will accommodate a maximum of three live-in students, any additional students will reside elsewhere and attend day classes.'

'We are very impressed,' said Giselle enviously.

I rang the builder who restored my own property, asking him to submit plans in order to carry out the necessary alterations. The month of December was unusually cold, work on the schoolhouse was scheduled to start in early January, the intervening weeks will be spent organising furnishings and essential kitchen items and the completion of my own home.

On the morning of their departure, Giselle and Gaston made one more tedious attempt to persuade me to move the diamonds to a more secure location, my expression told them both to avoid the subject.

'Mother, I wish you would take this seriously, don't be tempted to tell anyone about your jewels,' she said sharply.

I almost pushed them through the door.

'Come and stay for Christmas and stop worrying all will be fine,' I called after them, waving furiously as they drove off out of my life.

My relief at being alone was palpable, there had been so little time to acclimatise to my surroundings, nothing seemed safe or familiar, now I could relax into my new life.

As I turned to enter the house, a tall, dark-haired man entered my line of vision.

'Signora Roxberg, please forgive my taking the liberty of approaching you so directly, allow me to introduce myself, I am your late husband's closest friend, Guido Faconi.'

A stab of apprehension suffused my face with colour. His direct stare so disturbed me that my house keys fell from my hand onto the wet pavement, swift as a bird, he leaned down to retrieve them, tossing the keys back and forth between his hands. His eyes searched my face for signs of recoil as he continued to play with my house keys.

'How did you recognise me and find my address?' my voice rose in annoyance.

'Henry carried your photograph in his wallet,' he said smoothly. 'Your face is very familiar to me; Henry would often study your image.'

He shrugged, making an open gesture with his hands. 'Henry gave me your Menton address, and when I called, the new owners gave me your forwarding address, how fortunate to find you at home now your guests have departed,' he said glancing down the harbour.

'I see my presence has disturbed you.' He raised an eyebrow; it was more a statement than a question. 'Please accept my sincere apologies, it was not my intention to frighten you.'

His eyes are the colour of a raven's wing, this Machiavellian devil, whose sultry chiselled features would defy the most accomplished of artists to commit to oil paint and canvas, such is his magnetic allure.

I looked away, raising my chin to avoid his gaze. 'Henry never mentioned you.' My voice sounded sharp and defiant.

'My dear Inez... may I call you Inez?' He waited for my response.

'Yes, if you must.' He seemed almost amused by my impatience.

'Please allow me to tell you a short story,' he said, indicating to the bench outside my door. Avid for any information, I sat quietly and listened to what he had to say.

'Many years ago, Henry and I attended the wedding of a mutual friend, both you and your father were seated at our table. Unfortunately for me, I allowed Henry to out-manoeuvre me by eventually proposing marriage to you. In hindsight, perhaps you should have married me, as I would have been a far safer choice of husband and you would never have been allowed to leave me, as you left Henry.'

He leaned towards me a secret smile playing about his lips and whispered, 'So you see, Inez, I know everything about you.'

He took my hand and placed the keys in my outstretched palm.

'Will you join me for dinner this evening?' he said, still holding my hand.

'Thank you, I have a previous engagement,' I lied.

'Then perhaps we can meet for lunch tomorrow? I will call at 12 o'clock,' he said undeterred.

Lunch would be less threatening, so I agreed to his request. Why do I feel threatened by this man, who had proposed nothing more than friendship? Raising my hand, his face a mask of serious intent, he kissed my fingertips in a flamboyant gesture that was both embarrassing and unnecessary. Pulling away sharply, I turned to go indoors without a backward glance.

'Goodbye, Signore Faconi,' I called dismissively.

Hurrying indoors, I watched from the window as Guido sauntered off along the harbour, leaving me somewhat unnerved. My mother's cautionary words floated into my mind.

*When a dangerous panther in the guise of the human male enters your life, a woman of sense allows herself two choices, encourage and enjoy or destroy him before he destroys you.*

# Chapter Five

Standing there amongst the detritus left by Gaston and Giselle, my equilibrium shaken by this man who had the nerve to presume he knew everything about my life, propelled me into a frenzy of domestic activity.

Guido's addictive image followed me from room to room while I worked furiously to replace chaos with order and cleanliness. After seemingly endless hours of toil, I found sanctuary in a rose-oil-scented bath, a large glass of rouge and a bowl of olives, blissfully unaware of the dark figure dressed in black leaning against the harbour wall opposite my house, a mistral wind from the south whipping his coat and tearing at his scarf.

While eating an omelette supper at the kitchen table, my head fizzed with plans for the school, a reliable live-in cook/ housekeeper would be essential together with an efficient cleaner and one with a strong constitution, as one never knew what horrors might be found lurking under beds in student quarters.

After a while, exhaustion drew me to my favourite spot on the window seat, looking out to sea and focusing as if hypnotised as moonlit waves gently lapped the harbour walls, a veil of sea fret partially obscured my view of the stars. As I watched, my eyes became accustomed to the differing shapes of dog walkers and couples making their way home after a night on the town. One lonely figure caught my attention, pacing back and forth impatiently as if caged by some unknown force. I knew instinctively that man was Guido Faconi.

Eventually, a doze stole my consciousness. Some hours later, I woke to the sound of my own nightmare screams, beautiful people from another age walked by and laughed at me, then a man in a mask kidnapped and held me captive in a dungeon. Had I witnessed a vision of foreboding or had my vivid imagination played tricks on me? Trembling and fearful, I stumbled into bed and hid under the covers.

Next morning, feeling revived and primed to fire my verbal guns in Guido Faconi's direction, I read through my notes from the previous evening and checked my emails in the hope of receiving further applications from prospective housekeepers.

At 12 o'clock the doorbell rang, standing there was Guido, wearing a speculative expression, and a British plain-clothes detective, proffering confirmation of his identity. For a moment, the world stood still. The policeman introduced himself then asked to speak to me in private, he made no apology to either Guido or myself for his unscheduled intrusion.

Guido, sensing my unease, stepped back saying he would return in one hour.

With pulses racing, I almost ran downstairs into the kitchen, beckoning him to follow me. Having already guessed the purpose of his visit, I took a deep breath and began making coffee. He refused my offer of refreshments and went on to say that the purpose of his visit was to investigate a complaint made against me by Simone du Val.

'Madame Roxberg,' said the detective gravely, 'Miss du Val has accused you of stealing a quantity of diamonds from her home at Roxberg Gate. I am here to ask you directly if her accusations are correct,' he said sternly.

I turned to him, my face a study of frozen indifference. 'No, her accusations are not correct, they are pure fiction,' I retorted acidly. 'You are welcome to search the house if you have a warrant, however you will be wasting your time.'

He shifted his bony frame from one foot to another, looking nonplussed and rather embarrassed at my request to see a warrant.

'We did not consider it necessary to order one, we simply assumed you would be willing to cooperate, that said, Madame Roxberg, may we begin?'

'You may begin, I have an appointment,' I said defiantly, throwing a spare set of keys on the kitchen table, narrowly missing his hand. 'Post the keys through the letterbox on your way out, and please remember to wear gloves before touching my possessions.' Then I ran out, slamming the front door behind me before he could protest.

I ran straight into Guido who was loitering outside the door, deep in thought and frowning in concern. He looked up and laughed to see my face flaming with self-righteous indignation.

'I heard some of that, Henry was not lying when he called you a virago,' he said ruefully.

Just then my builder rang to say his current job had been postponed and would be able start work on the school when the notaries had completed the contract. Without preamble, I rang the notaries, asking them to complete my purchase within the next few days as my builder had become unexpectedly available to start work immediately.

'What a frenetic life you do lead,' said Guido with a hint of sarcasm.

My thoughts returned to Paris and to Sara, the owner of the drapery shop, her prediction had come true; Guido is a beautiful fiend, but one that will not be allowed to interfere in my life.

'Your plans sound fascinating,' said Guido gazing into my eyes. 'Almost as fascinating as you.' My face continued to flame under his scrutiny.

'My other subject of interest is architecture, perhaps you will permit me to look at the drawings when they are ready?' he asked in even tones.

As we walked, I began to wonder if his formal manner and mode of speech were natural and his own, or if he was just being overtly polite for my benefit.

'You dress like an accountant; artists are flamboyant, uncontrolled bohemians.' He laughed so much his shoulders shook.

'I do have uncontrolled moments occasionally,' he said silkily.

Guido had booked a secluded table with a harbour view in a nearby restaurant, my appetite had all but disappeared under the stress of having the house searched by a stranger, to have stayed and watched him trespassing through my possessions would have been too humiliating and I may have been tempted to make matters so much worse, by berating him for his cheek.

I was confident he would not discover my diamonds, but if by chance he was lucky enough to find them, I would deny all knowledge of their existence and blame Henry for his deceit.

Guido took his time studying the menu and wine list, giving me the opportunity of studying him. He wore an elegantly cut, black cashmere suit lined with silk of the darkest green to match his scarf, he smelled of some indefinable woody citrus fragrance possibly vetiver. We both ordered the fish; he was considerate enough not to enquire about the detective. If he had, I would have told him some ridiculous lie about home security. While sipping aperitifs, he tactfully enquired about my future plans.

'You will be unaware that I am a fully trained teacher of art and sculpture; this building will be transformed into a residential school of art.'

Guido looked at me intently, his eyes dancing with mischief.

'Oh that, yes, Henry told me all about your school at Honfleur, occasionally he would send one of his spies disguised as a student. He mentioned that some of these fortunate young men had become your lovers, we understood the liaisons had been passionate but all too brief, you are a heartbreaker, Inez,' he said relishing my discomfort.

At that moment I hated him and Henry for their conspiracies, is this Henry's revenge from beyond the grave, have I not been wounded enough, must they turn the knife until there is nothing left of me?

He sat opposite gloating as my confidence evaporated; had Henry really planted spies in my classes at Le Maison Bleu? Suddenly my world began dissolving around me, my marriage had been a worthless self-delusional mirage, for a moment tears of self-pity and suppressed emotion welled in my eyes. The look on Guido's face told me everything, he knew as did my late husband that I had been as guilty of infidelity as he with his serpent of a housekeeper.

Guido reached across the table and squeezed my hand.

'I am very sorry, Inez, but Henry knew everything; after you left Roxberg Gate, he employed a team of spies to follow your every move.'

'Are there more shocking disclosures?' I asked, dreading his answer.

Guido's unfathomable black eyes held mine and without a flicker of shame, he confessed to copying old master's commissioned by Henry for his wealthy foreign clients.

'I did nothing more than oblige Henry, he paid well, no questions asked. Naturally, our lucrative association ended with his death, a death brought about by your family's unwelcome intervention into his affairs. On his death the money he owed me died with him, for obvious reasons our contracts were never formalised in writing,' he said expectantly.

'After all that has happened, do you now expect me to honour Henry's debts without documentary proof that he owed you anything other than friendship. Guido, I am not obligated to you either personally or financially.' His expression hardened, he asked if I would care to hear more.

'Yes, I want to know everything.'

What other more damaging news could he tell me. The situation was becoming crystal clear, he had sought me out to collect his dues, his condolences were as fake as his paintings.

'Fine, Guido, let's not prevaricate; how much money did Henry owe you.'

He looked deep into my eyes, then and in level tones he continued. 'Oh, more than money, Inez, much more than mere coinage; however, for the moment it will remain my secret.'

My fears regarding Henry's business activities had troubled both my father and myself for the whole of our unconventional marriage.

'Guido, please tell me all you know, your information may help me reconcile those unhappy wasted years.' He hesitated.

'Are you sure? What I am about to tell you, you will find distasteful and extremely upsetting,' he said seriously.

'I am already upset so please continue.' *Will this nightmare never end?*

He called the waiter to order more wine and a dessert, while I sat waiting in trepidation for him to continue. When the waiter had served us and disappeared, Guido took my hands and held them tightly as if trying to steady himself.

'Our fathers, that is to say mine and Henry's, were also close friends, both maintained close links to certain groups both here and in Europe, for many years during that time, they became significant members of a far-right political party. Henry and I grew up together, we were awarded scholarships to study history of art and attended the same university, where radical thinking was accepted as normal.

'One evening, after a particularly drunken dinner party, our fathers spelled out in graphic detail the full extent of their involvement, including their past crimes in the name of separatism. Henry and I were sickened and disgusted by their actions, by then it was too late to rectify their crimes, instead we preferred to wipe the memory of that fateful night from our memories.

'Just six months later, Henry's father died, and he took up residence at Roxberg Gate and married you. I moved back to my native Venice, hoping to forget everything we had seen and heard. Henry and his Father had led dissolute lives, constantly avoiding the police or the tax authorities.

'Henry's mother suffered most, due to her delicate health and gentle nature. Adeline was abandoned, sometimes for months in that damp and freezing mausoleum of a house in England with only the staff for company. She was so unhappy; little wonder she lost her mind.' His pained expression together with his knowledge of Adeline's suffering brought tears to my eyes.

'I moved back to my family home in Venice where Henry and I entertained female models in secret and away from prying eyes. We learned to copy the great masters, however it soon became clear that I possessed a greater aptitude for forgery, while Henry was a more intuitive businessman.

'When he met you, he imagined his financial difficulties were over. He told me you were so besotted with him he could do almost anything, even keep that evil witch of a housekeeper as his mistress.'

I flinched at the memory of the women who had caused me a lifetime of anguish.

'She gave him homemade stimulants; he was completely addicted to them and made no secret of it.' He paused, reading my face, unsure of continuing.

'Your father saw through it all, he threatened Henry on several occasions in my hearing. At times, I even thought he might well resort to murder, so as to prevent your marriage taking place. He knew of Henry's many deceits and threatened to expose them if he upset you. When your children were born, his anger softened into a reluctant acceptance of your questionable choice of husband, he made payments, well bribes, to ensure Henry behaved himself.'

He raised his eyebrows and smiled.

'But then you now know some of this, after your ill-fated trip to Northumberland.'

'Yes, but only recently, I have lived in ignorance for years. Guido, tell me truthfully, did Henry ever love me?' He looked away searching for words.

'No, he only ever loved himself.' Guido looked at the floor in silence, hesitating as if still searching for words.

'Inez, there is something else.' His serious expression warned me to expect unwelcome news. 'I have a younger brother, Allesio. During your absence, he and your daughter Honoré became close, it was assumed they would make a splendid match had she lived.'

The blood pounded through my ears at hearing this, the most devastating revelation of all.

'Simone became increasingly resentful and envious of their relationship, she was a vixen like her mother, always making devious attempts to upset Honoré. Henry told me there were tears and tantrums almost every day. On that fateful day in Switzerland when Honoré lost her life in an avalanche, Allesio was there with them, he was their skiing instructor.'

A chill so bitter crept over me, penetrating my very core. I looked at him as shock and horror began to well up inside me.

'Did he witness the accident?' My voice rose in panic, his look told me the dreadful truth.

'Was she pushed, Guido? Tell me, did Simone push Honoré to her death?'

He looked downcast, his face a picture of compassion and pity, or guilt!

'Inez, we will never know the truth of what happened on that mountainside, the enquiry into the accident reached an obvious conclusion, that the tragedy was simply an act of God.'

'Both Allesio and Simone have strenuously denied any wrongdoing, if Simone was guilty of murder, then Allesio would be condemned as her accomplice, do you expect my brother to perjure himself to satisfy your revenge?'

'I want to know why they were skiing off-piste in bad weather.' My voice had risen to near hysteria. 'Had I known all of this, I would have asked him myself in Paris when he was caught stalking me.'

'Inez, calm yourself, you have nothing to gain by these accusations, you are just tormenting yourself, let your daughter be at peace,' said Guido in soothing tones.

'I will never be at peace until the truth is known and her killer brought to justice.' Bitter words constricted my throat.

He ordered coffee and cognacs while I sat in a state of shock and disbelief.

'Inez, you must believe that Allesio's account of what happened to Honoré is the only one that matters. Simone cannot be trusted with her own life and I should know, she and Allesio are to be married at the next Venice carnival.'

She had won, they had all won and left me to wallow in grief and bitterness.

*Well we shall see; this is not finished. Honoré will be avenged.*

'Now, Inez, there is another more pressing matter that I must discuss with you,' he said gravely, pausing for effect.

'Henry and I had a shareholding in a diamond mine out in Angola. I won't bore you with the details, however, suffice to say our investment proved extremely lucrative. Henry managed to keep our transactions under the radar, if you take my meaning. My share of the diamonds was kept at Roxberg Gate along with Henry's, but as you are now aware, they are missing. Naturally, Simone is the culprit, although she strenuously denies ever having ever seen them.'

At hearing this, I became speechless with dread and longed to escape to consider his revelations, fortunately he took my silence as shock.

'Will you be returning to Venice tonight?' I asked hopefully, my voice sounding unnaturally shrill.

'No, my flight leaves tomorrow at noon, may I prevail on your good nature and stay with you tonight, then we can discuss the future.'

*What future, there is no future for us, not even as friends.*

The waiters were looking in our direction, anxious to close for a few hours to prepare for the evening diners. Guido paid the bill and collected my coat, we left the restaurant and turned to walk back along the harbour, a damp mist sought the crevices of our coats and my broken heart. The sky had turned an ominous inky blue, white-capped waves threatened a storm, the brisk salt breeze tore at our faces leaving a healthy glow, or was it something else?

The detective had gone, nevertheless I felt violated, evidence of my unwelcome intruder had permeated every room. The detective had found nothing and had left a note of apology wrapped around my house keys.

*I am safe... for now.*

Guido made himself comfortable on a sofa in the sitting room and asked about my plans for the school. I offered him a drink and he opted for coffee and a cognac; on my return, he was standing next to the clock with a pearl face admiring my paintings.

'Why did Henry ask me to copy the old masters when he had your talents at his disposal?' he remarked admiringly.

His lighthearted attempt at making less of his life of crime and deception was lost in my disapproval of him.

'Inez, I am not in the least proud of my life's choices, we all need to earn a living and Henry provided me with a perfect solution. Admittedly, I would have continued taking his commissions had he lived. Incidentally, who was that man at your door when I arrived?'

'A security adviser,' I lied brightly.

Feeling playful, I mentioned the phone call from the British police informing me that Simone had made a string of accusations about my stealing some her property.' Now I had his full attention.

'Of course, her ridiculous claims are quite unfounded.' At this point my head was so full of alcohol and bonhomie that I would have taunted the devil had he been present.

'Simone is looking for some fictitious diamonds, she wants Henry's share. They were not mentioned in his will,' I said affably. He snorted with laughter.

'As I said earlier, the diamonds were kept under the radar, Allesio and Simone have conducted a thorough search of the building and found nothing.'

His eyes held mine as he spoke, my unease had grown to such proportions that lies slipped from my lips with consummate ease.

'Perhaps they are stashed in the church or buried in a grave. Who knows, they could be anywhere,' I replied, warming to my deceptions.

'No, I think not, Simone and Allesio have torn the place apart in an effort to find them.'

'How did Henry manage to smuggle them into England?'

'By sea, like every other item of value needing to be hidden from the authorities,' he said without a glimmer of remorse.

'Guido, I have a proposition for you. Disclose Honoré's killer, and in return I will help you to find your wretched diamonds.'

'My dear Inez, you have already disclaimed all knowledge of them and seriously, do you really expect me to accuse my own brother of such a crime?'

'If he was complicit in my daughter's murder then yes, he must suffer the consequences, family or money, Guido, your choice,' I said hotly. 'Think carefully, if these diamonds really do exist their lack of provenance means nothing, because as Henry's widow they will belong to me and all previous arrangements will be considered void, do you understand.'

He looked mollified and distinctly uneasy. My feeling of power increased with the knowledge that his precious diamonds lay less than four feet from his lap, a knowledge that pleased me beyond words.

I put a log on the fire and opened the drapes, stars lit the sea like fireflies, my earlier fear of him dissolved into my glass of cognac.

He relaxed, told me more of his early life but asked nothing of mine. As day lengthened into night, I found myself focusing on his seductively full lips; his close proximity and graceful gestures mesmerised me, and for a fleeting moment I wanted him desperately. Our warming cognac and heady scent of fir cones on the fire had accentuated the sexual tension between us.

No! No! Warning bells sounded in my head as he moved closer, lightly stroking my hair, his sumptuous lips found mine, as our kisses became more ardent, so my resolve began to fade.

'Shall we continue upstairs?' he asked huskily.

'Forgive me, Guido, you caught me unawares, it is far too soon.'

'Inez, please let me comfort you, comfort us both we can salve our sorrows together.' His need was becoming more urgent.

'No, Guido, please accept we have made a bargain, when you have kept your part, I will come to you willingly.'

Fortunately, he did not press me further, as we reached the upper hallway my heart quickened in anticipation of a struggle, he merely kissed my hand made a mock bow and retired to the guest room.

The fragrant sanctuary of my bedroom calmed my inflamed passions, Guido had provoked disturbing and unfamiliar feelings in me, the key to my bedroom door turned smoothly in the lock. Now I am safe from him, but am I safe from myself?

Slipping between the cool sheets, my naked body began to cool and relax, during my restless night, I imagined hearing strange noises coming from within the house.

Waking at midday feeling somewhat lethargic, I threw on my robe and ventured noiselessly out of my room and down to the kitchen, expecting to find Guido somewhere on route, there on the kitchen table was a note propped against a vase of flowers.

The note read.

*My love*
*I must leave you for now, your sensuous kisses will remain in my thoughts until we meet again next week.*
*Felicitations, Guido.*

Once again, my home had been invaded by a stranger, the house felt different this morning. On closer inspection, I found fingerprints on furniture which had been polished the previous day, moving from room to room there was further evidence of disturbance. Guido's hypnotic fragrance lingered in every room; my fears were confirmed when I saw the guest bed had not been slept in.

The clock with a pearl face had been moved, then returned to its former position in the alcove; the key had fallen behind the case. Had Guido attempted to retrieve it, he would almost certainly have found the lever to the secret drawer.

The clock face glittered in the weak midday sun; it had deceived its defiler, keeping its treasures safe for the moment.

Hearing a knock at the door, I raced downstairs to find my builder standing on the doorstep with masses of paperwork under his arm. We ate leftovers and drank a little wine; dusk had fallen before he had patiently agreed to my numerous alterations.

The landline phone rang as he was leaving, an officious male voice announced himself as an officer from Northumbrian Police. He asked if I would be at home the following day, as he would like to question me with regard to Simone's ludicrous accusation that I had stolen her diamonds from Roxberg Gate. It was five o clock in the afternoon, feeling depleted, short of temper and just a little tipsy from having finished off half a bottle of wine and the shared remains of a two-day-old fish pie with my builder.

'You are too late, one of your chaps has already searched my house and found nothing because there is nothing to find,' I said angrily then hung up.

When the phone rang again and displayed the same number, my first instinct was to ignore it.

'Hello, Inez speaking,' I said tersely.

'I think we were cut off,' said the policeman apologetically.

'No, I cut you off.' This man is infuriating.

'But, madam, no one from this department has visited or interviewed you,' he replied testily.

'Then who searched my house yesterday?' my voice trailed to a whisper.

'We cannot say, madam, I will visit you myself the day after tomorrow, until then goodbye.'

That evening Gaston and Giselle FaceTimed, we talked until our phone batteries had run low. Giselle, full of self-preoccupation, seemed to have forgotten about Guido, but unfortunately for me, Gaston had not.

He texted me the following day saying we had something to discuss, however it was not an urgent matter and could wait until we met later that week, apparently he had an appointment with a potential client in my area and asked if he might stay with me for a couple of nights.

This indeed was welcome news, Gaston's sound advice had over the past 10 years become an invaluable asset, hearing his humorous forthright opinions mattered to me a great deal, *but not his interference!*

Two days later the policeman from Northumberland stood at my door, a bespectacled putty-faced middle-aged man, shabbily dressed and reeking of cigarette smoke.

'Madame Roxberg?' he enquired, his transparent pale eyes seemed distant and unfocused.

He produced a soiled identification card and stood waiting while I peered through the stained plastic coating. His greasy hair was of an indescribable fawn colour and in my opinion, worn too long down his collar for a policeman. The aroma of an old cigarette left too long in an ashtray combined with a powerful scent of cheap aftershave, completed his nauseating toilette.

A threadbare burgundy scarf hid the collar of his ill-fitting tweed jacket, which appeared to have enjoyed a long and arduous life, and his nails were bitten to the quick. With great reluctance, I invited this English scarecrow into my home.

'Where would you like to start?' I barked at him.

His defeated expression told me he was in need of sustenance. Ushering him into the sitting room, I felt obliged to offer him a drink, he mistook my meaning and asked for a glass of white wine.

'Have you eaten today?' I enquired sharply.

'No just coffee, the buffet car was out of action, it has been rather a long journey.'

He looked around the room his eyes coming to rest on the clock with a pearl face. 'Nice bit of workmanship that,' he said examining the case closely.

My heartbeat quickened as he went down on all fours to further examine the engravings, finding him a sharp-eyed detective instead of a pathetic excuse for a man was very disappointing. I must remain vigilant as appearances can be deceptive.

'Would you care to stay to lunch?' I asked condescendingly, knowing he would accept. 'Meanwhile, you can conduct your search, you will find me downstairs in the kitchen when you have finished.'

He gave me a stern look of exasperation. 'Madame Roxberg, I have come here to interview you, not search your home; in any event, I do not have the requisite search warrant. As you are aware, Miss Du Val has made a serious accusation against you and we are obliged to hear your version of events.'

My growing sense of unease escalated as I prepared a lunch of ripe cheeses, pâté, a few olives and a newly baked loaf.

We ate sitting at the kitchen table, finding his pedestrian conversation rather tedious led me to think absentmindedly of Guido. After devouring his lunch and drinking another glass of wine, my patience began to fail. Finally, and in an effort to control my impatience, I broached the subject of my alleged iniquities, he looked at me in surprise.

'Oh, didn't I tell you? Miss du Val has dropped all charges. I have just received a text to say the diamonds have been located.'

Colour rose in my face. I had not checked the secret drawer since Guido's abrupt departure just a few days earlier. Struggling to keep my composure, I attempted to act normally in order to be rid of this man, who had duped me into providing him with lunch.

'Tell me, where were they found?' I asked breathlessly.

'In the chapel, just as you said.' His knowing smile told me that he suspected my deceit.

'How many stones were found? Have they been counted?'

'Does it matter now the investigation is over?' His searching look so unnerved me that he couldn't fail to notice my obvious discomfort.

He stood up, shook my hand, and thanked me for my hospitality, then went in search of his coat. At the door he turned to look at me.

'Why did you ask how many stones had been found? Your question suggests the stones had been divided, then secreted in more than one place.'

'Just curious, nothing more,' I lied.

No sooner the door was shut and with my heart thudding in my chest, I raced upstairs to the clock sparkling in the early afternoon sun. Easing the case from its position in the alcove, I pulled the brass lever releasing the secret drawer.

I found to my profound relief the diamonds had not been stolen. Night had fallen when finally I had completed my task and finished counting the precious stones. Had Guido discovered them and taken only a handful, it would have been extremely difficult to ascertain the quantity as foolishly I had no idea of the original number.

While counting the diamonds, many questions and very few answers presented themselves. Searching the chapel had been my suggestion; do they still suspect me of leaving a paltry number of gems to divert their attention from the main hoard, or had Henry himself divided them for some other purpose? And furthermore, who was the man claiming to be a policeman, who had searched the house two days earlier.

Guido received my good news without enthusiasm, Allesio had already told him about the insignificant amount of diamonds concealed in the chapel. Apparently, Simone was proving difficult as usual, in refusing to accept Guido's legitimate claim to at least some of them.

As the direction of blame had been laid squarely at my door, any unconvincing denials would be dismissed as false and nothing I could say or do would convince them to the contrary. Damn them all, enough was fast becoming too much. Henry had of his own volition bequeathed his diamonds to me, and I will keep them whatever the consequences.

Next morning my inbox contained the astonishing news, that Guido had contacted Gaston and arranged to meet in Villefranche within the next few days.

Marvellous, now I would be able to rely on Gaston to remedy the situation. But what of Guido? The man is a forger, would Gaston allow him to continue his illegal trade unhindered or would he expose him as a charlatan?

The thought of seeing Guido again so soon made my pulses quicken, his luscious lips, classical features and overtly formal manner intrigued me, he had aroused my curiosity, and now I felt an overwhelming desire to view and judge his abilities as a fellow artist, perhaps my curiosity will tempt me to visit his studio in Venice.

My earlier panic at having been interrogated by the seemingly complacent police officer had now subsided and with it the imminent danger of arrest. My response to any type of crisis is to immerse myself in scented bubbles, chocolate in one hand and a glass of wine in the other, followed by a peaceful evening on the window seat notebook in hand.

Next morning at seven am, the familiar calls of the sea birds around the harbour mingled with the hammering and banging coming from next door. My natural instinct would have been to rush in and help supervise the work, getting in the way and making myself a dreadful nuisance, instead of which, I inserted my earpieces and listened to the radio, with the firm intention of inspecting the day's progress each evening after the builders had left for the day.

The regular six asanas of my daily yoga practice had suffered in the weeks since moving house, at times my whole body ached from the strain of moving furniture from room to room in the hope of achieving a position that was both practical and decorative.

The new owner of my previous home at Honfleur had also bought most of my furniture, leaving me with hardly any with which to furnish the school. My search for unusual antiques would often take me along the coast, to markets on the Italian Riviera or Nice in search of suitable pieces.

When checking my emails later that evening, I was pleasantly surprised to find three responses for the position of housekeeper. The first an early retired army chef from England, who had travelled widely searching the world for exciting opportunities. The other two applicants were young females from the local area, this I found disconcerting as there would be a distinct probability of them circulating gossip around the neighbourhood.

Interviews were arranged at Gaston's convenience; he could make himself useful as my advisor in assessing the applicants' merits and disadvantages. The thought of a male housekeeper rather amused me, I began to imagine him as a submissive wearing a toga, but then perhaps not, considering his age and given the fact his role here would be to cook for the students, not me.

The next few days were spent in peaceful creativity, domesticity in all its many boring forms had been abandoned in preference for restaurant meals and the company of my new friends and neighbours. I painted my bedroom walls with figurative scenes from Greek mythology, the new lustrous soft furnishings purchased in Paris further accentuated an over contrived and somewhat pretentious atmosphere of otherworldliness, it was great fun and I loved it.

The following day my vastly amusing son-in-law arrived by car, he was impatient to meet Guido alone to talk over a business proposition without Giselle's continual interference, fortunately she was otherwise engaged in Menton, leaving him free to follow his own business pursuits for a few days.

When Giselle became pregnant, Gaston imagined her uncertain temperament would mellow into calm serenity, however to his disappointment the exact opposite occurred as her firecracker tendencies became ever more frequent and explosive.

Seemingly, young Flora was the only person within their household to have a sedative influence on her. Gaston referred to her as our sweet little Fleur. Giselle's pregnancy had been difficult from the outset, and while her daily bouts of morning sickness had lessened in severity, she bitterly resented the physical and emotional restrictions placed on her by complaining endlessly about the damage suffered to her career during 'the sprog hiatus' as she termed it.

Giselle had told me of her intention to return to the gallery soon as possible after the birth, leaving the child in the care of Flora, whom she considered a far more suitable choice of mother figure than herself.

Flora had proved herself extremely capable and trustworthy for one so young, she possessed a soft and gentle nature, which had been clearly demonstrated in her adoption and assiduous care of 'Thing' her little stray dog.

'Flora is the maternal type,' Giselle would often be heard to say, 'she will love caring for our baby boy.' A son for

Gaston, an only son as I will never subject myself to childbearing again,' she remarked adamantly.

During the course of my previous conversations with Gaston, his casual references to Flora had become more frequent, he spoke of her in such glowing terms and of his growing dependency on her to maintain Giselle's equilibrium.

Gaston and I enjoyed each other's company enormously, indulging ourselves in long walks, visits to cosy cafés, drinking coffee or hot chocolate. His knowledge of Villefranche and the surrounding district was far greater than mine, he escorted me to towns, villages and beautiful beaches, all of which would have taken me months to discover.

As a child, Gaston, having neither siblings nor friends of his own age, was invariably left in the care of elderly relatives or disinterested neighbours, while his parents pursued their own interests in Paris. When Giselle first introduced him to me, I felt a bond had been forged between us. We shared the same love of art, inventive cuisine peppered with foreign travel and long beach walks, he soon became the son I had longed for.

My concern that history might repeat itself was very real inasmuch as the Roxbergs, on the whole, took a distinct lack of interest in their offspring.

As her pregnancy progressed, Giselle relied on Flora to equip and organise the nursery, even the colour of the décor was to be Flora's choice. Any interference on my part would not have been well received in either camp, so I will worry alone and in silence.

One evening at the end of a particularly long walk, the sky purple with storm clouds, the air tasting of angostura bitters, my thoughts turned to the welcome pot of beef in red wine cooking in the range. *I must not forget to add oysters and chopped parsley,* I told myself.

We were almost home when a neighbour's door opened, she called out to us, eyeing Gaston speculatively. For the sake of propriety and to quell any salacious gossip, we accepted her kind invitation to join her for early evening drinks and canapés. Introducing Gaston as my son-in-law was met with furtive smirks and downcast smiles from the other guests.

Her home was furnished in the old French style of dark brocades and old lace, two elderly ginger cats perched on the arms of her chair, like tigers protecting their young. A complete bore of a man attempted to engage me in a conversation about local history, however my ear kept being drawn back to Gaston who was busy holding forth on his favourite subjects of painting, beaches and the countryside around his home at Menton. He was delighted at receiving so much attention from the ladies, who were fluttering around him like butterflies. We had not yet eaten a substantial meal that day and the drinks had been mixed with no thought to sobriety.

As the evening wore on, impertinent questions about our private family life became increasingly intrusive and ultimately the hot topic of the evening. To my profound relief, he refrained from announcing to the throng that he was meeting a former art forger associate of my late husband, who was due to arrive in Villefranche the following day.

Occasionally, I have the impression that Gaston revels in our family's indiscretions, as his own parents had led such conventionally dull lives and would be hardly worth a mention.

When we eventually arrived home, Gaston asked if he could look at the diamonds once more, the sitting room was chilly, and my only thoughts were of making supper. Glancing at the kitchen clock, I considered it was too late in the evening to light a fire.

'Be my guest, you will find the lever on the left-hand side,' I called as he disappeared up the stairs.

I had recently encased the diamonds in red velvet drawstring bags, enabling them to be transported easily should the need arise.

'Incidentally, why didn't Giselle join us this time, have you argued?' I called from the kitchen.

'Not at all, she has an old university friend staying for a few days, who is an absolute pain, so I escaped to find more convivial company.' He smiled.

'Creep, does everyone fall for your line of flattery.'

He gave me a coy look. 'Usually,' he replied, opening a bottle of rouge.

Over supper, Gaston explained that Guido had contacted him with a view to sell the remaining few paintings commissioned by Henry, prior to his death.

'I have been looking forward to meeting this rogue artist, he probably has a few fake Picassos to unload on some unsuspecting art lover with more money than knowledge. Rather an overconfident guy, don't you think? Who is to say I won't inform the authorities about his trickery?' he said thoughtfully sipping his wine.

'Gaston, there is something you need to know.' Taking a deep breath, I launched into my confession. 'Guido visited me quite unexpectedly just a short time ago and stayed the night.' A surprised smile played about his lips.

'You can think again, young man,' I retorted hotly. 'He slept in the guest suite and left without saying goodbye, furthermore close inspection of the house after his departure revealed a slight disturbance to every room, except my bedroom,' I answered truthfully.

'Well, Inez, what could he have been searching for?'

'Now, Gaston, do stop joking and listen carefully.'

I then proceeded to recount the conversation between Guido and myself regarding the diamond mine and Simone's reluctance to recognise his claim to a share in the gems, found in the chapel at Roxberg Gate. Also, the visits from two policemen, one of whom informed me that Simone had dropped all accusations against me as the gems had been found.

By this time Gaston had sobered up and was looking very concerned.

'If Guido suspects you of having more than your fair share, you could be in great danger. Please, Inez, let me remove them to a place of safety for your own sake. I have made a few discreet enquiries of my own before agreeing to meet him, however my investigations into his business affairs drew a complete blank. His residency in Venice is legitimate, he owns a large property not far from the Grand Canal, as a professional artist he lives completely under the radar, no one in the art world has ever heard of him. He may have bugged your house before leaving, you should not have allowed him to stay, anything could have happened,' he cautioned.

'Well I can assure you it didn't.' He was unconvinced by my firm reply.

'Are you attracted to him?' He saw me flush.

'Inez, you must beware, he is by his own admission a criminal. Giselle would be appalled at the prospect of having him for a stepfather.'

'Gaston, please, I hardly know the man, can we just drop the subject for now?'

'Fine, OK, but I will check the house for bugs tomorrow before leaving for Menton.'

It was getting late, Gaston said he would read for a while before heading for bed. Yet another man in my house with his own agenda. Prior to retiring, I checked my emails. Guido had sent an invitation to dine out next evening, by way of thanks for giving him a bed for the night on his previous visit.

Next morning, Gaston had risen early as usual and had just returned from a run as I was making an espresso.

'The dawn was fantastic, you should have seen it, marbled crimson more like a sunset.' He took out his phone to show me the picture.

'What time are you meeting, Guido?' I asked, ignoring his comments about beautiful dawns and sunsets.

'Oh, one o'clock at his hotel, how shall I recognise him?' he asked.

'No difficulties there, as I will be joining you.'

'No, Inez, you can join us for coffee, I will text you when we're finished.'

'You most definitely will not, I am coming with you.'

Gaston stood at the coffee machine with his back to me, suddenly he turned and saw my smile.

'OK, Inez, you win, you can act as witness to his proposals.'

After breakfast, we went our separate ways until just before one o'clock. Having already decided to throw caution through the window, I chose to dress to impress. My long, red-gold curls were left loose in a casual style that complemented a close-fitting, pale green cashmere dress and slinky suede boots the colour of autumn leaves.

'You are out to impress your favourite forger,' said Gaston whistling under his breath as I descended the stairs.

'Such nonsense,' I retorted, but of course he was right, as usual.

Guido had booked into a hotel just a short distance from my house. Gaston, having recently drunk two espressos, was fizzing with wicked humour and couldn't wait to meet a member of the criminal classes.

'Your family have provided me with unrivalled entertainment over the past year and I have a feeling another performance is about to begin,' he remarked gleefully. Conversely, I had the distinct impression this meeting of two volatile art lovers would feel like holding the reins of two stallions tethered to a go-cart.

On entering the restaurant, we saw Guido sitting in a bay window facing the sea, sipping mineral water and concentrating on his tablet. As we walked towards him, the harsh afternoon light fell directly onto his delicately lined face, making him look older than the picture of him etched in my memory. He stood up to greet us, my eyes fell upon the stylish cut of his navy cashmere suit and white linen shirt. Gaston received only a cursory glance, as his attention was entirely focused on me.

A fleeting smile crossed Guido's lips, his penetrating gaze bought a flame of colour to my face, at that moment my heart surrendered. Unfortunately for me, Gaston saw it too.

'We meet at last,' said Guido firmly shaking Gaston's hand. 'Henry always spoke very well of you.' At this, Gaston snorted with laughter.

'Regretfully, I am unable to return the sentiment, now all of that unsavoury business is in the past we can all move on. Tell us something of yourself and of your plans for the future,' said Gaston making himself comfortable.

Guido took my coat then courteously stood behind my chair until I was settled, much to Gaston's amusement. As Guido slid in beside me, he accidentally brushed my leg with his, a current of pure lust passed through me. I looked away to hide my embarrassment, just then the waiter arrived with our menus, my hunger had dissipated, leaving me feeling nervous and in need of a steadying glass of rouge.

When our food orders had been taken and the waiter had disappeared, Gaston launched into a well-rehearsed dialogue, sounding like a priest delivering a crushing sermon on the seven deadly sins.

'Guido, I will be happy to look at your paintings, however you must understand the arrangement you had with Henry can never become the one you may have in the future with me. Furthermore, I would appreciate your discretion when contacting my family, as quite frankly we consider you a worthless villain and entirely untrustworthy.' Gaston beamed at Guido whose faintly amused nonchalance at hearing Gaston's insults would surely have provoked violence under different circumstances.

'Enough said. What are you having to drink?' said Gaston amiably.

My face was a mixture of horror and mirth throughout Gaston's tirade. He never failed to successfully sum up awkward situations or to escape any verbal backlashes from the people on the receiving end of his wrath. I waited breathless while Guido absorbed Gaston's damming character assassination, he took it rather well, in fact he appeared slightly bored.

'Gaston, your pompous entry level attempts at pathetic sarcasm are childish at best and offensive at worst,' replied Guido evenly.

*Deuce.*

When our seafood casserole and crusty bread appeared, my hunger returned with a vengeance. I ate, while they discussed subjects ranging from the state of the art market to world politics, then heaven forbid, religion as they are both practising Catholics.

'Guido Faconi, shame on you, do you go to confession and tell the priest of your artistic deceptions,' I said playfully.

'The priest admires my work, he is well rewarded for his silence,' he answered blithely, opening his tablet to show us a small selection of his work.

Guido's astonishingly fine portraits of fifteenth-century nobles wearing fine costumes and semi-nudes, both male and female, were so impressive that Gaston agreed to take 12 paintings, providing Guido added his signature to the canvases. We talked of my plans for the school and of my intention to focus time and attention on its success.

'If you need an assistant, let me know,' said Guido smiling.

'Thank you, I am capable of organising my own nudes.'

'So I hear,' said Guido smoothly.

Guido will never let me forget that he thinks he knows everything about me. A bottle of wine or two led us through lunch, then on into the afternoon. He went on to elaborate about the arrangements for Allesio and Simone's nuptials.

'She has invited me to be her sponsor, I am certain Henry would have approved of her choice,' said Guido taking my hand in his and ignoring Gaston's look of surprised embarrassment.

'Inez, you must attend the wedding, Henry would have wanted you to be present, the poor girl has neither parent to support her.'

'Poor girl, such nonsense, she has Roxberg Gate, the diamonds, and the man she loves, what more could she wish for?'

'Do I detect a note of jealously?' he said inquiringly.

'Naturally you will stay with me, I will be your guide and show you a side to Venice that is unknown to tourists and one that only residents are allowed to enjoy.' His voice and manner were that of a consummate seducer.

He continued to elaborate on the cultural virtues of his home city in the most persuasive of terms, offering to obtain tickets for concerts and masked balls of my choice, all this made me feel very tempted to accept his generous offer.

Our easy discourse was maintained throughout the afternoon. Gaston wore a speculative expression, powerless to prevent a closer association between Guido and myself, he sat quietly listening to our conversation with an increasing awareness of the growing mutual attraction between Guido and myself.

Then suddenly with an air of sullen finality, he stood abruptly, announcing he was leaving immediately as Giselle would be fretting at his long absence.

'Gaston, we have interviews arranged for tomorrow,' I said, aghast.

'Cancel them or see these people yourself, you obviously don't need my help,' he said glaring at Guido.

As we left the restaurant, Guido offered Gaston his hand in a formal gesture of reconciliation, which Gaston rudely ignored and walked off saying he would call me later. After thanking Guido for lunch and apologising for Gaston's shocking lack of good manners, I ran to catch up with my impossible son-in-law and found him loitering on my doorstep, waiting to vent his considerable spleen.

'I think it's time for me to leave,' he said, then rounded on me fiercely. 'Inez, you are deluding yourself if you think he wants you for yourself.'

Gaston's grandiose overstatement sounded so ridiculous, I couldn't help laughing in his face.

'You sound like my father. Do you want a cognac to settle your ego?' I asked tauntingly.

'Don't be stupid, anyone can see Guido is a crook, he is only interested in your wealth, don't you see that? Maybe you lied to me, maybe you already have been intimate with him.'

My fingers twitched in fury, this time he had said too much.

'I would like to slap your face for that remark,' I retorted hotly. 'Gaston, what right have you to interfere in my affairs, when at times you yourself are a grade one, first-class, sanctimonious hypocrite; it's fine for you to consort with criminals, fine for you to do exactly as you please, your arrogance takes my breath, from now on it will be me and only me who decides what or who is important to me.'

No grudging apologies were offered on either side, too many truths had been voiced in anger.

'Now go if you wish, give Giselle my love and ask her to FaceTime me tomorrow please.'

His look of suppressed hurt and anger wounded me, but I was not prepared to offer him an apology. Simmering with rage, I stood until the car had hurtled away down the harbour and out of sight. Hearing footsteps behind me, I had no need to turn my head as Guido's arm slid sinuously around my waist. He had heard most of our heated argument and seen Gaston's hasty departure.

'Now we know from whom Giselle inherited her volatile temper, presumably the argument was about me?' enquired Guido as he took my hand.

'Just a difference of opinion,' I said briskly.

'That doesn't answer my question but then this is a family quarrel and I must not intrude,' he said placatingly. 'Are you going to invite me in for tea or something a little stronger?' His silky tones caressed my ears.

'We are meeting at your hotel for dinner remember, you emailed an invitation.'

'Indeed, however you didn't reply.' A rueful smile rippled around his lips.

'Until tonight,' I said firmly and turned to go indoors to fetch a warmer coat and hat, hoping a walk would bring clarity to the many disturbing questions spinning inside my head.

My argument with Gaston had upset me more than I cared to admit, he had simply tried to warn me about becoming too close to a morally bankrupt man like Guido Faconi. I will need to play this astute rogue carefully, he knows the truth I felt certain of that, Allesio would have told him the whole story of how Honoré met her death.

After an hour, I turned for home, a stiff breeze had whipped the sea into a frenzy of white-tipped waves and drops of rain had begun to fall. Hurrying indoors, feeling revived by the sea air, I went to the office to check for emails. The two female applicants for the position of housekeeper had agreed to revised appointments. The only other applicant, Alex Forbes, had not yet responded. In his original email, he had mentioned the possibility of staying with friends at Saint-Paul-de-Vence and would be temporarily offline due to their intermittent wi-fi.

Alex answered my phone call immediately, I explained there had been a problem and that his interview had been postponed until the following week, we arranged a mutually convenient date and time, then he abruptly rang off.

# Chapter Six

Guido arrived at seven pm as arranged, we set off to his hotel situated in a quaint side street leading up from the harbour. The rain had ceased, although the pavements were still wet and shining. We paused to look at the stars, was this the beginning of a magical evening? Sitting close together, I noticed his clothes had an aroma of some indefinable scent, reminiscent of the holy incense used at mass.

Having eaten only a few hours earlier, I ordered the cheese soufflé, while he delicately toyed with oyster linguine, seemingly neither of us had an appetite, except for each other's company.

We mused about our childhoods, which in many ways differed very little, his parents were successful in business, but not as parents due to their long absences abroad, leaving Guido and Allesio to run wild and remain practically uneducated.

'Our servants were left to oversee our education, which amounted to nothing more than reading and writing. Allesio and I would take a boat and escape to one of the islands on the lagoon, we were renegade boys searching for a mother's love.' His eyes took on a misty wistful expression that tugged at my heartstrings.

When I suggested coffee and dessert at home, his eyes immediately lost their far-off look and lit like stars in the night sky, perhaps he mistook my innocent suggestion for something more, he took my hand in his.

'Inez, my love, we both know we will soon become lovers, I see passion in your eyes and in your body language, the depths of my passion for you is tearing me apart, you are constantly in my thoughts.'

He looked at me across the table his black eyes glittering dangerously.

'Guido, contrary to your opinion, I am not a woman of easy virtue, a mere dalliance will not do, you have already admitted to being a criminal, my trust must be earned and your true motives made clear. We have made promises, give me proof of what happened to Honoré and you will have me and my wealth.'

*I will use his greed to trap him, will he protect his brother or expose Simone as a murderer?*

Walking back to the house, Guido seemed preoccupied, lost in thoughts which I couldn't bear to imagine. As he carried a tray with coffee, tiny pots of chocolate mousse and a bottle of chartreuse to the sitting room, I put a match to fire and closed the curtains, this picture of domestic bliss was not to last!

We sat on opposite sofas and prepared for a little verbal fencing, his potent masculinity emanated from every pore, I could hardly trust myself to remain in the room without inwardly squirming with desire.

'You appear to enjoy a convivial relationship with Gaston,' he said as we finished our desserts.

'He is the son I never had.'

Guido laughed. 'You are not old enough to be his mother, perhaps you are more than friends, perhaps you are lovers,' he said, raising his eyebrows expectantly. 'Your daughter is absent, it is not unknown, the ancient Greeks considered such a relationship commonplace.'

Now it was my turn to laugh as I was neither astonished nor insulted by his insinuation as it had been inferred many times in various guises.

'Guido, you and I do not share similar standards of honour, I could no more betray my daughter than sever my throat with a knife. However, I must confess that if Gaston were not my son-in-law, we would have definitely indulged in the relationship you so eloquently describe.' Guido made a sad face.

'Yes, he has warned me off by threatening to expose my dubious business dealings in order to prevent us becoming close, I assumed he was protecting his territory,' he said, still unconvinced.

'Guido, your moral compass needs a little readjustment.'

'I was rather hoping you might offer a little help in that department,' he replied seductively.

Ignoring his remark, I encouraged him to plumb the depths of his artistic endeavours and preferences and also, where his work sat in relation to the current fashion in France for natural landscapes and modernist art. He looked away to carefully consider his answer.

'Inez, my love, put quite simply my tastes and preferences belong to the Venetian renaissance period, a period when our iconic city was the centre of world trade, where merchants selling exotic spices, silks and velvets led decadent lives, commissioning paintings of their wives and mistresses in order to flaunt their wealth.' He paused; his eyes glazed with lust.

'I am a creature of the past, my greatest wish is that you will consent to join me in my world,' he said quietly.

This beautiful libertine has much to hide, such a pity and such a waste. As the hours lengthened and the fire blazed, my resistance to him began to melt. His languid manner and accented dulcet tone of voice assaulted my senses and fascinated my mind.

*Does nothing disturb his composure?*

Guido stood up to pour another cognac for us both, then sat beside me.

His narcotic scent assailed me, making my head feel light as if floating above my shoulders. I felt myself being slowly lifted by hands as light and soft as down.

I yearned to feel transported to my vision of perfect love, to pleasures of the flesh that were as yet unknown to me. He carried me to my bed and slowly removed my sweat-soaked garments. Taking slips of vividly coloured silk and a bottle of liquid from his jacket pocket, he proceeded to anoint my naked body with oil of spikenard.

His rhythmic, featherlight movements gradually induced a sensation of drowning in my own intense pleasure, like a floating sacrifice on the altar of his lust. Life stood still as I became his willing captive, my surreal existence did not extend beyond the edges of my sumptuous bed, my body became compliant and eager, his to coax, incite or dissipate at will.

My ability to move without his permission became lost to me, so entranced by his ministrations; a languorous lethargy of complete surrender seeped into my mind, dominating my focus, diverting my power to him that controlled it.

A sweet potion passed my eager lips, later when partial reality beckoned, I heard unfamiliar sounds and voices coming from a distant part of the house. I tried to move and found myself bound and secured to the bed by the very same slips of perfumed silk used earlier to arouse my passions.

With my awareness and clarity of mind still impaired by the residual effects of his scent, I sought evidence of a union between us and found none.

I am inviolate, and now, out of necessity, I had become his creature. Later when consciousness returned, I saw Guido sitting on the bedroom window seat staring beyond the harbour to the sea. When he turned and saw me watching him, he came to me with such a delicate look of humility that tears formed in my eyes, he stroked my brow as he spoke, his eyes never leaving mine.

'You are happy to be my captive?' He raised a questioning eyebrow.

'Yes, forever,' I lied.

Without hesitation, this falsehood slipped from my lips, his smile became my victory. He believes my every word; this man is easily duped. He sat on the edge of the bed and held my hand to his lips.

'Inez, last night you asked me why I had not married, so I will tell you once more, from our first meeting, my unwavering love for you has prevented me from forming serious attachments to other women.'

Then his tender expression hardened, the glitter in his eyes melted like snow in the sun. 'First Henry now Gaston, his threat to expose me will separate us once again unless you come to me in Venice.' He spoke with a frightening urgency.

He stood and turned towards the door, a sigh escaping his lips, his face merging into the semi-darkness of the room. I watched as his shadowy figure disappeared downstairs and realised my burgeoning lust for him was purely physical, as I could never bring myself to love or trust a man such as he.

My head ached slightly, falling back against the pillows, my thoughts returned to Gaston's threat. He must not be allowed to interfere, or we would never discover the events surrounding Honoré's so-called accident. Just then my phone rang, it was Giselle asking if it was convenient to FaceTime, as I had completely forgotten my promise to call her.

'Gaston told me your news, has Guido gone yet?' she asked accusingly.

'No not yet, we still have much to discuss, he had known your father since childhood, and I would like to learn more of his early life.'

'Mother, have you been intimate with Guido? I won't tell Gaston.'

'Darling, you ask too many questions, my private life is precisely that... private. The builders next door are making such an unholy noise, let me call you later.'

'Fine, don't forget, and don't consort with that man.'

'Giselle, it is of vital importance that you say nothing to Gaston of my association with Guido, or you will risk jeopardising my plan, now promise.'

'Yes, fine, just call me later.' A click and she was gone.

Guido appeared after some 20 minutes with a pot of strong coffee and slices of toasted chocolate brioche. We sat in completive silence while eating our breakfasts, me languishing in bed and Guido taut as a bowstring on the window seat.

In a corner of the room stood an ornate dark blue marble fireplace, which had the pristine appearance of little use, fortunately my builder had had the foresight to have all of the chimneys in the house swept prior to my moving in. Guido carried firelighters, twigs and logs in the hope of setting a blaze, the gesture and his assiduous charm was quite unlike that of any man known to me, with the exception of Gaston.

As the flames danced before our eyes, we talked endlessly of the past, and for my part, I was grateful to unburden myself to someone who held a deep understanding of my early life, having met both my parents and had the dubious advantage of lifelong friendship with Henry.

Unlike Guido, my life after leaving Henry had been filled with laughter, creativity and family pleasures with Gaston and Giselle both in my former home at Honfleur and at their home at Café Villande at Menton, while Guido had lived the life of a grandiose semi-recluse, regretting every fake picture he had ever painted and every half-hearted failed relationship he had attempted.

He was tired of life, portraiture and the ever-constant fear of arrest. He wanted to paint land and seascapes with me by his side. How could I tell him his hopes were futile, my very real fear of his reaction to my schemes would result in violence or murder.

'We could rent a house on Capri and paint together,' he enthused.

'I have my school to organise,' I protested. 'My love of teaching others self-expression through art is worthwhile and extremely rewarding,' I counter-enthused.

'Mmm, I can clearly remember the reports of your pleasures from Henry's spies, my jealousy knew no bounds in those days. I once asked Henry's permission to become one of your students in the hope of seducing you, but he flatly refused,' he said wickedly.

'Do you realise,' I said interrupting him, 'if we had married, Henry and Margo might still be alive today.'

He took my face in his hands.

'My faithful darling,' he said tenderly, 'Margo had been falling over a cliff of insanity for years. Henry knew of her illness; he just didn't know how to resolve the problem short of killing her.' My blood ran cold at hearing his words.

'Did you think him capable of murder?' He looked away.

'We are all capable of murder given the right circumstances,' he answered gravely.

'When do you intend to leave?' I asked anxiously.

'I would like to say never,' he said, tickling my nose. 'Unfortunately, I do have legitimate commissions to complete, also Allesio and Simone are staying with me next week to finalise their wedding plans.'

On hearing Simone's name, my heart sank. How could I countenance the women who had caused so much dissent within my family? Guido read my pained expression and took me in his arms.

'Inez, forget a past you can never change, move on, there is no alternative if you seek happiness,' he said compassionately.

As the dawn rose, he prepared to leave the house, as we kissed goodbye, I caught his sleeve.

'Remember, we have a bargain, if you love me you will keep your promise then I will pay what Henry owed you.'

'Is that it?' he said sadly. 'Is that all we mean to each other, a bargain?'

'For the present, yes, you can hardly expect me to fall at your feet in gratitude after so short an acquaintance.'

'You disappoint me, Inez, I mistook your kindness for something deeper.' He nodded respectfully.

'Until we meet in Venice.' Guido walked away, out of my life without a backward glance.

# Chapter Seven

Later the following evening, when the builders had left for the day, I ventured into my new schoolhouse. The transformation in so short a time was nothing less than a miracle. A new kitchen had been fitted, the old scullery was now a capacious boot room with an adjacent lavatory, each of the four bedrooms had their own en-suite, and new heating and electrical systems had been installed. Now I could begin placing advertisements in the locality for adult students hoping to expand their artistic repertoire.

At bedtime after being faced with an unappetising supper of chilled salmon and a two-day-old mixed salad, I opted for a bar of chocolate and a large glass of rouge on my bedroom window seat, planning the next moves for both Guido and the school of art. Of the well-written responses received for the position as housekeeper, there still remained only three with relevant qualifications, and as Gaston had let me down by departing in a huff, I would have to interview them alone and without the benefit of his sound judgment.

After emailing my apologies to all three applicants for the delayed interviews, I reconfirmed their appointments then promptly fell asleep. My dreams soon descended into the recurring nightmare of running panic-stricken from an unknown figure chasing me through dark unlit passages, where damp green mould covered the walls leaving stains on my nightdress, rancid shallow water covered my feet, undeterred I continued searching this strange place for my lost diamonds.

Waking with a start, breathless with relief at finding myself safe in my own bed, a feeling of trepidation and an inexplicable urge to look at the diamonds overcame me. Bleary eyed and anxious, I hurried downstairs to the sitting room.

The clock felt feather light and moved easily in my grasp, my fingers chilled with cold searched for the lever to the secret drawer, a prickle of dread crawled over my skin as blood pounded in my ears. I pulled the lever and held my breath as the secret drawer opened, revealing an empty space where Henry's diamonds had been.

For a moment, time stood still, my limbs froze, and spears of panic clenched my stomach, rendering me sick with fear and misery. A veil of red mist floated over my eyes as perspiration coated my brow, I gasped for breath in order to control my anger, and at that moment my feelings for Guido left me like a soul leaving the dead.

Gaston had warned me to keep my distance, if only I had listened to his advice.

Guido is a devil, he duped me in order to steal the diamonds he considers are rightfully his. How could I now claim ownership of them when no authority knew of their existence, notwithstanding their lack of provenance.

My feelings of anguish were soon replaced by anger and an overwhelming desire for revenge. Brimming with nervous energy, I paced the floor in search of a plan, my mind a vortex of unconnected words. I rehearsed a cutting accusatory speech, to be delivered when Guido's searing betrayal of me had dissipated. But then, how could I accuse him of stealing the diamonds when I had denied all knowledge of them, let alone having them in my possession. Then it would be my turn to admit I had lied and deceived him from the outset, my high ground principles would be cast down to mirror his.

But what if I am mistaken and someone else had stolen the diamonds? Not only would I lose Henry's legacy, but possibly my only chance of finding Honoré's murderer. Steeling myself for battle, I logged into FaceTime.

Guido answered immediately, he looked and sounded lighthearted, there was no trace of evasiveness in his eyes or manner. He made polite conversational enquiries about the progress of the school and asked permission to visit me when he had finished his current commissions, any references to Allesio and Simone's visit were carefully avoided.

He walked phone in hand around his large south-facing studio, which benefited from full height windows allowing maximum light penetration. He showed me his paintings and unusual furniture, revelling in my admiration of his palatial home.

'I will make a workspace for you here in my studio, we can paint together in peaceful harmony away from prying eyes,' he said with false sincerity.

Strange though. Why return to me if he already had my diamonds in his possession? There would be nothing to gain by alerting him to my suspicions or by accusing the cheating liar of grand theft, as this would simply alienate him completely.

The builders progress in the schoolhouse moved at pace. As each tradesman completed his work and departed, I would spend hours deliberating on the next stage of the conversion, much to the irritation of the build manager, who covertly resented any suggestions other than his own. Admittedly, his project management was second to none, even so my input and concise instructions regarding the placement of permanent fixtures and fittings would not only save time but minimise potential mistakes, therefore the need for my involvement was constant and demanding.

All that remained was for me to purchase household items such as cutlery, crockery, cooking utensils and bedclothes, as the shutters, blinds and floor coverings had already arrived and were stored in the well-insulated cellar.

Two days later in the afternoon, Guido returned unexpectedly while Giselle and I were chatting on FaceTime. As I opened the door, she caught sight of him on my screen, and after a few moments of embarrassed silence, Gaston who had heard Giselle's gasp, grabbed the phone and told me to shut the door in Guido's face. I pressed the end call button then switched off. Minutes later, Guido's phone rang, Gaston could be overheard ordering Guido to leave my house immediately, issuing a rant of threats in such terms and language unbecoming to him and embarrassing for me to hear.

'Not the most auspicious welcome,' said Guido lightly kissing the top of my head. 'That son-in-law of yours should mind his own business if he knows what's good for him,' he continued absentmindedly.

I felt Guido's casual dismissal of Gaston's threats were for my benefit, although he did look rather shaken. Within the hour, our conversation was interrupted by a loud knocking on the front door. Two gendarmes stood there impatiently flashing their identification cards and a warrant for Guido's arrest, they stepped into the hall without invitation and demanded to see Guido; saying they had received vital information regarding his alleged fraudulent activities.

Guido had gone to the bathroom, so in an effort to aid his escape, I kept them talking with weak protestations of feigned outrage at their unwelcome intrusion.

'What is happening here?' I demanded indignantly. 'How dare you burst into my home unannounced.'

'Madame, we believe Guido Faconi is staying here, we have orders to bring him in for questioning, this man has been accused of many crimes, now please I must ask you to tell us where he is, or be arrested yourself for obstructing our enquiries.'

The horror of Guido's predicament stole over me like a creeping shroud of fear. I needed him to find Honoré's killer, which would prove impossible if he were imprisoned. Gaston had seen Guido on my tablet screen as I opened the door, drawn his own conclusions then kept his promise to expose Guido to the authorities if he ever contacted me again.

Guido on hearing the commotion in the hall, sauntered downstairs with the stealth of a cat, his face a study in nonchalance.

'Good afternoon, gentleman,' he said imperiously, surveying them with a degree of hauteur, which was completely lost on the gendarmes. The senior of the two men came forward, his penetrating stare boring into Guido's defiant black eyes.

'You are Guido Faconi,' said the gendarmes moving forward.

'I am he; how can I assist you?' said Guido without any trace of apprehension.

'We are here to escort you to the gendarmerie for questioning with regard to a complaint we have received regarding your fraudulent activities.'

'As you wish, please lead on.' He gestured towards the door.

The look he threw in my direction spoke volumes, no doubt he regretted ever having sought me out. I stood watching as they handed Guido into an unmarked car and wondered if my neighbours had seen or heard this disastrous turn of events.

In the space of 24 hours, my life had become unbearably complicated, now it was Gaston's turn to become the recipient of *my* mountainous wrath, that snitch of a son-in-law had ruined everything, and now I will make him pay for his iniquity. Had Henry lived he would have taken his revenge as I will, with a cold heart calculated to wound the one man in whom I had placed my trust.

Picking up the phone, my simmering rage at boiling point, I FaceTimed Gaston. He answered immediately, the triumphant broad grin on his face left me in no doubt he was still revelling in Guido's arrest. The sight of his gloating face on my screen sickened me beyond words, his inflated ego and manner of speech revolted me to my core.

'You do realise, Inez, had I not had the foresight to take your diamonds into my safekeeping, Guido could have stolen the lot. You were so obviously in thrall to him; you would have done anything to please him.'

*A flush of relief came over me. Guido is innocent, my diamonds are safe.*

Looking at him intently on my screen, I ordered Giselle to leave the room and close the door behind her, as my conversation with Gaston would not be suitable for her ears. Once again, a red mist clouded my vision, but this time my intense anger had reached a crescendo akin to hate. My breaths became laboured and difficult to control such was my animosity towards him.

'Sit down and don't interrupt me,' I ordered scathingly.

'My dear Gaston, since your marriage to my daughter, I have treated you as a son, however your recent unwelcome interference in my life has irrevocably changed my feeling towards you.' He attempted to intervene, but I was having none of it.

'You *will* return here tomorrow before noon with my diamonds, you *will* also accompany me to the gendarmerie and withdraw your spurious accusations regarding Guido's activities, which incidentally are none of your business. Should you fail to comply with my wishes, I will disinherit Giselle and leave my considerable fortune to your unborn son or some nameless charity. Please understand me when I say this is no idle threat, you have overstepped the threshold of my patience, your intrusion into my affairs must cease immediately.'

Ashen-faced, Gaston attempted to apologise but I had had enough of him, reaching for my tablet and pressing the off switch imbued me with a curious feeling of liberation. No one would ever be allowed to interfere in my life again, not even my family.

Looking down, I saw my hands were covered in tension scratches, spots of blood began oozing onto my clothes. Rushing to the bathroom to search for a first-aid kit, I almost tripped over Guido's overnight bag, which he had forgotten to take with him in the confusion. No doubt the bag was packed full of essentials, so I decided to deliver the bag to the gendarmerie in person, hoping to hear if Guido had been charged and more importantly would he be allowed to leave.

The gauzy amber daylight was fading as I walked out along the harbour, a biting north wind stung my cheeks and tugged at my coat. The leather bag was heavy, which necessitated several pauses to catch my breath. Striding purposefully towards the gendarmerie, I noticed a crowd of people leaving and wondered if visiting time was over and my journey wasted. Finding this was the case, I pleaded with the officer on the front desk to relax the rules and was rudely refused.

'Rules are rules, Madame Roxberg,' the desk officer confirmed.

'Return tomorrow at the correct time and you will be admitted,' said the officious officer. I left the bag and departed in a foul temper.

Walking home, I pushed any defeatist thoughts from my mind by resolving to remedy Guido's situation in his favour. Turning onto the harbour, my eyes caught the bright lights of a café run by a local family who served deliciously rustic food, the scent of which made my mouth salivate in anticipation of a tasty meal.

On entering, the welcoming warmth of their petite dining room enveloped me like a blanket, an attentive waiter came forward with bread, olives and a half carafe of rouge from their set menu. I accepted his recommendation of the pork escalopes in mustard and caramelised onion sauce.

The owner's children arrived home from school, throwing their coats in all directions and demanding a high tea of kitchen leftovers. In the hour that followed, I sat watching the family eat together and catch up with the day's news.

I missed Honoré's gentle stoic nature and the way she tempered Giselle's violent outbursts, two sisters could not have differed more and now after time, as Honoré's loss had become less acute, my only chance of discovering the truth surrounding her death was slipping away. There must be a way of ensuring Guido's release, thus enabling me to attend Simone's wedding. I had decided to employ any method of entrapment to expose Honoré's killer.

After yet another turbulent white night of ruined sleep, Gaston appeared shortly after breakfast carrying a small suitcase and wearing a facial expression that could beat eggs at a glance. On entering the house, he asked what had happened to my hands as they were covered in plasters.

'During our heated exchange yesterday, I pressed my nails so far into my palms they bled, had you been present at the time, the wounds would have been inflicted on your neck and, Gaston, just imagine this scenario. If I had alerted the gendarmerie about my missing diamonds, you might also be held custody right now for theft, of course the difference is that you really *are* a thief.' He moved towards me intending to give me a hug.

'We really are very sorry—'

I stopped him mid-sentence. 'Gaston, leave my daughter out of this, you alone are the architect of this mess so beware my patience is waning, now go and restore my diamonds to their rightful place. You can buy me lunch, then later you will accompany me to the gendarmerie, where you will retract your accusations, citing incorrect information as the reason, then we will both offer Guido our sincere apologies.'

'I would rather choke on the diamonds than apologise to that snake,' said Gaston, swallowing hard.

'Nevertheless, Gaston, revenge, as they say in England, is definitely a dish best served cold, and I intend to serve you an enormous portion.'

'So tell me, does Guido know you have the diamonds?'

'You idiot, of course he doesn't, and furthermore he will never know from me.'

Throughout our delectable lunch of lobster linguini, followed by individual orange and cardamom custards, washed down with ice-cold Chablis, Gaston employed every implement in his extensive toolbox of charm and persuasion to resurrect our previously cordial relationship. We indulged ourselves with coffee laced with a strong measure of cognac, to fortify ourselves for the approaching ordeal of facing Guido.

'Time to go, Gaston, prepare yourself and don't let yourself down again.'

Leaving the restaurant, we joined the throngs of Christmas shoppers in their frantic quest to overstock with food and gifts in preparation for the following week of festivities. Children, faces pink with excitement, ran amok and became detached from their parents, then shrieked in terror when realising they were lost.

The outdoor decorations, both official and those of the residents, were being tossed and tugged by a mild but restless southerly breeze, damp salty air formed droplets of moisture on my hat and coat as we strode purposefully battling the elements.

'Let's get this over with as quickly as possible,' said Gaston grudgingly.

As we walked, I smiled quietly to myself at his obvious discomfort at having to recant his statement and face the possibility of being charged with wasting police time. On entering the station, a powerful sanitary smell of disinfectant greeted us at the door. Holding a scarf over my nose, we went straight to the welcome desk where an officer sat perusing a pile of untidy paperwork. Looking up as we entered, his sharp eyes scrutinised us as we waited for him to speak.

'Good afternoon, Madame Roxberg, you are prompt today, who is your companion?' he enquired, staring at Gaston.

Gaston stepped forward to present himself and asked if he might have a word with the officer in private.

'To what purpose?' enquired the officer,

'A private matter; is there somewhere we can talk?' said Gaston sounding impatient.

The officer pointed his finger toward a room at the end of the corridor.

'Will you join us, Inez?' said Gaston stiffly.

'No, thank you,' I replied dismissively.

Declining Gaston's offer to join the pantomime that was to follow, would not only save me from further embarrassment, but my noire sense of humour might have overcome me had I been forced to witness his attempt to weasel out of his earlier statement regarding Guido's alleged misdeeds.

The unheated building was virtually empty and silent, the ill-fitting door to the tiny office where Gaston and the officer sat failed to close properly, which enabled me to overhear Gaston's ludicrous explanations as to why he had mistakenly accused Guido of criminal malpractice. His wheedling voice resembled that of a well-practised confession to a priest.

The officer gave Gaston a severe lecture for wasting police time, threatening to fabricate and charge him with any offence that came to mind should his reprehensible behaviour ever be repeated. He also informed him, that Guido would not be released until his lawyer had applied for bail, as additional evidence had been uncovered during their routine investigations.

Gaston's face was red with mortification as he emerged from the room, he was unaware that I had recorded his humiliating retraction in full on my phone, this would in effect hold him to account for the rest of his life, else be branded a foolish liar.

Unfortunately, the initial damage caused to Guido by Gaston's accusations were fast becoming irreparable as the gendarmerie, their suspicions alerted, had contacted their Venetian counterparts, who in turn had made extensive enquiries regarding Guido's business activities.

The French authorities had also passed their evidence to the Italian police department dealing with fraud and tax evasion, which on closer inspection revealed considerable discrepancies in Guido's tax affairs. Having no legal representation would result in the likelihood of Guido remaining behind bars until after Christmas. On hearing this, I rang my own lawyer asking for immediate assistance, only to be told that he was out of the country and subsequently unavailable, fortunately for Guido a junior member of staff could be made available and would join us within the hour.

We were ordered to wait while Guido was transferred from his cell to the visiting room. He walked in proudly erect, his face pale with exhaustion and my heart went out to him, rushing over and without any embarrassment, I kissed him full on the mouth, thereby revealing to all present the depth of my affection for him.

'Be patient; you will soon be released; a lawyer is on her way.' I tried to sound encouraging, Guido's eyes brightened momentarily.

'Thank you, Inez,' he said with gratitude.

'Incidentally, Gaston has something to say to you,' I said glaring at Gaston.

'Yes.' He hesitated, a pained flush staining his cheeks.

'My apologies, Guido, for now.' Gaston's apology was short, terse and totally devoid of sincerity.

'We will meet sooner than you think,' said Guido, his voice laden with menace.

Gaston shrugged his shoulders and turned away, my fingers itched to slap his petulant face, time was fast running out on my short fuse. When the lawyer appeared at the door, she paused, surveying the scene before her, then sailed towards us arms outstretched like an opera singer about to perform.

She had the formidable appearance of a school matron; her commanding vocal delivery combined the dominant with the amusing. I felt drawn to her aura of power and comedic presence and wondered if indeed she had been an actress.

She took control of the proceedings by politely but firmly asking us to withdraw, thus allowing time to familiarise herself with Guido's case in privacy and without interruption from Gaston or myself.

On reaching the dismal waiting room, which was painted in a revolting lurid green and still smelling of disinfectant, my simmering temper could no longer be contained. Turning on Gaston, I launched into yet another tirade.

'That was the most insincere apology I have ever heard, you really are the limit, perhaps you should leave and return to Menton right now. Giselle needs you, and I most definitely do not.' Unrepentant, he stood up, gathered his dignity and prepared to leave.

'As you wish, Inez, I will wait outside,' he said, unperturbed by my anger.

After 40 long minutes of drumming my nails and pacing the floor, I was invited back into the visiting room where Guido, my lawyer, and a young man sitting with his back to me, sat in close conversation.

Guido stood up as I entered and came forward to thank me for rescuing him, his black eyes glittered in appreciation of my support, my heart soared at the sight of him. He smiled reassuringly and gave me the news that he would be released in a matter of hours pending deportation to Venice.

Then he turned and beckoned the young man, who was staring fixedly at me from the corner of the room. I felt the blood drain from my face, in recognition of the man I had encountered at my hotel in Paris.

'Inez, my love, may I introduce my young brother Allesio, he has journeyed here from England to lend me moral support.'

'We need no introduction as we have already met in Paris,' came my icy response. As I walked towards him, my eyes never left his, but this coward looked away, unable to meet my gaze.

'I have waited many years to make your acquaintance and hear your explanation of how my Honoré met her death on that treacherous mountain, while in your care.' His eyes flickered to Guido as he registered my insinuation.

'An unavoidable tragedy, Madame Roxberg, every day that Simone lives is a reminder of the tragic death of her sister.'

'Step-sister.' My correction was swift and cutting. I met his cowardly downcast look with blazing eyes. 'You are aware that Simone is the daughter of my late husband and his housekeeper, a fact that can never be erased.'

'Nevertheless, she is the daughter who inherited Roxberg Gate, that also is a fact that can never be erased,' he replied calmly.

My loathing of him increased with every second, his downcast serpent eyes and false puppet smile chilled my marrow, how could Simone love this hateful creature.

'Madame Roxberg, you must accept my heartfelt apologies, if it had been in my power to save Honoré on that fateful day, she would be alive today.'

'Not if you played God and chose to save your lover instead of my daughter.' His face froze as he took my meaning.

'Madame, you are accusing me of negligence and murder, when in fact you were guilty of being an absent mother, therefore don't blame me for an accident of which you know less than nothing.'

'May I remind you that Honoré chose to live with her father and Simone, in preference to a more convivial life in France with Giselle and myself, it was her decision entirely which does not excuse your neglect.'

He shifted from one foot to the other clearly unsettled, in another time or place I felt my relentless questioning would eventually have provoked him into revealing more than he would have wished. Allesio shrugged and turned to his brother.

'I will return to Venice immediately and remove your private papers to Roxberg Gate, you have my word the authorities will find nothing, no thanks to Gaston, who I will deal with in my own way and in my own time,' he said quietly, shaking Guido's hand then turned back to me.

He smiled, his false puppet face alight with mischief, stepping closer, he held out his hand in a gesture of reconciliation. My hand automatically slipped into the pocket of my coat. Ignoring my snub, he continued as though our previous conversation had not taken place.

'Simone and I are to be married at the Venice carnival, we would both be honoured if you and your family would join us in our celebrations.'

'Thank you, Allesio, but I think it unwise under current circumstances,' my swift response left him in no doubt that my feelings of animosity toward him would never be altered.

Guido had stood listening helplessly as our heated exchange escalated from whispers to raised voices and gesticulations.

'Inez, please calm yourself,' said Guido placatingly.

'Come with me to Venice, we can discuss this further, our differences can be resolved,' he implored.

'Guido, my school is nearing completion and Christmas is almost here.' Guido gave a sigh of resignation.

'Look, Inez, I fully understand you have pressing commitments but when will we be together?'

'Be patient, Guido, I will see you before the school opens, in the meantime keep a low profile and stay out of trouble.'

'Trouble, I wouldn't be in trouble if your family hadn't interfered in my life.'

Meanwhile, the lawyer watching from a safe distance began huffing and kept impatiently crossing and uncrossing her legs. I needed air, the combination of obnoxious disinfectant, Guido's pleading and Allesio's pathetic excuses were stretching my nerves to breaking point.

A welcoming cool breeze caught in my throat as I stepped from the building, twinkling Christmas lights momentarily blurred my vision. Gaston emerged from the darkness asking what had kept me, seeing my tears, he proffered a handkerchief.

'Inez,' he began gently, 'you seem fatally attracted to this man. While I realise we cannot choose whom we love, it pains me to say that you have once again chosen a villain.'

I was in no mood to be scolded like a naughty schoolgirl and told him so, as we reached the doorstep, I thanked him for returning my diamonds, which was ridiculous as they are my property, then bid him farewell.

'Expect me at Christmas, this year I will visit you and Giselle at Menton, my own well of hospitality has temporarily dried up and I have no inclination to refill it at present.'

'Are you actually asking me to leave?' said Gaston incredulously.

'Yes, Gaston, my opinion of you has lowered somewhat over the past few days, go away and take lessons in humanity, not to mention good manners.'

He looked stunned, my usually indulgent attitude toward him had lately descended into a form of matriarchal censure. Collecting his case from the corner of the hall without a word, he strode dejectedly out into the darkness and was gone, and I was glad to be rid of him, for now.

Heading to the kitchen, I poured myself a large glass of rouge, took a bowl of queen olives from the fridge and FaceTimed Giselle to tell her the whole sordid tale. Simone's wedding was of much more interest to her than my association with Guido.

'Mother, you should attend Simone and Allesio's nuptials,' she urged. 'It's the only way to catch them out, and I want to know more of their past, well and their present activities.'

The very thought of meeting Simone again would certainly bring my ill-concealed dislike of her to the surface and possibly ruin the wedding, however it was worth considering if only to confirm my suspicions about Allesio.

# Chapter Eight

Giselle rang early the following morning to say Gaston had still not arrived home and was not answering his phone, she asked why he had decided to leave at night and in stormy weather when the sensible option would have been to travel the following day. Feelings of guilt flooded over me as I told her of our acrimonious parting.

'Well, Mother,' she said tearfully, 'if he is found dead in a ravine it will be your fault.' She was beyond consolation, and that also was my fault.

Gaston's tendency to sulk had been well documented in letters from his mother to Giselle prior to their marriage, she had over-indulged him as a child by allowing him to do exactly as he pleased and say whatever entered his head, without considering the consequences of his actions.

We agreed to report Gaston's disappearance to the gendarmerie in both Villefranche and Menton. The officer at the front desk, who only yesterday sanctioned my visit to Guido, was now faced with the mysterious disappearance of Guido's accuser.

'Indeed, Madame Roxberg, what interesting friends you have,' he said sarcastically.

I considered his sarcasm unwarranted and tactless in the circumstances, ignoring his obvious lack of interest in my concerns, I attempted to explain that initially we thought Gaston may have interrupted his journey home by simply retreating to a hotel or possibly a secluded beach to heal his wounded ego with only a bottle alcohol for company.

The officer made various notes, then asked me to go home and wait for news.

While walking in the direction of home, feeling guilty and dejected, a sudden thought struck me, why hadn't I thought of this earlier? Making a detour around the house, I saw to my horror Gaston's car parked exactly where he had left it just a few days earlier. I rang Giselle to give her the news about finding Gaston's car.

'I will be with you as soon as possible, Flora will drive me,' she said tearfully, then put the phone down.

After five days of torment spent searching the town, carrying out my own house-to-house enquiries and listening to media bulletins, our anxious waiting period was about to come to an end. On the morning of day five, I answered the door to find a stocky middle-aged man standing there with his sleeves rolled up, looking ready for arduous work. He asked my name and if I *had* a son named Gaston; his use of the past tense sent me into a spiral of apprehension.

'Please come in, what information do you have? Where is he?' I said hopefully.

'My mother found him five days ago, you'd better come and see for yourself,' he replied, stepping aside.

Grabbing my coat, I followed him around the back of the house where Gaston's car was parked.

'There that's where she found him,' he said pointing to an area between Gaston's car and the rubbish bins.

'On the floor, lying in a pool of blood, he'd been stabbed in the back and covered in old newspapers, a note had been pinned to his jacket warning anyone who found him not to tell the gendarmes, or they themselves would be murdered.

We have prided ourselves on being a non-violent community until you moved in,' he said accusingly.

'Where is he now, please take me to him,' I replied testily, feeling stung by his comment.

Just then a petite woman with tightly curled grey hair appeared, she cast furtive glances up and down the wide passageway before asking if I was Gaston's mother.

'Well not his biological mother, he is my son-in-law, please take me to him,' I implored.

'He is asleep and must not be disturbed but come in and I will tell you what happened,' she said kindly. We introduced ourselves and agreed not to stand on ceremony due to having found ourselves in such perilous circumstances. Agnes, a retired nurse, invited me into her cosy sitting room filled with family photographs and mementos of her past sporting achievements.

'Sit down, Inez, and stop worrying; Gaston will recover in time,' she said reassuringly. Then disappeared to make refreshments, she returned after a short time with a tray of coffee and biscuits.

'How long will it take him to recover?' I asked nervously, wishing she would stop fussing with the coffee pot and biscuits. She looked at me over her spectacles, a look of studied preoccupation clouding her soft face as if she was debating with herself how to couch Gaston's dire situation.

'Inez, I must tell you plainly that Gaston has been gravely ill, although there has been a marked improvement in his condition over the past 24 hours, so much so that he now feels ready to leave as you live close by, which will enable me to check on him daily with your permission.'

'Of course, Agnes, we would all be relieved if you would continue to advise us,' I replied gratefully.

She poured the coffee and insisted on me trying her homemade nutmeg and chocolate biscuits, before regaling me with the events of that fateful night when she found Gaston.

'On the night in question, I went out in the late evening with my rubbish, most unusual for me to venture out after dark, but, my dear, how fortunate that I did, because your son would not have survived the night after such a considerable loss of blood. He was semi-delirious with infection from the rusty blade used in the attack and so close to death, the warning note pinned to his jacket prevented me from contacting a hospital or a gendarme. Inez, just imagine my dilemma, how could I move such a well-made young man by myself, so I rang my son who came immediately with a cart, there was so much blood, I feared Gaston would die right there in our arms.

'As luck would have it, I had replenished my first-aid chest that week. Over the past few days, I have been dosing him with out-of-date prescription antibiotics, tending his wound and feeding him small pieces of baguette dipped in homemade chicken broth. He should have been taken to hospital, he should have reported the crime to the gendarmes, my son is very angry at my refusal to disobey the threatening note, but you understand, Inez, I could not ignore the note for my own sake and that of my son and his family. This morning he felt well enough to ring his wife, offering the most bizarre of explanations of being *off his head for days* to excuse his absence, then he asked me to contact you.'

'You are an angel, now may I see him, please,' I said impatiently.

Finding Gaston asleep, we crept out, leaving him undisturbed. Agnes made more coffee then continued to regale me with the finer points of the whole sorry tale. During the first two days following the incident, this sainted women had questioned neither Gaston's identity nor his state of mind, she had calmly continued caring for him, as she had cared for countless other patients in hospital over her 30-year career. She told me that a worrying 48 hours had passed before he became fully conscious and able to speak or stand alone.

'He begged me not to inform the authorities, as his recent involvement with the gendarmes might result in charges of wasting their time, in any event he felt unable in his condition to face more interrogation.'

Just then Gaston appeared, clearly in pain and in no mood for censure.

Agnes informed us that the deep wound near his left shoulder blade had begun to heal, however she was still concerned about the possibility of permanent muscle damage, due to the depth of his wound and advised him to seek medical advice when he eventually reported the incident to the gendarmes.

'How can I tell them?' he scoffed. 'They will lock me up as a time-waster. No, I will get the bastard who did this, and I won't have to look too far to find him,' he said bitterly.

Agnes arranged to visit Gaston daily until she was sure there would be no further complications, as previously agreed. We departed soon after, with Gaston loosely dressed in old pyjamas covered by a long overcoat for his short but painful walk back to my house. I wondered how we could ever repay Agnes's kind fortitude, mere words seemed grossly inadequate however sincere the sentiment.

Over the following two weeks, Giselle and Flora adopted the roles of alternate nursemaids. Agnes visited Gaston every day to supervise our care of him, we followed her precise instructions to the letter, her stoic kindness had touched our hearts we would be forever indebted to her.

Christmas here in Villefranche was a subdued affair, the absence of gifts and festive ornaments meant nothing to us, as Gaston's wellbeing became our only concern. Agnes joined us for lunch as her son had departed south to spend the holidays with his wife's parents.

Our daily lives began to follow the familiar pattern of caring for Gaston between periods of painting, reading or long walks, taking turns to sit with him to deflect negative thoughts and prevent him from brooding about his attacker. One night after dinner I broached the thorny subject of our own safety.

'Speaking personally, I feel rather vulnerable, the authorities have no idea there is a villain at large who may strike again. Gaston, when are you going to report the attack?'

'Inez, this was no random incident. Giselle and I are convinced that Allesio was the perpetrator, in an act of revenge for betraying Guido to the gendarmes. You witnessed his reaction at the gendarmerie, the guy is unhinged, also my wallet was untouched, so you can rule out theft as a motivation,' he said irritably.

Gaston's increasingly dangerous desire to wreak revenge on Allesio had begun to grow in strength and conviction, as the days passed his strength also began to return, but the memory of his close encounter with death had left deep invisible scars in his mind, an all-consuming anger glowed menacingly inside him.

'I will take my revenge, Allesio has miscalculated, he will pay with interest for his murderous attempt on my life.'

'Gaston, cast your mind back and tell us exactly what happened, did you see anything that would help incriminate Allesio,' said Giselle looking anguished.

He sat in silence for a few moments, wrestling with tears of unspent anger.

'I have been through the events of that night, turning them over and over in my mind. The passageway was deserted, he must have been hiding, waiting for me to leave your house, Inez.' He looked at me intently, did I hear a hint of accusation in his voice?

'If you hadn't asked me to leave, this unfortunate incident may have been avoided.' My paper-thin patience snapped at his cruel remark.

'Gaston, in truth, your misfortunes are of your own making, you take it upon yourself to sit judge and jury on matters beyond your understanding and business that is no concern of yours.' Gaston flushed and gave me a look of blatant hostility.

'Stop it please, stop arguing you are all making me ill,' wailed Giselle plaintively.

'I am going for a walk... alone,' she said, heading for the door.

Upsetting Giselle during her pregnancy was unforgivable, the poor girl had been through enough trauma, so in her absence we resolved to cheer up for her benefit.

'Fine for you,' said Gaston pointedly. 'You're not the one with Allesio's brand burned into your back.' I took his point and wished they would all go home and leave me in peace.

My stock of fresh food ebbed and flowed like the tide, constant visits to the market and valuable time spent cooking for three extra people had become a chore. Occasionally, we would eat previously prepared dishes and, horror of all horrors, bread from the freezer! Frozen bread is considered an abomination in France and something no self-respecting French woman would admit to serving, however, as I am Spanish, the rules do not apply in this household. My previously well-stocked wine cellar had also come under attack and was almost empty. That evening at dinner, I made tentative enquiries as to how much longer they intended staying with me.

'For purposes of catering,' I explained lightly.

'I think we just heard a hint,' said Gaston glancing around the table.

'Not at all,' I lied.

'Let us greet the new year together, then I really must turn my attention to the school, we are opening at Easter, and as yet, we have no staff.'

Agnes joined us for dinner most evenings, her vegan food preferences were severely limiting to cater for, she also abstains from drinking alcohol even at celebrations and her sensible conversation invariably contrasted with our riotous jokes and bohemian lifestyles. Nevertheless, over the past few weeks, she had become an essential part of our family group, none of us could imagine life without her.

After dinner, we would take our coffee into the sitting room to relax and watch the firelight reflecting on the clock with a pearl face, or watch the January sea and sky in an ever-changing scene from turbulence to tranquillity. Giselle would sit transfixed, meditating on the clock's pearlescent face.

'Agnes, did you know that our family is cursed?' she said one evening as she caressed the child growing inside her. 'Our child must be shielded from our family's dark secrets,' she whispered theatrically.

My thoughts turned to Giselle's grandmother, Adeline, imprisoned by her cruel husband for 20 lonely years in a high turret inside Roxberg Gate, for her presumed insanity.

Agnes gave Giselle a thoughtful look. 'My dear young woman, you dwell too much in the past, when the future holds a treasure trove of happiness for you and Gaston, happiness is a gift to cherish not a right to squander,' chided Agnes wisely. She had spoken the truth, but for those of us who have either squandered or hidden from true happiness, how do we recognise this the greatest gift of all, when presented with a myriad of tempting choices?

With Giselle and Flora's help and my hospitality, Gaston gradually began to recover his equilibrium and sense of humour. As they prepared to leave, I felt my true worth as a mother had been tested to its limits, by helping them avoid a potentially tragic situation.

# Chapter Nine

The whole week after their departure was spent restoring the house to my usual standard of order and cleanliness, not one meal would be cooked in my pristine kitchen for the time being as I intended to drift aimlessly through the month of January on restaurant meals and a cloud of self-indulgent idleness.

Guido FaceTimed with his annoying news; apparently, he had been ordered to pay thousands of euros and a fine for his evasion offences. The tax authorities in Italy had carried out a forensic investigation and had subsequently placed the blame squarely at the door of his accountants, who had been subverting large portions of Guido's income into their own pockets. In my opinion, any discussions involving personal finance with a potential lover is the ultimate turn off. I thought it curious that not once had he mentioned the diamonds, neither Simone's paltry few that had been discovered in the church at Roxberg Gate or the main hoard, of which he suspected were still in my possession.

If Guido was able to produce clear evidence that he was entitled to part of my hoard, then I would have albeit reluctantly shared some of my diamonds with him. But then he would know that I had deceived him and more importantly, everyone would know that I had riches worth more than my life.

Guido, like ourselves, must have suspected or had prior knowledge of Allesio's past crimes, including the attempt on

Gaston's life. His daily FaceTime calls invariably began with enquiries after Gaston's progress, and on every occasion, I scrutinised his facial expressions and saw no flicker of guilt in his dark eyes or discernible change in his usual easy manner.

On one particular occasion, I casually mentioned Gaston's burning anger and firm intention to find and wreak vengeance on the culprit, then seek retribution by turning him in to the authorities. Hearing this, Guido immediately changed the subject by continuing to persuade me to visit him in Venice.

It had occurred to me that by agreeing to attend the nuptials, I would be better placed to indulge in a little detective work of my own. My faith in human nature desperately wanted to believe that Allesio was not the iniquitous little snake who stabbed Gaston, but for whose sake? My own or the fascinating man who is his elder brother.

# Chapter Ten

My burgeoning school of art had been all but forgotten in the chaos of Christmas and what we now referred to as 'Gaston's situation'.

The weather had turned unusually mild for early February, giving me an ideal opportunity to scratch my gardening itch. Dressed in old jeans and a jersey that wouldn't pass muster at a flea market, I went out into the new kitchen garden at the rear of the schoolhouse to dig the areas intended for herbs and house flowers. That evening while luxuriating in attar of rose-scented water, a cognac and a dish of dark chocolate balanced precariously on the edge of the bathtub, feeling satisfied with my day's toil, I felt myself gradually descending into a drowsy stupor.

Some time later, the cooling water woke me, the room was cloaked in velvet darkness, above my head twinkling stars pierced the heavens with diamond light reminding me to check my own precious diamonds.

Wrapped in a bathrobe and feeling famished, I made my way down to the kitchen in search of a hasty supper. On the hall floor lay an envelope with my name and a message written in bold red ink, stating the letter had been delivered by hand.

My builder's final account perhaps, I thought, putting the envelope in my pocket. Resuming my culinary investigations, well, imagine my disappointment at finding the fridge almost empty apart from vegetables of a questionable age and three eggs. Switching on my music playlist, I opened a small bottle of dry champagne, then turned my attention to making an indulgent dark chocolate and cardamom soufflé. While the soufflé was cooking, I FaceTimed Guido, who was busy rearranging his studio to make space for me.

'We will paint together,' he said, a broad smile of satisfaction for his efforts lifting his beautiful features.

Naturally, he was assuming too much. Evading his remark, I changed the subject by asking if he would face further enquiries into his tax discrepancies.

'No, but my so-called accountant will, he has been charged with theft, the blame has been rightfully laid at his door. Apparently, I am not his only victim; he is by all accounts a practised thief. *If you will forgive the pun.*'

Nothing more was mentioned about the trip to Venice, giving me time to reflect before making a final decision. My curiosity had been aroused, as I had never seen the carnival, and this may be my only opportunity to discover the truth of how Honoré died. The only disadvantage in my opinion was in being forced to witness Simone's farcical marriage to a man my family have accused of stabbing Gaston!

Guido poured himself a glass of wine then watched on screen as I ate my soufflé, wearing the most salacious look I had ever seen on any man.

'You really are the most alluring creature I have ever encountered.' His heightened colour and short breaths told me he needed a little private time, so I said goodnight and switched off, feeling rather pleased that my arrow of female potency had hit Guido's target. There were to be no more dilemmas, Guido was a pawn to my queen, I just needed to make sure the winning hand would always be mine. I took my refilled glass up to the sitting room and gazed at my diamonds.

The night sky could never sparkle more brightly than the gems laid before me, even my warm hands became chilled by their icy brilliance. Returning them to the drawer, I pressed the leaf-shaped lever under the clock and watched as they disappeared from sight, safe for now in my keeping. That night I slept on the window seat and dreamed of Guido's eyes covered by a devil's mask.

At dawn, feeling chilled and hungry, I decided to go for a run, followed by a delicious breakfast at a harbourside cafe. Later, walking home exhausted in the soft morning light, I called into the schoolroom hoping to see if anyone was working and to ascertain if the conversion was nearing completion.

The building echoed to my rattle of the door knocker; all was quiet, so I went indoors to find the key. To my delight, the rooms had been finished to perfection. The architect had described the project as an authentic restoration for residential and commercial use, both he and the builder had more than adequately fulfilled his description to the letter. A new restaurant-style kitchen filled the whole of the lower ground floor, so that in the event of the school failing, I could with permission change the business into a bijou hotel.

Fireplaces of Italian marble, heritage joinery, ornate plaster coving and wall colours from the period in which the house was originally constructed complemented the common rooms. All that remained was the installation of mosaic flooring in the hall, parquet in the ground-floor rooms and hotel grade Berber carpet elsewhere with the exception of bathrooms. Sturdy wooden shutters were fitted to every window in order to secure privacy and provide shade when required.

The architect had suggested a connecting door between the two properties, to be installed in the upper floor of the school for my convenience and to be used as an additional fire escape. The sheer thrill of beginning this new project filled my head with innovative ideas. I had researched and made copious notes about every aspect from the availability of using new technology to the latest artisan paint and printing techniques.

The view of the bay from the top floor was simply stunning, as it appeared to have a wider perspective.

'Lucky students,' I murmured to myself.

Suddenly I was shaken from my reverie by a loud hammering on the front door, running headlong down two flights of stairs, I expected to find the builder or architect waiting on the doorstep. To my surprise, there was a grinning muscular framed man dressed in a long navy overcoat, dark red corduroy trousers and carrying a rucksack leaning on the door frame, smoking a cigarette.

'Inez Roxberg,' he said a wide grin dividing his face in half.

'Madame Roxberg,' I corrected, 'How can I help you?'

'Oh, yes, sorry, you French are so formal,' he replied, grinning from the depths of his verbal hole, smoke billowing from his mouth.

'Being a native of Spain, I really wouldn't know about French formality, so tell me who are you?' I enquired testily.

'My name is Alex Forbes, I posted a letter through your door yesterday, you emailed me regarding the position of housekeeper at Maison des Artistes.'

*Not like any housekeeper of my acquaintance.*

He stepped back to read the sign above the door.

'So this is your new art school.' His grin faded on seeing the empty rooms beyond the open door. 'It doesn't look finished,' he remarked, looking vaguely disappointed.

'Come in see for yourself, but first extinguish your cigarette, we will be a non-smoking establishment,' I emphasised pointedly.

Leaping over the threshold, he bounded upstairs two at a time, strode purposefully around the top floor rooms, leaving me standing in my own hallway rooted to the floor in astonishment.

'Come on, Inez, chop chop,' he said, disappearing into the basement.

'Nice kitchen, I'll be very happy down here,' he called from the basement.

'The successful applicant would no doubt agree with you,' I replied sarcastically.

He raked his fingers through his hair, a habit I deplored in kitchen staff.

'You must have read my CV by now, I emailed it before Christmas,' he said, sounding somewhat miffed.

*What a presumptuous nerve this man has, turning up unannounced and assuming he will be employed without references.*

Ignoring the remark about his CV, I invited him to follow me next door for an impromptu interview or, in his case, a lecture on employer and employee protocol from me. My pressing need for staff persuaded me to consider him, if he passed my rigorous tests, then perhaps he might do, eventually.

'Alex, you will need to tell me all about yourself, the information contained on your CV was scant and may be a complete fiction.'

'Ring my referees they will vouch for me,' he said while opening the kitchen cupboards and drawers.

I launched into my second lecture in the space of half an hour. 'Alex, this is a live-in position, we may take very young and impressionable students, you will be required to demonstrate not only an ability to produce fine cuisine but also a sensible and trustworthy character. Should your application prove successful, you will find good manners and honourable behaviour are prerequisites in my world. Now, I would like you to make breakfast for two persons, using any ingredients you choose from my kitchen stock.'

He hesitated. 'Well, go on, prove yourself,' I said nastily.

'OK, Inez, calm down and stop the schoolmarm act it looks fake.'

Speechless with indignation, I swallowed a cutting retort, made coffee for us both and waited. Alex washed his hands then opened every cupboard and drawer, then inspected the contents of the fridge, freezer and larder.

'Familiarisation,' he said, holding a finger in the air as I watched with growing fascination his deft handling of my kitchen equipment.

The range cooker posed no significant problem, he juiced my fruit, made excellent coffee and perfect eggs Benedict. While cooking, he gave me a short résumé of his career after leaving the armed services, more recently he had managed a small hotel in Lyon. After reading my online job vacancy, he jumped at the chance of working with food in an artistic environment. As a keen portraitist himself, the combination of his two passions had sounded like an irresistible opportunity.

I questioned him on his choice of referees, one of whom was a police officer situated in the north of England. He explained they had both served in the same regiment and had known each other for many years, then changed the subject.

Throughout breakfast, he bombarded me with questions, both personal and professional that I was unable or in turn unwilling to answer.

'Excuse me, Alex, this is your interview, not mine,' I said wearily, bringing his interrogation of me to an end.

Alex then had the temerity to suggest my original plan of opening the school at Easter be moved forward to February.

'Absolutely out of the question,' I said flatly holding my palms up in finality.

'I will be away so, please, no more argument, now that will do for today.' He looked slightly crestfallen.

'Tomorrow you will cook for me again, please be here at 10am prompt.'

'OK, boss, understood,' he said reluctantly.

As I watched him walk away a thought occurred to me, I had told Alex about my proposed absence.

'Decision made; I am going to Venice.'

# Chapter Eleven

Next day, as instructed, Alex hammered on my door at 10am precisely, holding a petite bouquet of seasonal flowers.

'These are for the table, so don't get the wrong idea,' he said, holding the bouquet aloft.

'Glad to hear, and no, I never get the wrong idea, as you put it.' This is not going well, I thought, inviting him in.

'Now, Alex, you know where the kitchen is, the menu and requisite ingredients are on the table, you will serve lunch at one o clock please.'

'Right ho, boss, prepare to be swept off your culinary feet,' he said with a grin.

'I think not,' I replied swiftly.

'I did mean the food, not you,' he said, realising his mistake.

A few minutes later a loud expletive previously unknown to me could be heard, followed by the clatter of cooking pots. Rising early to buy fresh ingredients from the food market for Alex's second and final test, had filled me with renewed enthusiasm to experiment with innovative dishes myself.

The prospect of making progress in the staff department pleased me, albeit staff with a forthright gift of repartee, the kitchen was overflowing with fresh local produce, all waiting for Alex to impress me with his culinary expertise. I had asked Alex to make a cheese soufflé, boeuf bourguignon and a citron tart, all simple French dishes, which any chef worth his reputation would easily accomplish. If he fails to impress me with this menu there is no hope for him.

Closing the door to my study, I rang Alex's first referee, a policeman from the north of England, whose accent was uncannily familiar to me from my early years at Roxberg Gate. More disturbingly, he informed me that not only was he still a serving officer but recognised my name and had detailed knowledge of the ongoing investigation into Henry's criminal activities.

I asked if he had heard of Simone du Val's spurious accusations against me with regard to the diamonds. He confirmed, in confidence, that he had and that the case was now closed.

'Madame Roxberg,' he began sternly. 'Our mutual connection to Alex Forbes is simply a fortunate coincidence, fortunate for you that is, his flippant attitude hides a resourceful and trustworthy character, he will protect both you and your property,' he said stiffly.

'I need a chef not a watchdog,' I replied without humour.

'Nevertheless, Madame, you would be well advised to employ Alex, he is a fine chef and who knows what future misfortunes await any one of us.'

I thought his advice was rather poetic for a policeman. Replacing the phone, my earlier resolve not to interrupt Alex was proving difficult due to a mouth-watering aroma of cooked food that had permeated the whole house. Resisting the temptation to take a quick peek in the kitchen, I found refuge in my favourite spot on the window seat, my thoughts lingered on the police officer's advice, his close friendship with Alex was too great a coincidence to be believed, perhaps they too were conspiring to locate and relieve me of my diamonds.

A dark veil of deceit is surrounding me, webs of hidden agendas and people with selfish motives are invisible, except to my enemies. First Guido and Allesio, especially Allesio, his crime against Gaston must not go unpunished and now Alex and his policeman friend. Are they all conspiring against me, all intent on discovering the whereabouts of my diamonds? They pry into my affairs, search my house without permission, and I have stood by and allowed their interference to continue unchallenged. Well, no longer, now I will become their enemy, use their tactics, mirror their unprincipled modus operandi, then tell them all to go to hell and stay there.

At one pm exactly, Alex called up from the kitchen.

'Lunch is served, Madame.'

To my utter amazement, he had cooked the required dishes to perfection, albeit there was room for improvement in his presentation skills, but equally as important, my kitchen was spotlessly clean.

In my absence and to my amusement, he had changed into chef's whites, complete with hat and knee-skimming dark pink corduroy shorts. He darted around my kitchen with the speed and accuracy required for a busy service. My old pine kitchen table was clothed in a snowy damask cloth, crystal glasses shone spotlessly in the sunlight, the hallmarks on my old silver cutlery which had not been seen for years, were now visible.

Tasting his dishes pen in hand, I made notes as to where improvements were needed. During this silent examination, his face grew pink with embarrassment.

'Don't you like my cooking?' he asked defensively.

'Just a little refinement, to excite our students' palettes, you understand me? Any adverse comments are designed to be constructive not destructive. The robust palettes of your Lyonnaise diners contrast sharply with our own more delicate tastes here in the south, naturally my own recipes will be at your disposal.' He seemed mollified, but not altogether convinced.

'Take my advice, accept our regional differences, this is your opportunity to learn new flavour combinations, forget the past and start experimenting with new culinary experiences.'

'Thanks for the sermon. Can I have a strong drink now please?' His expression resembled that of a scolded schoolboy.

'My sermon, as you so inelegantly put it, has not ended so please pay attention, this enterprise is not a whim to be discarded at will if it proves unsuccessful.'

Moving on to more mundane matters, I explained the full job description, salary and accommodation etc. 'Additional help will be provided by two part-time ladies from the village, who will work on alternate days,' I explained.

'Oh great, I was beginning to think it would be down to just you and me.'

'No, Alex, it will be you and your staff, as my time will be devoted to our students.'

'I'm starting to feel like a manager already,' said Alex brightly.

'Good man. Now we have our first booking to consider, and it's worth remembering that a dim view will be taken if you are caught fraternising with students in their rooms, which also includes mild flirting and flippant personal remarks.' Alex's face was a picture of mock outrage.

'Steady on there, Inez, I never mix business with pleasure, never needed to,' he said cheekily while looking me straight in the eye.

'Right, we understand each other, now let us return to the subject in hand. An art society from northern Italy has booked six children between the ages of 14 and 16 for my first two-day course in watercolours, beginning in early April.'

'Is there anything else? This job is beginning to feel like my old army life,' he said, refilling my glass.

'Well, actually, there is something else, a very important something else, occasionally some of our students may be lacking in less than perfect table manners. Our younger residential students in particular will be required to display, or if not, learn and practice the rudiments of exemplary behaviour. Our daily rhythm of life is ruled by mealtimes, the quality of your dishes will literally serve to further enhance the school's ambience of artistic and culinary endeavour. My efforts to convey a sense of achievement and personal confidence in our students will require your dedicated contribution, as in my absence you will be the purveyor of our reputation. If you feel incapable or unwilling to comply with my standards, then this position is not for you.' He stood to attention saluting me.

'Yes, boss,' he said loudly. The man behaves like an incorrigible adolescent, what am I to do?

'When you have cleared, join me for coffee in the sitting room.' He looked rather pleased with himself as we both knew he would be offered the position. After 20 minutes, he appeared with a tray of coffee and chocolates, poured our coffee then settled down to tell me something of his life, his travels and his parentage.

Alex's father, a single-minded fiercely patriotic Scot, owned a small family-run whisky distillery, situated on a remote island off the north coast of Scotland. While visiting friends in Edinburgh one summer, he was introduced to Alex's mother, an equally fervent French patriot from Lyon. They married in Scotland at Christmas of the same year and Alex was born nine months later. Home-schooled in academic subjects by his mother, a trained linguist whose passion for French cuisine she passed on to her son.

Albeit a true Scot, Alex had spent his childhood years between his homeland and lengthy visits to France, where he holidayed several times a year with various aunts and cousins. Growing up between two cultures had imbued him with a thirst for adventure. At the age of 18, he exchanged the stifling disciplines of academia, for a more adventurous life in the British army, for the next 15 years, he rose through the ranks, fulfilling his ambitions on his own terms.

The day he was ambushed, beaten and left for dead while on secondment abroad, was the day he decided to leave the army to begin a new life.

'I have revelled in civilised vagrancy ever since.' His infectious laugh masked something deeper, something undefinable. Alex's eclectic appearance and unconventional manner gave him an affable charm, which may be a well-contrived smokescreen for mental anguish.

'Where did you live this vagrant existence?' I asked with genuine interest.

His expression changed to one of wistful pathos. 'I have been living as a goatherd under the vast skies of the Andorran mountains, when quite unexpectedly my life became rather complicated.' He hesitated.

'So, you ran away,' I interjected.

'Inez, you wouldn't understand,' he said, raking his hair. 'You have read my CV, sadly all too late one realises there is precious little to show for my selfish life. It's time to get real and start again.'

'Thank you for your honest candour, a quality I wholeheartedly approve of.'

'What about you, how has your life panned out?' he asked companionably.

'Alex, don't ask; you will find out soon enough,' I said, putting my hand up to stop his questioning.

'This seemingly cosy tête-à-tête forms part of your interview, my ultimate trust in you will be a vital part of our business relationship and you still have some way to go to instil my complete confidence in you.' His smoky blue eyes clouded momentarily.

'Shall we agree on a probationary period of six months, to commence on the first of March, during which we can assess our compatibility.'

He looked relieved.

'Great thanks, boss, you won't regret it. I will be staying with my cousins at St-Paul-de-Vence if you need help before then, let me know.'

As Alex stood up to leave, my phone rang. Seeing Guido's image and number, I allowed it to continue unanswered.

'Boyfriend eh, lucky guy,' he said with a chuckle.

'It is customary for employees to have some respect for their employers, by refraining from familiar comments,' I said with a wry smile.

'Don't worry, you'll soon get used to me.' Alex saluted, bid me adieu then departed.

I watched him walk away in the same direction Gaston had taken on that fateful day when he was attacked and wondered uneasily if the house was under surveillance.

Just then my landline phone started ringing. Looking at the caller display and seeing Guido's number filled me with a surge of apprehension, rushing back into the school to escape the incessant ringing of both phones, I found the build manager with two chaps discussing the finer points of their work.

'Ah, Madame Roxberg, we are here to conduct a final heating test before the flooring is fitted later this week,' he informed me with a look of confident satisfaction.

So now I must begin the daunting task of foraging for furniture once again. Why hadn't I put the contents of my previous school at Honfleur into storage thereby saving myself time and money, instead of selling it all with the house? In conclusion, the easiest solution would be to install the entire contents of my adjoining house into the school, then buy new furniture in Venice.

The late afternoon light was fading as we left the school, a light salty mist coated my hair as I walked along the narrow streets lost in thought, pausing in doorways of small restaurants to read their varied menus. Then I saw a familiar face through a window. Seated in the furthest corner of the bar was Alex, his back to me engrossed in a book, with the remains of a meal and a glass of beer in front of him. The busy restaurant was almost full of early diners conversing loudly, which enabled me to enter and secret myself at a corner table for one person, allowing me to observe Alex unnoticed. He looked somewhat older and more serious when alone.

As the waiter took my order, the other diners began to pay their bills and disperse, leaving the restaurant half empty. When the waiter returned with my meagre order of a small cognac and coffee, hearing my voice, Alex turned around.

'Hello, boss, are you stalking me?' he said a wicked smile crossing his lips. The waiter looked away in an effort to hide his amusement at hearing Alex's cheeky retort, then covered his mouth with a menu to hide his laughter.

'Would you care to join me?' I said, ignoring his impudence.

'Thank you,' he said, bringing a chair to my tiny table. 'Are you offering me a drink now or has the interview moved to a different venue?'

*This man is impossibly cheeky.*

Alex's muscular frame filled our small corner of the restaurant. We sat almost elbow to elbow and knee to knee, he finished his beer then ordered another. I found his easy, affable manner relaxing and unpretentious, while he sat regarding me with a look of curious amusement.

'Do you have sporting interests?' I asked conversationally.

'Sure do, fencing and deep-sea diving, although there has not been much opportunity to enjoy either in the past two years. Now your turn,' he said with raised eyebrows.

'Save your curiosity for another occasion, I am in no mood for confessions.' He looked up sharply, thinking he had offended me in some way.

'OK, sorry, you obviously have unresolved issues that are none of my business, but hear this, while I am in your employ, no harm will come to you.'

'Thank you, Alex, you are most kind, but your concern is quite unnecessary.' This seemingly impoverished fool possesses the insightful mind of a gifted artist, a quality that resonates with my own temperament.

We finished our drinks then stepped out into the cool air and fading light of late afternoon. Walking around the harbour, we watched the sea hurling white-tipped waves against the harbour wall, his jovial comments becoming lost on the wind. At my door, he thanked me for his beer.

'See you later and take care,' he said, raising both thumbs in salute.

Hurrying indoors, my mind buzzing with plans for the future, I noticed three missed calls from Guido. While waiting for FaceTime to load, I speculated as to his reaction to me having a male housekeeper.

'My love, you look flushed with excitement,' he said, immediately detecting my mood and asked the reason for my elation. Like a silly schoolgirl, I confessed my relief at finding a suitable housekeeper but avoided any mention of gender.

Guido listened intently to my news, his main objection was of Alex's referee being a serving police officer and wrongly assumed that Alex was a female.

'Guido, why should this concern you? You have nothing to fear from the British police.' His face became tense and uncertain.

'No, Inez, you are wrong, we have everything to fear until the lawyers have sorted out the complexities of Henry's estate. Grant of probate could take months to resolve and who the hell knows what his private documents will reveal, as a former associate, the police may regard me as having been complicit in his nefarious activities.'

He asked if my time-starved life would leave space for him in the coming weeks.

'Guido, my preparations are way behind schedule, we have a booking and must be ready by April, which only leaves me just a few short weeks to complete my tasks.'

'Excellent, then you will need my help,' he replied eagerly.

'Guido, I have all the help required, thank you, perhaps in a couple of weeks when things calm down, I will be able to give you my full attention.'

Looking suspicious, he rang off, leaving me feeling guilty. Had I offended him and damaged our arrangement in the process? He had made a promise to investigate Honoré's death and I will do anything to ensure he keeps it. That night, as my romantic dreams of unrequited love for Guido became the now familiar nightmare of never-ending, dim, airless corridors, leading to austere sumptuously furnished rooms, bereft of their owner's personal belongings, like a museum of lifeless objects to be admired but never touched. My desperate screams went unanswered, as unyielding window shutters resisted my frantic efforts to escape.

I woke in darkness, shaking and bathed in perspiration to the sound of my own screams catching in my throat. Slipping out of bed, I took a glass of fruit juice to my refuge on the sitting room window seat, vivid images seen in my nightmare continued to flicker through my mind like a horror film. Were they reminders of the past, or of some threat yet to befall me, in a house I had never seen?

That morning, I showered and dressed with little enthusiasm for the day ahead, the ordeal of a marathon two-day shopping expedition to buy items for the school left me feeling exhausted before I had even begun. The thought of seeing Giselle again so soon and in more pleasant circumstances uplifted my mood. We had arranged to meet at my hotel, situated close to the opera house in Nice for an early supper and a catch-up chat.

At five pm, a taxi drew up outside the hotel, my beautiful daughter alighted looking fabulous, wearing a winter-white coat and long, vermilion-coloured suede boots. Giselle, now six months pregnant, greeted me with a kiss, slipping her arm through mine she whispered, 'Mother, you sly cat, you look radiant, what is your secret?'

I'm not sure you'll approve; however, I will tell you anyway over dinner. My darling, if anyone looks radiant it is you.' She has settled down now her sickness has gone, I thought gratefully.

We walked to the old market area where numerous excellent restaurants are to be found, once seated we ordered our dishes and a half carafe of rouge for me.

'Well, Mother, I have heard Gaston's version of events since Flora and I left you at Villefranche, perhaps you would care to volunteer yours, however we both agree that Guido and his snake of a brother will forever be persona non grata.' Her quiet vehemence took my breath away.

'Yes, of course, it's understandable given the circumstances, are you and Gaston certain that Allesio was responsible for Gaston's attack?'

'Yes absolutely, it must have been him. Mother, if you are thinking of attending Allesio and Simone's wedding, I would seriously urge you to think again, you will be alone and unprotected in that serpent's nest of violence and intrigue.'

'Giselle, please stop, Guido will be there, so you have no need to worry on my account,' I replied firmly.

'That is exactly what concerns me, your blind trust in that man is misplaced and quite frankly dangerous. Gaston has been making enquiries of his own,' she continued warming to her theme.

'He has discovered to our astonishment, that although Guido complied with the court order to present himself to the Carabinieri on his arrival in Venice, he promptly took himself off to Roxberg Gate two days later. Mother, he is still there with Allesio and Simone, no doubt plotting their next move in order to steal your diamonds.' I was very shocked to hear of this turn of events, Guido had not exactly deceived me regarding his whereabouts, he simply allowed me to assume he was still in Venice.

'Darling, please, let's change the subject, *now* let me tell you all about my new member of staff.' She looked at me in surprise.

'You *are* a sly cat, who is she?'

'I have recently engaged a housekeeper and two part-time domestic staff, enabling me to teach undisturbed by the day to day mundane aspects of running a residential school. The staff will comprise of two ladies from the town and a housekeeper who is an excellent ex-army chef.' I waited for her to assimilate my words.

'Mother, are you telling me you employed a man as housekeeper?' she giggled.

'He was the only applicant with the relevant experience, he is on a mutually agreed six months' probation, he is also a keen artist, so he tells me,' I said in an attempt to sound convincing and deflect the conversation away from Guido. 'You will like him, he is quite the bohemian, dresses like a circus clown and has the behaviours of an adolescent. Gaston will think I have lost my senses employing such an oddity.' Prattling on, I managed to avoid telling her the source of Alex's reference, as any mention of the north of England would send her into a vortex of vitriol against Simone and Allesio.

'But can he cook to your exacting standards?' she asked.

'Oh yes, but equally important he leaves the kitchen in spotless good order.'

'This I must see; when does he start?' she asked eagerly.

'Not until March, giving him ample time to organise himself before our first booking in April.'

When her onslaught of questions had been answered, she turned her attention to Gaston's fixation with his attack.

'Gaston is in danger of becoming a self-obsessed bore,' she said uncharitably. 'He intends to avenge himself, he has a plan but won't tell, thankfully, as I would prefer my pregnancy to continue to full term! He has become more erratic and unpredictable recently. I really shouldn't be telling you all this.' She paused, looking around for eavesdroppers, her expression now worryingly serious.

'Gaston plans to visit Roxberg Gate when Allesio and Simone are away in Venice organising their wedding, he wants to burn the place to the ground.' She held her hands up despairingly. 'Unbeknown to me, he kept a set of keys to the sea gate on the north side of the bay. In the few short weeks since the stabbing, his temperament has changed, my husband has become a stranger, his only goal in life is to avenge his assailant who he firmly believes was Allesio.'

She was clearly concerned about Gaston's state of mind, I felt myself being drawn into their problems, instinct told me to listen without comment or interference.

The following evening, as I drove in darkness along the rugged coast road towards home, my anxiety levels began to rise. The prospect of meeting Guido again after learning of his illicit visit to Roxberg Gate filled me with unreasonable anger, he was not obliged to inform me of his movements, but nonetheless I felt excluded and suspicious.

Salty tears fell into my lap like autumn drizzle as I drove on through the night, tree branches shaped like fan-vaulted cathedral ceilings hid the stars twinkling in the clear night sky. Foxes barked and owls hooted as the night creatures emerged from their daytime lairs. Many lonely hours later, with a car filled to the brim with household goods; I saw to my profound relief the road sign for Villefranche come into view.

After parking my car in the unlit passageway where Gaston's attack took place, my heart beating fast, shivering with cold and fear of anyone lurking, I looked around into the darkness. As I walked along the path to the garden door with only the light from my phone for guidance, I made a mental note to have a security light installed as soon as possible. When safely indoors, I quickly locked and bolted the kitchen door behind me, leaving my purchases in the car until daylight.

The house felt warm and safe after the long journey, my first thought was the clock with the pearl face and the treasure contained within. There it stood in the alcove, glowing like the moon in my starlit sitting room, the hands read twenty minutes to three. Gently easing the lever toward me, the drawer slid forward silently.

My diamond hoard was safe... for now.

'Time to move you to a place of safety,' I murmured into the darkness.

Later that morning, after spending the remainder of the night curled up fully dressed on the window seat, I made arrangements to have a safety deposit box in a local bank. My preference for keeping the diamonds at home appeared now to be somewhat irresponsible, especially as their existence was known to the criminal underworld.

Taking the diamonds from their hiding place and placing them in the light, I selected two pinkish brilliant-cut stones with the intention of having them fashioned into rings for myself and Giselle as a reminder of her father's generosity in entrusting the gems to me. After a hasty breakfast and hearing activity next door, I wrapped a scarf around my shoulders and went to investigate. The school flooring had arrived and was being unloaded from the back of a lorry parked nearby, the build manager waved and walked over.

'Ah, Madame Roxberg, good morning,' he called striding towards me.

'Our job here is almost finished, come and see for yourself.' Of course, he was unaware of my regular night-time progress checks. My pleasure in allowing him to unveil the nearly completed interior of the school building, a project that had given him considerable satisfaction to transform, was his to reveal and mine to congratulate.

Three days later the builder handed me his keys in ceremonial style, a completion party had been arranged for the many artisan craftsmen responsible for breathing new life and purpose into this historic old building, a building that would become a place to develop skills of artistic endeavour for both young and mature students.

Neighbours and friends were introduced to my two female helpers, they toasted each other and wished me every success in hoping the school would bring prosperity and prestige to the town. Champagne flowed as the caterers warmed to their task of keeping our glasses filled and plates full. We all fizzed with laughter and good conversation when suddenly Alex walked into the room, flamboyantly dressed as usual in a mustard coloured jersey, an elderly brown leather bomber jacket and bright red jeans, his tanned face alive with the prospect of enjoying himself.

On receiving his invitation, he had initially thought it too long a journey to make for a party, then evidently had a change of mind. After introductions had been made, he seated himself with his female helpers to discuss their future working lives together and completely ignored me. Hours later as the crowd began to disperse, he sauntered over.

'Great party, boss, perhaps we should throw one every night for the students.'

'Alex, be assured you will be too tired to party, we will all be too tired for anything except our beds.' His smile slipped.

Yours or mine?' he whispered quietly into my ear.

As we were draining the remnants of champagne from each discarded bottle into our glasses, I felt a shiver of tension down my spine. Unbeknown to me, a tall figure, immaculately dressed entirely in black, had entered the room. To my astonishment, Guido stepped between us, turning his back on Alex. Had he been standing watching Alex and myself, inebriated and engaging in a little innocent repartee?

Putting my glass on the table, I threw myself into Guido's arms, he held me tightly and kissed the top of my head. Alex stepped away in surprise, excusing himself, he started clearing the tables.

'No don't leave, allow me to introduce Guido Faconi, a very close friend,' I said, trying not to slur my words.

'Guido, may I introduce Alex, my new housekeeper.'

A few moments of shocked silence were followed by the sound of shattering glass as Alex lost control of the tray he had been holding. Stepping forward, Alex shook hands with Guido and offered him a celebratory drink. Guido thanked him but declined the offer, turning to me he asked if he might have a word in the privacy of my sitting room. One of the staff asked if we would like coffee to be sent up.

'Yes, leave it black and make it strong please,' said Guido glaring at me, as if I had just won the first prize in a drunk of the year competition. On reaching the sitting room, my drunken passion drove me to an attempted seduction, only to be repelled by Guido's insistence that we would not make love until I was capable of a meaningful response.

'You are a cold fish, have fun,' I whispered, sliding my hand up the warm flesh of his back.

'Look, Inez, I have flouted the authorities by coming here, and you have some explaining to do when you've sobered up,' said Guido raising his voice.

Hearing these words placed me firmly on a path to sobriety, and after drinking half a pot of black coffee, reality began to clear my head.

'Has Alex gone? I need to speak to him.' Reaching for my phone, I pressed his number, he answered immediately.

'Alex, there is little point in your returning home today, your rooms are ready so why not stay and begin organising the household.' He agreed, thanked me and hung up. Guido looked a little uneasy.

'I do hope the household will not include you, my love,' he said firmly.

'Guido, I just want to teach and paint, domesticating is for others and having a man around imbues me with a feeling of safety, more especially after Gaston's attack.'

He flinched at my retort, and although my insensitive words had wounded his feelings, they also held grains of truth which could not be denied. Inviting a man into the household had clearly upset Guido, he looked pensive as if searching for a tactful way of expressing his displeasure.

'Personally, I think a relatively youthful male housekeeper may prove wholly unacceptable to parents of younger female students, I would urge you to think again, Inez.'

'Guido,' I whispered in a voice that was barely audible, 'my home will be run as I see fit. Alex is a highly competent chef, it's true his organisational abilities have yet to be tested, however, I feel his help will be invaluable to the future success of the school.' Guido interrupted me.

'How do you know? He may be an imposter, out to rob you of your valuables,' he said coyly, any mention of valuables was guaranteed to send my pulses racing.

'There *are* no valuables kept here, it would be inappropriate to put temptation in the way of my students or any other visitor to the house,' I retorted sharply.

'Alex's reference came from an impeccable police source, even if he were a thief there is nothing of real value here for him to steal and the accounts will be my sole responsibility, furthermore Alex is not your rival, he is simply not my type, his bohemian tastes make me shudder. Now please stop this petty jealousy and take me for a walk to clear my head.'

This unwelcome insight into the deeper layers of Guido's character both alarmed and excited me. His transparent display of jealousy gave me a frisson of power, a power

I intend to maintain. He took me into his arms and gave me a lingering kiss.

'Truce,' he suggested.

'Yes, on condition you stop this pointless jealousy,' I said firmly.

Grabbing our coats, we walked arms linked along the harbour, gusts of bracing sea air captured our breath as we struggled on towards the beach.

'How long will you be staying?' I shouted into the rising wind.

'Two days maximum,' he shouted back.

We walked on, continuing our shouty conversation against a backdrop of leaden skies and the pungent scent of newly grown seaweed, sea-soaked sand squelched under our boots, making our footholds ungainly and difficult, at last as we turned for home, Guido grasped me tightly around the waist.

'Just remember, Inez, that whatever happens in the future, I have always loved you and will go on loving you forever,' he said with feeling.

Hearing these words reduced me to tears, no man had ever declared themselves to me with such raw feeling, and although this beautiful man had undoubtedly made a welcome intrusion into my life, there were still fragments of doubt in my mind as to the authenticity of his motives. Simone will soon become his sister-in-law, together with Allesio they might all be plotting to steal my diamonds.

We called into a bar on the way home and sipped warmed cognacs to revive us. Sitting close together, my head felt light and dizzy with desire, his almond-shaped dark eyes burned into mine as we held hands over the table. In the hearth, a blazing fire sent sparks flying past us, watching the flames seemed to subdue his natural tension and he began to relax, becoming more open and talkative, he told me about his recent lucrative commissions, painting family groups of pompous entrepreneurs wishing to be immortalised for posterity.

I thought it wise not to ask where he had journeyed from as I was in no mood to hear a lie. As the pleasurable warmth from the cognac circulated our bodies, we relaxed by the fireside and spoke at length of our fears and dreams for the future. 'Allesio's move to England has left me feeling lost,' confessed Guido sadly.

'He and Simone intend to live permanently at Roxberg Gate, how can they bear to endure such brutal weather when our family palazzo in Venice is large enough to accommodate them, many of the rooms have not been occupied in years.' He grimaced.

'I hear Roxberg Gate has a history tainted by the evil crimes of its past inhabitants, my brother has an impulsive nature, he does not always think before he acts. I am concerned that his hedonism will lead to trouble if not contained by Simone. His life will change irrevocably when he takes up permanent residence in England, my greatest hope is that Simone will be able to cope with his moods.'

Guido's frank disclosures brought us closer together, I wanted to share his concerns and offer words of reassurance.

'My darling, Allesio's love for Simone will no doubt transcend any reserves he may have about life in England. He has been living in the house throughout the winter, surely he will have acclimatised by now, he is after all a skiing instructor and accustomed to harsh weather.'

'I hope you're right; dry ski slopes are being installed as we speak, apparently Allesio has a syndicate of backers who are all keen to convert the house into a hotel,' he said, looking doubtful.

'Have you visited Allesio in England?' He looked away.

I couldn't help asking, I needed to know if would lie to me.

'Yes, in fact I recommended the companies about to carry out the conversion,' he replied, looking slightly discomforted.

He turned to me his eyes searching mine and asked why I had not inherited Roxberg Gate from Henry. Was he suggesting that I had inherited something of greater value than a crumbling house? He watched as my face flamed with colour, for a few mute unguarded moments of confusion, I was in danger of revealing the truth.

'Guido, you know I inherited a considerable fortune from my parents, perhaps Henry felt it necessary to look after Simone. Like us, he was unaware of her relationship with Allesio at the time of his death.'

'He must have left you something,' Guido enquired cautiously.

'Some memento of his love for you, jewellery perhaps?' Blood coursed through my eardrums, my heart beat so loudly I imagined he could hear it. Turning away in confusion, I dropped my handbag, then made a fuss of retrieving it to avoid his penetrating gaze.

'Yes, he did leave me something.' I paused long enough to gauge his reaction. 'The old long-case clock in the sitting room, it belonged to his grandmother and is more precious to me than wealth.'

*He knows I have the diamonds.*

All the signals were there, he was sure to make a move at some point, his fake protestations of love were simply designed to subdue my suspicions. Well, he can think again if he imagines me as a weak female to be seduced with empty words.

My relief in knowing the diamonds were safely concealed in a deposit box at the bank did much to calm my nerves.

Some of my neighbours had gathered in the bar, they called out inviting us to join them. Guido's wary expression told me of his unwillingness to be sociable.

'We are never alone,' he said in exasperation.

'I enjoy stimulating company,' I said, squeezing between two ladies in order to join their conversation. Guido sat looking bored, his monosyllabic responses were greeted with curious looks; clearly, he was in no mood to socialise with anyone except me. We arrived home late and found a note from Alex on the hall table. After removing the party debris, he had thoughtfully left a bowl of leftovers neatly arranged in my fridge, with another note saying midnight feast to be consumed within 24 hours.

Guido seemed preoccupied, distant and completely out of his depth. On reaching the upper landing, we found the connecting door to the school wide open, snoring as soft as a cat's purr could be heard emanating from the school hallway. We looked at each other, I giggled covering my mouth to stifle more laughter. The emotional storm clouds that had been circling Guido's head all evening exploded in temper, he slammed the door shut with such force the sound reverberated around the building, then turned on me with breathtaking vehemence.

'Why did you employ that joker, it's obvious he is out for what he can get, he will try to joke his way into your bed when my back is turned.'

Now it was my turn to lose my temper. 'Guido, do you think me so stupid as to conduct an affair with a penniless chef, please accept that our arrangement is purely business.'

My anger flowed like molten lava over Guido's head.

'Just remember this is my house, my rules and my staff, so please put away your false jealousy and stop wasting my time with insincere declarations of love.'

Furious at myself for losing control, I stood hands on hips in anticipation of a stinging rejoinder from Guido, when we were interrupted by Alex bleary eyed and wearing nothing more than black boxer shorts!

'Keep the noise down, folks, some of us are trying to get some shut eye, oh and as you're both here, what time would you like breakfast?' he asked innocently. Guido's face turned white and taut as a mask.

'No breakfast for me, thank you. However, I will need to speak with you in private before leaving.' Alex looked at me expectantly.

'Alex, please just go back to bed.' He shrugged and gave Guido a venomous look.

'OK, if *you* say so, Inez. Call me if he gives you any trouble,' he said, walking away.

# Chapter Twelve

Guido took his anger and foul mood to the guest room while I went to my bedroom feeling deprived and miserable. A barrier had been burned in the flames of temper, open warfare had begun, and I was the central figure, everything was all about me. Guido wanted the diamonds, and, in return, I wanted Honoré's murderer. My life had become a chess game of uncertainty, with each player holding pieces relevant to their hidden agendas, waiting for each other to make the first move.

As I came out of the bathroom, I heard the stair treads creak as Guido padded downstairs, minutes later he returned with two large cognacs which he placed on the nightstands. A smile of reconciliation had replaced his earlier scowl of anger as quickly as a cloud passing the sun.

'Must you employ that man? He has already begun to assume command, I fear what will happen when I leave here,' he coaxed.

'Guido, please can we hear no more of this. Alex is an accomplished chef, his organisational skills will be needed to free my time, you know how passionate I am about my work.'

'Talking of passion,' he said smoothly while taking me in his arms.

My cognac tasted of musky rose, or was it something more dangerous? What did I care, this devil will keep me alive until my diamonds are in his possession. My eyes lost their focus as a delicious languor seeped into my mind, the now familiar scent of spikenard oil filled my nostrils, my voice appeared to revolve around the room as I slipped undisturbed into unconsciousness.

Waking early to see a pinkish grey dawn threading soft light through my open shutters, I gazed out on the tranquil sea and wondered what or who had woken me so early. Hearing raised voices coming from the direction of the schoolhouse, I leapt from my bed, stumbled through the connecting door and downstairs into the kitchen where a violent exchange between Alex and Guido, was rapidly descending into an ugly display of testosterone-fuelled aggression. Blood coursed down Guido's face as Alex held him tightly by the throat, pushing him against the wall.

'Stop this madness now,' I screamed. Alex released his grip, pushing Guido towards the door.

'Your boyfriend came down here and started throwing his weight around, he needed a lesson in manners, and I have just given him his first session,' said Alex breathing heavily in an effort to control himself.

'Get out of here,' I cried imperiously, 'return to your quarters. I will deal with you later.' Then Alex rounded on me.

'May I remind you that this *is* my kitchen, and these *are* my quarters,' he said standing his ground.

Guido ignored him and spoke to me. 'Inez, I would seriously suggest you take control of your staff now before more harm is done, or I shall report this idiot to a gendarme.'

Alex scoffed at his remark. 'You wouldn't have the courage, and anyway you're in enough trouble already, so I hear,' sneered Alex.

Guido gave me an accusatory look and wiped his bloodied nose on a tea towel. 'We need to talk in private, get dressed we're getting out of here,' he ordered.

Guido neither spoke nor looked in my direction until we were seated outside a café with a double espresso in front of us.

'Let me speak first without interruption,' I began, staring at the lapel of his coat.

'Your arrogant assumption that I disclosed personal information regarding your background and present difficulties to Alex is wholly incorrect, he most likely received the information via his English policeman friend, so next time – and there will be a next time – you accuse me of anything, do yourself a favour and do your homework first.'

'Let's go inside and have breakfast it's freezing out here,' he said, squeezing my arm.

Guido's mood had miraculously changed from hurt and resentment to one of contrition in the blink of an eye, his capacity for self-control was almost inhuman.

'Once again I feel the need to explain my true feelings for you, because if Alex's insidious erosion of our relationship proves successful, you and I are on a collision course before any permanent relationship can begin.'

Again, he was assuming too much, however I allowed him to continue.

Guido's deeply accented voice made his every word sound convincing, like a travel writer ardently describing the beauty of his native Venice.

'My love, please come to me, I want to show you my secret places, to where my escape from Henry's constant demands for more pictures gave me space and time to recover and reminisce. Henry and his kind have corrupted my sense of honour, I envied everything he had, family life, careless freedom and of course most of all, you. In contrast, my unnatural existence has consisted of selfish indulgence and hard work, with only an exorbitant tax bill to salve my conscience. Henry's distant domination of you ended with his death, your domination of my heart will never end.' He glanced around the room in an effort to find more words to describe his feelings and reconcile the emptiness of his past life.

'Whatever possessed me to overlook my own life in favour of Henry's demands? Well... money, of course,' he conceded ruefully.

'I guess you were beguiled by his charm and eloquent mode of speech, whereas my choice was made for me, paint Henry's pictures or lose my family home.'

He looked into my eyes. Was it compassion or self-pity clouding his dark, troubled eyes?

'Go on, please tell me more, I need to hear the truth,' I coaxed.

'Henry was an accomplished crook, he thought everyone regarded him as a caring landowner, committed to looking after the families living on his estate. In reality the place was crumbling under the weight of serious neglect, he was a fake, his whole life was a sham, both his father and yours knew it.

'When Henry's more wealthy clients were low on funds, they would knowingly substitute my copy of an old master into their art collection, then brazenly hang them on the walls of their expensive villas, passing them off to their family and friends as authentic works of art in order to sell the originals, thereby morally defrauding themselves, the original artist, and their insurance companies.

'When time allowed, I found solace in the company of beautiful women. Like strangers passing through revolving doors, they never lingered long enough to form a permanent relationship, now after years of transitory superficial excitement, even they have begun to bore me. My longing for a new rhythm to shape my life has finally been realised after meeting you again, your infectious enthusiasm for the art school gives me hope for the future. Only this time, I am not prepared to lose you again and especially not to a worthless joker like Alex.'

I had listened and understood the sentiments in his words but cared nothing for them. However, my own concealed indifference to his revelations gave me an unwelcome insight into my own deceitful character, which disturbed me more than I cared to admit.

Guido's revelations about his past confirmed my first impression of him as a man to be feared, my misplaced trust in him had dissolved like a dying sunset. His confession was simply the morbid recollections of a man who had failed from a personal perspective to lead a life of his choosing, he is a parasite seeking a free ride to artificial happiness, he attempts to enrich his own life by becoming dependent on the object of his desire for every enjoyment life has to offer, then blames them if things go wrong.

Despite my feelings of self-disgust at the honey trap set to tempt Guido into betraying Allesio and Simone's murder of Honoré, my physical attraction to him continued to excite me. Arriving home later that evening, after spending the day perusing the town, we saw no sign of Alex and found the connecting door to the school locked.

'Gone off in a huff, I expect; no matter,' I remarked, wondering if the resentment between Alex and Guido had damaged our working relationship.

Gaston remained convinced that any one of my many visitors over the past month could easily have installed surveillance equipment when my back was turned. Before retiring, we checked the weather forecast and made plans to take our sketchbooks and pastels to the Alps Maritimes the following day. Tonight, I will pour my evening cognac and sleep undisturbed in my favourite spot on the sitting room window seat.

Next morning, we rose early and drove out along the narrow roads leading to the majestic snow-capped Alps. A picnic basket, safely stored in the boot of my car, brimmed with a variety of cheeses, pots of organic meat infused in fruit jelly for ease of spreading on fresh baguettes, dark chocolate pots topped with lavender and an obligatory bottle of champagne to complete our al fresco lunch.

The exhilarating crystal-clear mountain air mingled with the heady scent of damp moss; lichen-coated rocks where aconites and windflowers nestled into deep crevices became our artistic subject matter.

Dishevelled and wind-blown, we ate, drank and sketched like children on a carefree day out devoid of parental interference, we made love with words and gestures unsullied by physical desires and untainted by his as yet, undisclosed plan to steal my diamonds. Despite my fears, I felt myself drawn once again by the intriguing nature of this man, his calm, detached manner proved an effective antidote to my own fiery persona.

A burgeoning acceptance of Guido's intense feelings had blossomed inside me during our time together. Had I regained some affection for him or is my affection a mirage and one that will dissipate when he departs for Venice?

Two days became three, then four as Guido showed no signs of leaving until one evening a phone call from Allesio, who had arrived in Venice expecting to find his brother at home and not visiting me at Villefranche, demanded he leave immediately. The wedding was now just three weeks away, a celebratory dinner for a mere 30 guests had been arranged and was to be held in the privacy of their family home.

As Guido prepared to leave so grew my sense of loss. I would miss his courteous protestations of love, be they true or false, his flattering attention and our like-minded interests had forged a rapport between us.

'You are coming to me in Venice,' he said, his hands tightly gripping my shoulders.

'Yes, Guido, but don't expect too much of me where Simone is concerned, our recent intimacy has changed nothing and remember we have an agreement.'

He studied me closely, then looked away before uttering the words I had waited 10 long years to hear.

'I already know the truth of how Honoré died, but, my love, do you know where the diamonds are?' He kissed me so forcibly my lips bled, stepping back he laughed and was gone.

# Chapter Thirteen

I had mentioned to Alex in passing, on the first morning of Guido's visit, that various pieces of furniture from my house would need to be transferred to the school, as our opening deadline was fast approaching and we had very little furniture with which to accommodate the students.

Imagine my surprise, after arriving home with Guido each evening, to find the house contained less furniture than when we had left that morning. Letting myself into the school after Guido's abrupt departure, I was amazed to find the students' bedrooms had the required amount of furniture, complete with bedding and a desk!

On ringing Alex, I heard a ringtone coming from the direction of the garden, there I found him, spade in hand, double digging the entire garden. Alex greeted me with a weak smile and a wave then carried on digging.

'I have already dug the school kitchen garden,' I called out.

'Yes, not deep enough though, I have just re-dug it,' he called back without looking up.

'Where did you acquire such lovely furniture?' I called from the terrace.

'Oh yes, a guy in the pub said he was clearing a house in Antibes, so I helped and bought most of the furniture, didn't cost a great deal. I will give you the paperwork later, assuming lover boy has gone,' he called back, still concentrating his efforts on the task in hand.

'If you mean Guido, yes and no,' I called over.

'Yes, he has gone, and no, he is not my lover.'

'Glad to hear it, that guy is a fake,' he replied stone-faced.

'You hardly know him,' I shouted defensively.

'I know a fake when I see one,' he said with conviction.

'Alex, I can look after myself. Look here, to save me having a sore throat would you join me for dinner, then we can continue our argument in comfort.'

'Fine, thanks, give me a shout when you're ready.' His voice sounded offhand and unlike his usual cheery self.

I hurried indoors out of the mud and squally rain that had begun to dampen my clothes but not my spirits and started to prepare our meal, occasionally lifting my gaze from the chopping board to the window to watch Alex making light work of removing the most invasive of weeds and brambles.

After an hour he disappeared inside, presumably to shower and change for dinner. Calling him just after seven, he appeared carrying a large file overstuffed with papers, wearing black jeans, a crisp white shirt which bore signs of age to both the collar and cuffs, the first three buttons were missing revealing a disconcerting expanse of tanned muscles.

Having laid the dining table in formal style fit for royalty, in honour of his outstanding achievements, I asked him to open a bottle of my best champagne.

'Are we celebrating something?' he asked, eyeing me suspiciously.

'Yes, your salary increase, congratulations!' I crowed, raising my glass.

Alex flushed with appreciation, then looked crestfallen on hearing separate wines were to be served with each course, his contribution would be to choose a wine appropriate for each course.

'Oh, thanks. I imagined a staff kitchen supper, not a banquet contrived to test my qualities as a sommelier,' he said with a wry smile and looking baffled at the array of bottles before him.

We sipped roasted vegetable consommé, followed by sea bream with a dill and citron sauce, accompanied by crisp fondant potatoes and asparagus. My favourite pear and cherry charlotte topped with frangipane cream was an absolute triumph. As we ate, Alex's dread of the wine challenge posed no obstacle to his enjoyment of the meal; of course, he already knew which wines suited each course and the correct temperature at which they should be served. In fact, he left me feeling rather ashamed of having wrongly assumed his unsophisticated manner and mode of dress concealed little knowledge of the finer aspects of life.

My pompous assumptions of him must stop here and now, I told myself as we sat drinking champagne and organising student menus.

'So, boss, are you ready to confide in me?' said Alex as we took our cognacs to the sitting room.

'How long have you got, isn't that the term you English use?'

'All night or as long as it takes.' A serious note had crept into his voice.

I told him everything, my lonely childhood, Henry's resident mistress and his shameful criminal activities.

'While accepting the past can never be changed, you will come to realise that revenge is an intrinsic part of my nature. Honoré deserves justice and with Guido's help, I will ensure justice is served on Allesio and Simone.' My voice broke with emotion.

'You can never be certain they planned Honoré's death; if Guido and his family have conspired in one murder, they won't think twice about arranging your death,' said Alex urgently.

'I have to try, they killed her, I know it, I feel it in here,' I said holding my hand to my breast.

'You must not go to Venice, forget this folly it's just too dangerous.'

'Alex, thank you for your concern, but no harm will come to me while they think I have the diamonds.'

'And do you have them?' He held his breath.

'No.' I was lying, and he knew it.

'OK, Inez, have it your way but let me help. Before you leave, I will conceal surveillance equipment in your belongings, they are tiny, so you won't notice them – and take two phones. Oh, and how long in your estimation will it take for your amateur detective work to prove effective, given you have little knowledge of the language and will be alone in a foreign country?' said Alex with raised eyebrows.

'Now you are laughing at me and sounding like an army man, or a policeman.' He darted me an unreadable look.

As the evening progressed my understanding of Alex's true character evolved, there was nothing I could teach this intuitive ex-army officer, in fact my profound underestimation of him would have constituted insubordination, had I served under him in a professional capacity.

The few days spent with Guido seemed to have erased the real world from my mind. In my absence, Alex had invited his two lady under-housekeepers, as he preferred to describe them, to join him for lunch in the schoolhouse kitchen in order to better acquaint themselves with both himself and their roles within the school. He had built a website and taken images of them all laughing together, posted them online and had received many likes and a few enquiries with regard to the types of courses we intended to offer. At three am we said goodnight and parted as firm allies and co-conspirators.

# Chapter Fourteen

Next day, Giselle rang with alarming news. Apparently, Gaston, who was still thirsting for revenge, had just returned from England having caused havoc at Roxberg Gate, safe in the knowledge that Allesio and Simone would be away in Venice until after their wedding.

'He told me not to say anything as he wanted to tell you himself, he even tried to insist on phone silence if you please,' she wailed. 'Must see your face when Gaston tells you about his escapade, it's unbelievably funny, he will FaceTime you later, bye for now.'

Now it was my turn to worry in silence, Gaston's inventive mind and reckless courage had often given me cause for concern since he married my daughter.

I spent the whole day domesticating in the schoolhouse, Alex had arranged the furniture to no one's advantage and minded not a jot having to rearrange it all again to my liking. My own house looked like a recent burglary had taken place, the last few pieces of furniture and most of my elderly kitchen equipment had all found their way into the school kitchen. A newly installed navy and sky-blue sign swung on its well-oiled hinges above the front door announcing Maison des Artistes.

Alex offered to cook that evening, but I was more interested in what news Gaston had to impart about his adventure in England. It was tempting to allow Alex the pleasure of hearing what I suspected would be an hilarious account of his humiliation of Allesio.

Still undecided, I chose a lone rustic supper of cassoulet at a local café. In all probability, Alex, who had yet to be formally introduced to Gaston, might think him a coward for not facing Allesio in person. Walking home exhausted and happy, I leaned over the harbour wall to watch the waves lap the algae-coated stone steps leading down to a slippery walkway, steps that became treacherous and impassable in winter.

A fine sea fret dampened my hair, the scent of wet seaweed filled my nostrils with its salty scent. This is raw nature, this is real, my students will be taught to appreciate every aspect of these natural changes in light and colour; hopefully, under my tutelage they will feel inspired to express themselves through their art.

My long red-gold curls were dripping with salt water by the time I eventually reached the house. While hanging my wet coat near the range to dry, Alex walked into the kitchen.

'Your phones have been ringing for hours, I could hear them through the wall. Thinking it might be urgent, I went through to answer it and spoke with Gaston, he asked if you would call him when you arrived home.'

'Thanks, perhaps you should listen in, whatever he has done will be cringeworthy and not to be missed,' I said, having undergone a spectacular change of mind about involving Alex in our dramas.

'Fine if you are sure Gaston won't mind,' said Alex warily.

Alex and I settled down with cognacs and chocolate nibs, then waited for the connection to load.

'Inez, where have you been?' said the person on screen.

'Wrong connection,' I said in sheer disbelief, reaching for the off button.

'No, it's me Gaston, I have paid that bastard back for stabbing me,' he said jubilantly waving his arms around.

'What do you think of my disguise?' he said, stepping back, bowing and waving his hat in a triumphant flourish.

'You look like an itinerant sailor,' I said giggling.

'Do pay attention, Inez, this is my impersonation of a rogue pirate,' he said with mock severity.

'Rather good eh, don't you think?' He grinned from ear to ear.

'Gaston, stop dancing around and take that smug look off your face.'

He sat down reached for a glass of Chablis and told us the whole story, including his turbulent flight to Newcastle, which had left him feeling sick on arrival. He had hired a car large enough to sleep in, as staying at the village hotel nearest to Roxberg Gate would have been too risky, as he would undoubtedly have been recognised by the locals as a familiar face seen in the bar on his last visit with Giselle just a few short months ago.

Early the following morning as dawn was breaking, he stole a small boat from the jetty and rowed with a life-size plastic monkey around the headland on an incoming tide, aiming for the spit of a beach which lay on the north side of Roxberg Gate. Fortunately for him, the sea was calm that morning, however his arms were still aching from the effort of defeating the currents.

At this point Alex, who had been listening with an expression of incredulity on his face, choked on his chocolate nibs.

'This guy is unreal, and you're related to him,' he chuckled.

'Only by marriage.' We laughed till our sides ached and waited for the next instalment.

'Pay attention please, you haven't heard the best part yet,' said Gaston on screen after refilling his glass.

Gaston reminded me about a natural inlet through the rocks, leading to a cave under the house, which had for many years been used as a makeshift boathouse, this convenient route was also used to bring stolen goods into the house unseen.

As he rowed into the cave, he saw a red motorboat half covered with a tarpaulin with *Allesio*, written in red lettering clearly visible on her hull. First, he cut the ties holding the tarpaulin, then taking the monkey, he wedged it firmly in the driver's seat and tied the monkey's ankles to the steering wheel.

On their disastrous visit a few months earlier, Gaston had taken the unwise precaution of having door keys copied for future use, if ever the need arose. He had no idea of what to expect on opening the door leading from the wine cellar to the main staircase. The house was ominously silent, there was no sign of life, perhaps the staff were lazing in their beds while their employers were away.

Gaston tiptoed across the great hall, pausing occasionally to listen for any signs of life. Hearing no sound, he crept down into the game kitchen, the freezers were switched off their lids left open like crocodile's jaws. The pantry shelves, where homemade preserves and pickles had been stored, lay bare and unused. Creeping up six steps to a once spotless main kitchen, he saw layers of grime on the work surfaces, the floor was covered in mouse or bat droppings while rusted iron cooking pots hung forlornly on their hooks. A dank smell of decay permeated the whole building, leaving Gaston with feelings of utter disgust; this once noble castle had in a matter of months been reduced to semi-dereliction by its new owner Simone du Val.

Upstairs he found the north wing in a similar state of decay, mullioned bay windows looking out onto treacherous rocks and the sea beyond were now caked in salt. Gaston was appalled by the neglect he found in virtually every room, the building was half empty of furniture and what remained, he would have been too ashamed of donating to charity. The south wing, judging by the detritus of discarded clothes and other personal items, was where Simone and Allesio lived in a state of semi-squalor.

He called out while climbing the steep stone steps to the attic, his words echoing eerily around the tower. Making his way along a windowless hallway, he came to the suite of rooms where Giselle's grandmother, Adeline, the first owner of the clock with a pearl face had been imprisoned for her helpless insanity. The rooms that had been lovingly maintained as a shrine in Henry's lifetime were layered in dust, and now only the resident spiders held the privilege of spinning their webs around the ceiling light and lampshades in this once beautiful room. Gaston took images that he would never have the courage to show Giselle, as her heart would break at the sight of them.

Moving to the bathroom, he hesitated before turning the taps full on, watching in fascination as water gushed over the top of the bath and hand basin. In the south wing, no such hesitation halted his progress as he again turned on every tap in the upper floors, thereby causing maximum damage as the water flowed downwards through the building.

Simone, in Gaston's hearing, had often mentioned her fear of the day a great storm would claim the house and bury it in the sea. Gaston ran downstairs unafraid of the enormity of his crime; the malevolent spectre of this house and its occupants had hovered like the grim reaper over his 10-year marriage to Giselle, but no longer, it ends here and now at his hand.

The tide was against him on the return journey, but eventually after a herculean effort he prevailed, only to see figures on the harbour pontoon shouting to each other about the loss of a boat. He called to them asking for help. When he and the boat were safe and secure, he apologised by saying he had seen a surfer in distress and took the first available boat to rescue him, the fact that he was alone did nothing to confirm their belief in this lame excuse until he lied by saying that he had mistaken a large log for a man as his contact lenses had fallen out!

The two men exchanged sceptical glances, their boat was undamaged; however, they would have viewed Gaston with suspicion as unusually he was wearing a pirate costume over his wetsuit! The men accepted Gaston's generous payment of two hundred pounds for the loan of the boat and his grateful thanks for their help in rescuing him. His journey home was fraught with indecision. Should he confide the whole story of his adventurous misdeeds, thereby making his family complicit and liable for prosecution, or should he tell an abridged version, leaving out the flood, which he was certain would destroy Roxberg Gate forever.

Alex and I looked at each other in amazement, then fell about in uproarious laughter at hearing Gaston's unsound reasoning as to why he felt justified in destroying an ancient monument for the sake of personal revenge.

'Quite a character, your son-in-law, he could be put away for a long time if this gets out,' said Alex officiously.

'Alex, forget you ever heard of Roxberg Gate and concentrate on your career, it is Allesio who needs to be put away, as you term it.' Alex shrugged bid me goodnight, then disappeared into the schoolhouse.

Gaston, I want your opinion of Alex. Can you get away without upsetting Giselle? I will be leaving for Venice next week and need to see you before leaving. Alex has suggested me carrying surveillance equipment, which is too ridiculous to contemplate, please do come soon.'

As January drifted into February, my mood lightened, the weather was unseasonably mild, and the daylight hours had begun to lengthen, giving me more time to prepare the garden for planting on my return from Venice.

Alex had taken to his new career in housekeeping with seemingly effortless ease, his relaxed, unobtrusive presence around the schoolhouse had a calming effect on me, resulting in a gradual change in the dynamics of our working relationship. After having spent time in his company testing recipes, discussing day to day management and house rules, I came to the conclusion that his flamboyant mode of dress and unsophisticated manner concealed a conventional cast-iron character.

Two days after my conversation with Gaston, I arrived home after a day shopping for something suitable to wear at Simone and Allesio's nuptials, to a note left on the kitchen table saying: 'Have abducted your housekeeper, see you later.'

How typical of Gaston to wade into situations without preamble. After an hour had passed, I rang him and received no response, a few minutes later my phone rang.

'Inez we are sitting in your favourite restaurant along the quay, contemplating an early dinner; come and join us.'

I had expected to hold a private conversation with Gaston prior to his introduction to Alex, to warn against his predilection for gossiping about our family's unsavoury past.

'When did you arrive?' I asked, taking my place at their table.

'Just after you left,' he replied brightly.

'I have done as you asked and interrogated your esteemed housekeeper,' he added cheekily, darting a glance in Alex's direction. At this point, Alex shifted in his seat, looking distinctly uncomfortable.

'Gaston, you really are the limit, not to mention being quite drunk,' I replied, trying not to smile.

'Oh, come on, Inez, where is your sense of humour? I have waited all day to tell you more of my escapade at Roxberg Gate, and I guarantee you will both howl.'

We all ordered fish of the day and a bottle of Chablis. When the waiter disappeared, I held my breath as Gaston launched into a lurid account of his misdeeds.

'Of course, it's Allesio's fault entirely, brought it on himself,' said Gaston his face a picture of self-righteous outrage. Once again Gaston's hedonistic actions had jeopardised my plans.

'Does Simone know that her inheritance has crumbled into the North Sea? Because if she does, my visit to Venice will be all the more dangerous as she will no doubt guess who is responsible.'

Alex, who had sat in stunned silence throughout my heated exchange with Gaston, held his hands in the air despairingly. 'Stop this bickering,' he said, clearly annoyed at Gaston's thoughtless act of vandalism. 'Look, mate, I can fully understand why you did this but your timing was out, you should have waited until after the wedding, then with Inez safely home I could have gone with you.' Now it was my turn to be stunned.

'Gone with him! We have a school to run and furthermore one miscreant in the family is quite enough, thank you.'

Gaston's sickly drunken smile told me further remonstrations would prove fruitless, given his condition. 'Hear that?' He grinned at Alex. 'You're family now.'

Later that evening after listening to endless male banter, Alex virtually carried Gaston to bed he was so far gone, tucking him in fully clothed. He shut the door firmly and came downstairs to find me, leaving Gaston comatose and snoring loudly.

I made hot chocolate laced with cassis, we sat in silence for a few minutes collecting our thoughts and opinions in an effort to assimilate the more foolhardy aspects of Gaston's mission to England.

He turned to me a look of concern creasing his brow.

'You shouldn't go to Venice, it's too dangerous, especially now as Gaston has ruined your plan, your lover boy will do anything to get his hands on those diamonds. Sorry, Inez, I am afraid Gaston told me all about the diamonds and that was before he started to drink,' said Alex ruefully. He looked at me fixedly holding my gaze.

'Your wealth doesn't interest me, however your safety does, in fact it interests me a lot,' he said quietly.

His eyes burned with unspoken emotion. Feeling confused not knowing how to respond to his subtle declaration of affection, I thanked him for his concern then reiterated my previous assertion that no harm would befall me while the whereabouts of the diamonds remained a secret.

'Alex, you have an unfounded dislike of Guido, he would never harm me, of that I am sure.' He gave me the pained and restless look of a man with a well of undisclosed secrets of his own, clawing at his lips desperate to escape.

'No, Inez, you are mistaken; the guy is dangerous, and his brother is a psychopath and well-paired to his intended wife by all accounts.'

'Alex, he knows how Honoré met her death, he told me as much. You must understand, I will never find peace until I hear the truth and avenge her death.' Tears welled in my eyes.

'If you think he would condemn his own brother you are naïve at best and foolhardy at worst, he wants your diamonds and he will stop at nothing to get them. I have had him checked out, the guy operates so far under the radar he hardly exists at all, do you really want to live your life in the shadows or laze forever in the sunshine of my affection,' said Alex meaningfully.

'Kind sentiments don't alter the fact that you yourself may not be telling me the whole truth.' He flinched visibly as the words left my lips.

'Tell me, Alex, are *you* genuine or are you just like the others, with their lies and hidden agendas.'

'No, I am not like the others, but I do have issues to resolve and they are confidential matters which cannot be shared,' he said with a determined air of finality.

My face flushed in temper, he leaned forward and dropped a brotherly kiss on my lips.

'Just trust me,' he said firmly, setting two cognac glasses in front of us, the liquid flowed like molten gold from his steady hand.

'You might need a snifter right now,' he said, studying my face for any adverse reaction to his kiss.

'Will you look after everything here in my absence?'

'That's what you're paying me for,' said Alex sighing in irritation at his advice being ignored.

Somewhere between us a line had been crossed from which there was no retreat, now or in the future. We must either restore our business relationship and maintain boundaries of proprietary or part as friends.

That night vivid dreams taunted me as two horned masks floated before my eyes, one a devil with glowing ebony eyes, the other a puckish character holding my diamonds in his hand, throwing them one by one into a pool that became Alex's eyes.

# Chapter Fifteen

By the following afternoon, my few garments made from silk or velvet had been carefully packed in tissue paper to minimise creasing. A much-loved cashmere coat with matching stole and hat will be my only source of warmth for the next two days. Guido had purchased a cloak and mask for me to wear at the wedding ceremony, being held in traditional style on the first day of the carnival.

On hearing Alex's robust singing voice emanating from the schoolhouse garden, I went out to find him making raised beds in which to plant spring flowers and vegetables. Oblivious to my scrutiny, I watched as his strong hands, smeared to the wrists in verdigris, cut damp wood into the required lengths, releasing a woody scent of newly cut timber into the air.

'If you're going to stand there spying on me you might as well make yourself useful. Hand me those nails please.' He stood hands on hips smiling broadly, while I flushed with embarrassment at being caught assessing him, an electric current of undiluted pleasure passed through my fingers, as he took each nail from my grasp.

'You are a happy gardener; how fortunate I am to have a man with such a wealth of expertise in such a wide range of subjects at his fingertips.'

'Have a man.' He snorted with laughter. 'What century are you living in? Yes, indeed I am a very happy gardener when left in peace to finish the job. Incidentally, what time are we leaving for the airport tomorrow?'

'Eleven am or thereabouts, my flight leaves at four in the afternoon.'

He turned his back to me and continued sawing furiously. 'OK, fine, see you in the morning,' he said dismissively.

Feeling rather deflated, I walked off through the gate into my own garden. Alex had turned the soil, added fertiliser and weeded; together we would create a tranquil wildlife haven, somewhere for our students to unwind and meditate. The garden faced north, so a camomile lawn would be out of the question; however, there would be alternative options to explore on my return from Venice.

That night my recurring nightmare returned; satanic masks floated before my eyes chasing me down seemingly endless dark corridors. Once again, I woke to the sound of my own screams, coated in rivulets of perspiration, terrified that my nightmares would become real.

Taking my wrap and a blanket to the sanctuary of the sitting room window seat, I glanced at the clock with a pearl face and wondered for the umpteenth time, if the clock was a bad omen. After a few minutes of deep breathing, my composure began to return. Hearing footsteps on the landing, my panic returned, then Alex called out from the kitchen. 'Just making you a hot drink,' he yelled up the stairs.

A few minutes later he appeared wearing a black tee shirt and boxer shorts, carrying two mugs of hot chocolate. As he handed me a steaming mug, the aroma of cognac filled my aching head.

'May I join you?' he said, his eyes full of concern. 'You don't want to go to Venice.' His statement of fact confirmed my secret fears.

'You're frightened, frightened of what might happen, because when you hear the truth you have been dreading for so long, you will be forced to confront the dilemma of how to avenge your daughter. Of course, I could lock you in the cellar to prevent you running off to meet lover boy,' teased Alex.

I moved over to allow him space to curl up beside me, he opened the top half of the shutters in order to reveal a star-filled sky and the first full moon of the month. He piled several cushions against the bottom shutters then tucked the blanket snugly around us.

'How extensive is your knowledge of the constellations,' I murmured drowsily.

Gently placing my head on his chest, he stroked my temples until I fell asleep, lulled by the rhythm of his breathing.

I woke at daybreak, chilled and alone on the window seat, where just a few hours earlier Alex and I had communed like children in a tree house, looking up into the heavens hoping to spy a unicorn, or perhaps in my case a phoenix would be more appropriate. Looking out to sea, I wondered how many days would pass before I looked upon the familiar scene before me, and how many lives would change irrevocably in Venice.

# Chapter Sixteen

As I prepared for the journey, my thoughts turned to Guido. Had my fascination for him lessened during his absence and would he be less, or more threatening in his home city? These and many other unanswered questions hung suspended in the air like a kite tied to a mountain peak, billowing in a fierce breeze of uncertainty unable to move forward, never progressing beyond the limits of the string that holds it fast. But now the time had come to resolve the painful personal issues preventing me from moving my life forward, now I must find the strength to face the woman suspected of pushing Honoré to her death. Simone du Val, a name soon to be consigned to history by becoming a Faconi wife.

Next morning Alex drove the car round to the front door, I put my luggage in the boot then slipped behind the wheel and started the engine.

'Independent as usual,' he commented wryly.

'I am accustomed to looking after myself, but thank you, driving will occupy my mind,' I replied nervously.

A recent shower of rain had left rivulets of moisture on the car; the trees and bushes lining the roadside were soaked and dripping, their newly formed buds holding the promise of an early spring, migrating birds, having returned early from their winter resting grounds in warmer climes, sang in our ears through the open window.

Driving out onto the busy main roads in the direction of the airport, my mind and focus were in turmoil, the wind from the open window tugged at my hair and stung my eyes. Simone: my only thoughts were of Simone and of her unpredictable reaction when I accused her of murder.

'Crying? Surely not,' said Alex in a failed attempt at levity. Ignoring his remark, I drove on at speed, disregarding the limits.

His offhand manner, so different from that of the previous evening increased the tension between us as my foot depressed the pedal still further.

'Stop this. You're driving like a bloody maniac, pull over and let me drive,' he shouted against the wind.

Breaking suddenly, I lost control of the car and skidded to a halt facing in the opposite direction, just inches from a huge tree.

'You stupid idiot; you could have killed us both,' screamed Alex loudly.

Shaken and trembling, I turned away hiding angry tears. Alex slammed his fists into the dashboard.

'Don't go; feign illness, anything, but don't go, the thought of you being at the mercy of that villain makes my blood boil,' shouted Alex angrily.

'Alex, this is my only chance, I must take it,' I replied resignedly.

We spent the remainder of the journey in reflective silence, at the airport he leaned over and kissed me gently on the forehead.

'Call me twice a day, I will be tracking your every move.'

Thanking him, I headed for departures, determined and unafraid of what the future held.

The flight was on time and uneventful. At Marco Polo airport, Guido stood waiting for my plane to arrive, craning his sunburned neck searching the crowds of carnival-goers leaving the arrivals lounge, their suitcases no doubt laden with sumptuous costumes and warm clothes to cosset themselves against the freezing damp air circling the lagoon and seeping through the canals.

I stood momentarily watching him before waving to catch his eye, he stood apart from the others and was instantly recognisable, being unusually tall for an Italian, he stood head and shoulders above the other passengers standing nearby.

He was formally dressed as usual in a black cashmere suit under a long black overcoat, his crisp white shirt left open at the neck relieved his somewhat sombre appearance, his anxious facial expression served to accentuate the melancholic beauty of his dark features. He appeared younger and less threatening than the man in my memory. Walking towards him, I felt my heart lurch at the sight of him and hated myself for it. This man represented everything I despised in people of his tribe, the untrustworthy, the sly self-seeking individuals who care for nothing except the accumulation of personal wealth.

As he caught sight me, his face lit with relief, a broad smile transforming his features; like lifting the lid of a casket containing long-forgotten heirlooms. Striding purposefully towards me, his smile grew wider, his eyes shone like jet beads in his tanned face, until at last I felt the warmth of his body against mine, clasping my cold, gloved hands to his lips.

'Inez, my love, we have been apart for too long,' he murmured into my chilled palms. 'My people are waiting; everything has been arranged for your comfort,' he said silkily.

We stepped out of the airport and walked towards the waiting car holding hands like lovers, the purpose of my visit remained clear and steadfast in my mind, it did not include love in any guise.

The late afternoon mist rolled in off the lagoon, shrouding the buildings and coating our coats and hair in moisture.

Suddenly, a shudder and a feeling of impending doom enveloped me. Noticing my disquiet, Guido slid his arm around my shoulders, pulling me to him.

'My love, you need to feel the warmth of a fire and glass a warming cognac,' he said lovingly. Throughout our journey, Guido held my hand in his vice-like grip, almost crushing my fingers.

'Ouch! Stop squeezing me,' I squealed wriggling my hand free.

Guido kissed my fingers, then rubbed them vigorously in order to restore my circulation. 'My apologies, Inez. I don't wish to lose you, I want you to stay here with me and never leave,' he said wistfully.

What could I say without insulting him, tell him a lie, or simply varnish the truth?

'Guido, you go too fast for me,' I whispered gently in his ear.

The car pulled up to a quay, where a black motorboat carrying a crest depicting two foxes rampant, facing each other over four swords, was swaying at its mooring. Once aboard, Guido nodded to the surly boatman as he started the engine. As we progressed slowly along the canals, minding our wash and avoiding carnival-goers slumped on cushions in their gondolas, I became completely entranced by the romantic magnificence of the city.

'Damn this fog,' I said irritably.

'Patience, my love, the weather will improve next month, then I will show you my Venice, the Venice of my childhood and tell you about the stories linked to the islands in the lagoon and of their rich and ancient history.'

'You sound like a tour guide,' I said cheekily.

His expression changed to one of hurtful disdain.

'Do not mock me, no one is allowed to mock me or our proud and glorious city,' said Guido sharply.

The boatman glanced in my direction, nodded to Guido, then averted his eyes. I shrugged, turning my gaze to hide a smile, not caring if I had injured his feelings.

*Pompous man.*

Guido took a mobile phone from his coat pocket and tapped a number from the log.

'Arno, we have arrived, open the watergate,' said Guido without civility.

As I watched his movements, his haughty manner and lack of civility towards his staff, a feeling of unease settled in the pit of my stomach. Alex's opinion of Guido was correct, this man is dangerous, this man is capable of anything. I will take care while staying under his roof and in his domain or else he might take against me, hurt me or even kill me. Or is my vivid imagination leading me along the wrong path? Guido is a proud Venetian, offering me every hospitality his city has to offer, and I am wary and suspecting of his gracious hospitality because I know at heart he is a callous criminal.

# Chapter Seventeen

The impenetrable mist and incoming tide made navigation difficult as we turned off the Grand Canal into a narrow side canal, at the end of which stood the private watergate leading to Guido's family home. The boatman shouted to Arno, an elderly servant who stood waiting while the boatman skilfully navigated the entrance to the open watergate. On entering the berth, he threw a mooring rope to Arno, who then secured it to an iron loop set into the side of a tiny quay.

The boatman turned and spoke to Guido in his native tongue, thereby excluding me from their conversation, as my schoolgirl knowledge of their language was no match for their Venetian dialect. When their conversation had ended, they both nodded in agreement, then threw an unsmiling speculative glance in my direction.

'Forgive our rudeness, Inez, my cousin understands very little of the outside world, let alone civilised manners.'

Guido's cousin sprang out onto the quay in order to steady the boat, ensuring our safety on alighting. I hesitated on the edge before stepping out; smiling up at him as I held his arm for support. Once again that look in his dark reptilian eyes, a look of undisguised malice, and in that moment, a potent sense of danger enveloped me; trapped and terrified, I struggled with the impulse to turn and run, looking around I realised there was no path or pavement only water, everywhere just water.

A faint odour of rotting vegetation combined with salt air caught my nostrils as I waited for Guido to alight, his heavy tread sending ripples of iridescent water slapping against the stone walls of the quay.

'My love, look at you pale and pinched, you are cold and hungry, come, come, let me look after you,' said Guido drawing me towards his tall imposing home. Raising my eyes, I saw intricate weatherworn stonework relieved by grotesques in the shape of foxes heads encircled by serpents, all leering devilishly over an ornately carved wooden front door, its heavy brass knocker fashioned into the head of a fox.

'Welcome to your new home,' said Guido a beatific smile curving his lips.

'I have a home, in fact two homes,' I replied firmly.

'Yes, my love, so you do, you also have my share of the Angolan diamonds.'

He looked down on me, gauging my reaction to his audacious statement, then drew my hand to his poisonous lips, now curved in a sly smile.

*I am trapped and in his power; there is no turning back.*

Ignoring my astonished silence, Guido proceeded to elaborate on the finer points of his home by recounting a potted history of the building and of the previous members of the Faconi dynasty who had lived here.

Pausing momentarily to absorb the scene, my attention was drawn to a movement above my line of vision, a window shutter on the first floor opened slightly, someone was watching me! I know that face, it is the face of the woman who pushed my daughter to her death down a mountainside. She is here watching, waiting, her evil presence writhing and twitching like her mother before her. Glaring up unflinchingly at her malevolent profile instilled me with a newfound reserve of courage, a courage that will be needed when I stand and accuse her of Honoré's murder.

My leather weekend bag, heavy with clothes and jewellery, contained one other comfort, a well-concealed small silver-handled gun and two rounds of ammunition, given to me by Henry soon after our marriage in view of his dubious trade in anything that would secure a profit, consorting with criminals *and* keeping a mistress who regularly poisoned anyone who crossed her.

Guido caressed my arm, guiding me towards the entrance door.

'Welcome to Palazzo Faconi,' he said proudly, standing aside, both arms held outwards in an extravagant flourish. Smiling up at him, I glanced around desperately looking for a memorable landmark, anything to pinpoint my location should the need arise for me to make a hasty escape.

The suffocating grey mist continued to swirl up the side canal and around the palazzo, merging into the darkness and partly obscuring the lower floors of the building. A solitary vespers bell tolled somewhere in the distance, within seconds the first bell was joined by another, then another until a deafening crescendo rang out across the city.

The front door opened into a vast marble-floored dining hall, a painted minstrels gallery at the far end supported by stone pillars stood opposite tall east-facing windows, which looked out onto our private side canal. My eyes drifted upwards to several large portraits lining the walls, paintings so large that one imagined the sitters could speak and come to life before our eyes. Bellini, Titian, Tintoretto and the fearsome Caravaggio, all copies and presumably the work of Guido himself.

As my gaze moved across the paintings, a curtain in the gallery parted, the gleam of a mirror threw a fragment of light on the wall behind me.

*She is here watching.*

Composing myself, I continued walking around the room, asking questions, commending Guido on his fine brushwork and making a pretence of inspecting the marmorino, a decorative mixture of oil and paint used in these parts to discourage damp penetration in the walls of buildings situated close to water.

*The hair on my neck is rising, I am afraid.*

Tension fine as a spiders web laced the atmosphere in this oppressively decorated room, the Venetian red silk upholstery and window drapes were edged with waterfalls of tassels and fringes that grazed the floor laid with mosaic tiles in colours of gold and lapis lazuli.

Bouquets of white flowers stood on tall stands in each corner of the room, my feverish eyes scanned their foliage for Michaelmas daisies, their sickly scent more obnoxious to me than lilies. Perfumed oil burners, lit and smoking, scented the air with the now familiar scent of spikenard, a scent that once stirred my yearnings and delighted my senses and had now become the scent of fear. A gleaming ebony table with 40 matching chairs occupied the centre of the dining hall.

'This room is now reserved for grand occasions,' announced Guido, a ring of pleasure in his tone. 'The privilege of living in such a place, owned by my family for three generations is marred only by mother nature herself, the smell of damp is part of our everyday existence here in Venice, our every breath serves to remind us of the transitory nature of our own lives.' He stole a sideward glance in my direction from under lowered eyelids, was this a philosophical observation or a warning?

Guido invited me to approve the wedding table settings. Silver-lidded serving dishes and cutlery had been placed with military precision on the ebony table, plain red Murano glass plates sat in readiness for the 30 guests invited to the formal wedding breakfast.

The ornate grandeur of Guido's home took me quite by surprise, I had imagined a crumbling loft or dingy cellar away from the prying eyes of the Carabinieri, instead of which I found an artist's lair where dignified luxury was a prerequisite of daily life. Guido was amused at my expressions of amazement.

'I never imagined such splendour; you live like a royal duke.'

'Inez, my love, did you really consider me an impoverished artist eagerly awaiting your dead husband's next commission? No, I have many customers; in fact, there is hardly a gallery in the world that does not knowingly or unknowingly exhibit my work.'

Guido rang a tiny silver bell, and after a few minutes, a small gaunt-faced male servant dressed like a penguin in a long black tailcoat appeared from a door concealed within the folds of a wooden wall panel. The poor man had a pronounced limp and wore a resigned expression. His bony strangler's fingers were clasped together as if in prayer, his oiled grey hair worn too long over his collar gave him the look of a stoat.

'Arno, take Signora Roxberg to the Caravaggio suite, wait for her to refresh herself then bring her to my apartment,' said Guido, watching me intently, gauging my reaction to his orders.

'Very good, signore.' Arno bowed then turned his sharp eyes to me.

'If you would be so good as to follow me, Signora Roxberg.'

'Thank you,' I said, turning to collect my bag.

'Signora, your luggage will be taken care of, please this way,' said Arno quietly.

He gestured towards a lift hidden behind a stone pillar.

'Are there no stairs on the ground floor?' Alarm sounded in my voice.

'No, signora, they were consumed by a damp infestation and removed several years ago.' He sniffed haughtily.

'What if guests have an aversion to confined spaces, is there a fire escape?' My anxious tone climbed to a crescendo.

He eyed me with disdain then shrugged his shoulders.

'Signora, our guests usually remain in the hall; if you are nervous, I would recommend the use of a mask to cover your eyes when accessing the rooms above,' he advised in heavily accented English.

As Arno stepped aside for me to enter the velvet padded lift, a faint musty odour of decay wafted from his clothes. On reaching the third floor of the building, he turned to me.

'The master has ordered me to watch over you, be your guide around our large palazzo, previous visitors have strayed into private areas kept exclusively for the family, favoured guests such as yourself will in time become accustomed to our home and customs.'

He opened a door and stood aside for me to pass.

'You will find everything you need; I will wait here. Please, signora, take your time.' He limped over to a chair placed opposite my door, sat down and closed his eyes.

'Thank you, Arno,' I murmured uneasily.

'At your service, signora,' he said, nodding his head.

The large bedroom was richly furnished in the elegant empire style of Napoleon.

*This room is a room reserved exclusively for females.*

Black painted furniture relieved by gold motifs in the shape of fish and flowers had been painted in exquisite detail by an expert hand. A half tester bed hung with faded magenta velvet draperies and matching coverlet smelled slightly of mildew. From the tall windows an uninspiring view of a walkway along a side canal at the rear of neighbouring properties could be seen when standing on tiptoe. In the bathroom, neatly arranged on a gilt tray, lay toiletries scented with spikenard, as legend would have it this precious oil was used by Mary Magdalene when bathing the feet of Jesus Christ at the last supper.

After hanging my few belongings in the huge gold and black painted wardrobe, I brushed my hair, applied a coat of lipstick, and hurried to the door in my eagerness to see all of the palazzo. To my astonishment, I found the door locked, a mistake surely, a forgetful sleight of hand by an old man whose habits are fixed, not intentional, not here in the home of a friend.

'Arno! Arno! Let me out,' I said, banging my fist on the door.

I heard a shuffling of feet and a key scraping in the lock. As the door opened, Guido's cousin stood there, dressed in black jeans and polo neck jersey.

'Come, signora, follow me,' he said without deference or manners.

'Where is Arno?' I demanded.

'Here asleep, you want me to wake him?' he said tersely.

Arno had dozed off, the large, upholstered chair outside my door had welcomed his frail body and lulled him to sleep, a soft whistling snore emanated from his open mouth.

'No, I will wake him, please go, you are not needed here.' My rudeness was intentional as I found it impossible to conceal my dislike of this man.

Squeezing Arno's arm, I whispered in his ear until the poor old fellow woke with a start, he looked around with unfocused eyes glazed with sleep.

'Scusa, signora,' he said, visibly embarrassed. Placing my hand under his arm for support, he managed to stand. I waited patiently while he straightened his clothes and recovered his dignity, clearly the man was exhausted and in need of rest not servitude.

The odious cousin hovered silently in the background as Arno led me along a dimly lit hallway through a modern steel door, which opened into a small lift, this apparently was the only method of entry to Guido's suite of rooms on the top floor of the palazzo. Arno pressed a button then stepped back as the door closed and the lift began its ascent.

Guido was sitting at his desk with a pile of paperwork pushed to one side. He came forward to greet me, his eyes scrutinising my face for any sign of discontent.

'Inez, my love, come here, let me look at you.'

Walking towards him, my eyes were immediately drawn to the portrait of a reclining nude above the fireplace, he stood aside a smile curling his lips.

'Here, Inez, is the depth of my devotion to you made real, do you like my version of your younger self? Naturally, I prefer your living, breathing flesh and now you are here, forever my captive.'

Stepping forward to examine the picture, I considered the image of my younger self. He had captured every nuance, every line, crease and fold, even the colour of my skin to perfection. Sliding his arm around my waist, he kissed my neck.

'Henry took a photograph of you sleeping on your wedding night then commissioned this portrait, it hung in his dressing room for more than 20 years, unsurprisingly the painting drove that mistress of his wild with jealousy.' He gazed into my eyes.

'How do you feel knowing both Henry and I loved and lusted after you for all of our adult lives.'

*This is not why I came here.*

I turned from him abruptly in an attempt to distance myself and escape his increasingly firm grip around my waist.

'For once words fail me, tell me truthfully, Guido, how long has my picture hung in this position?'

'Since my own copy of the painting was completed some 20 years ago,' he replied, staring obsessively at the picture.

Releasing me suddenly, he walked to the window and stood there, keeping his back to me.

'There is a matter of some urgency that I must discuss with you, please sit down,' he said, gesturing towards a long banquet covered with cushions and throws. On a small marquetry table stood a silver tray bearing a chilled bottle of French champagne, two glasses and a plate of Turkish delight.

'Let's drink to our future,' he said opening the champagne and filling our glasses.

'Salute,' he said adopting a more persuasive tone.

'Salute,' I replied, eyeing him suspiciously.

While sipping our drinks, we exchanged banal conversation about the current state of the art market and fluctuations in buyer preferences. At length as the room darkened and the cries of the carnival-goers became louder, having emerged in their elaborate costumes from the many hotels situated along the labyrinth of canals and waterways in the city, I broached the subject of his *matter to be urgently discussed*.

Suddenly he stood up and began pacing back and forth, adopting a mode of speech similar to that of a lecturer addressing his students.

'Inez, hear what I have to say without interruption,' he said imperiously.

*Fascinating, I wonder how he will couch his claim to my diamonds.*

'I know that Henry entrusted his diamonds, our diamonds to you, had he lived he would have honoured my valid claim to half of them.' His jaw clenched in determination.

'It is a matter of principle for Allesio and more especially for Simone, funds are urgently needed to repair the damage caused to Roxberg Gate.' I looked at him in dismay.

'What can you mean, any damage to that house is no concern of mine,' I said dismissively.

'Please, Inez, hear me out,' he said scowling.

'Someone broke into the castle and turned every stopcock in the attics full on, causing an almighty flood that almost destroyed the whole building, in fact most of the north wing has since fallen into the sea.'

He seemed agitated, consumed by conflicting emotions, he had just professed his love for me, but as he stepped closer his eyes boring into mine, the old saying that love and hate are close companions was never truer than at this moment.

'Of course, Gaston was the culprit, who else would have his knowledge of the building and keys, yes, Inez, keys! Not one door or window had been forced. The two members of staff that had remained to look after the place heard nothing until they were woken by the sound of rushing water.' Angry, rasping breaths heaved in his chest. 'Someone could have been killed, but no, Gaston cared for nothing, nothing except revenge.'

A coldness, an air of indifference stole over me while listening to his tirade.

'An assumption; why would Gaston commit such an act of foolish vandalism?' I scoffed airily.

'Foolish indeed, he even left his calling card in the shape of a blow-up monkey wedged into the driver's seat of Allesio's boat to ensure we all knew he had taken his revenge,' he replied, savagely running his fingers through his hair.

'You exaggerate, what has Allesio done to incur Gaston's wrath?'

'Inez,' he said rolling his eyes in exasperation. 'Stop this farcical act of innocence; we both know there is bad blood between them, Allesio and Gaston have impetuous natures, they are the type of men who nurture their grudges.'

He waited expectantly for my reply but what could I say? It is true, all of it is true.

'What do I care for the arguments of others, they are none of my business, you know the purpose of my visit, when shall I be allowed to question Simone?' I replied, changing the subject.

'Simone will speak with us after her wedding and at a time of her choosing, Allesio does not want her upset before the nuptials,' he said firmly.

He held out a hand of reconciliation to me.

'Come let me show you my rooms, let's not quarrel, we can talk and make plans for our life together after our wedding.'

*Wedding, whose wedding?*

'I have plans of my own,' I said lightly.

He shot me a questioning look but said nothing.

Guido's light-filled studio occupied two thirds of the palazzos top floor. Oil paintings of various sizes were stacked against the walls in stages of near completion, among his more recent commissions of modern portraits, both male and female, standing or sitting alone or in family groups with their children, there were copies of religious medieval figures in the dramatic yet tortuous styles of Giotto and Caravaggio.

My stomach lurched, sickened at the sight of such beautifully executed work no doubt commissioned by unscrupulous dealers with fraudulent intentions, who prey on unsuspecting art collectors with more money than knowledge.

A plump chaise, piled with silk and velvet cushions in a myriad of colours, lay resplendent under tall, rectangular south-easterly facing windows that reached the ornately plastered ceiling. A pungent smell of oil paint and solvent filled my head with longing for my own oils and brushes.

On my knees sifting through half-finished canvases reduced me to tears, such was the arresting beauty of Guido's paintings of women, every generation, type and colour had been captured in different stages of their lives, all now abandoned and left to litter the floor of his studio.

'You have a sympathetic eye when painting older women,' I said in complimentary tones.

*This man is shredding my emotions.*

'I will paint you again nude for my own delectation, only this time your soft, yielding flesh will be immortalised in soft watercolours,' said Guido raising my hand to his lips and drawing me through the first of four rooms.

The first a spacious salon, decorated from wall to ceiling in frescoes depicting scenes of medieval Venice, the effect was surreal, like stepping back into the fifteenth century, an era when unconventional Venetian society lived by their own rules.

In one corner stood a silk screen concealing the doorway to a small anteroom furnished in the oriental style, leading on to the first of Guido's two bedrooms.

On the threshold, I took a sharp intake of breath, the room was sparsely furnished with ancient rustic wooden furniture, course threadbare linens draped the windows and covered the single wooden bed, a monk's pallet would have offered more comfort. Noting my surprise, he began to elaborate on his theory of *living in the moment.*

'In order to create beauty, one must live in some small way like the painters of the thirteenth and fourteenth century, experiencing the hardship and deprivation of their miserable lives in order to feel what they felt in a time of plague and political uncertainty, these things ignite my imagination.' His voice held deeply felt emotion.

'Does a forger need an imagination?' I said cruelly.

He looked at me through narrowed eyes, my barbed comment had obviously found its target, he continued, ignoring my impertinent question.

'This room is such a contrast to other parts of the house; how can you bear to live like a beggar monk when luxury lies beyond this door?'

'Discipline, my love, discipline,' he replied sternly.

Through yet another connecting door was the bedroom I had expected to find. As Guido stepped aside for me to enter, the hairs on the nape of my neck began to rise as a shiver of fear ran up my spine, a potent atmosphere of sanctity tinged with impending evil abounded in this room, furnished like my own in the Napoleonic style, dark, austere and formally grand... rather like Guido himself.

This is the lair of a deeply religious man fixated by one woman above all others, a woman castigated by some who have little interest or understanding of her life, the woman who adorns every wall of Guido's innermost sanctuary. A picture of his beloved Mary Magdalene stood on a tiny rosewood prayer stool beside the bed, two silver candlesticks and a posy of dried lavender lay under her picture.

'Your devotion to her astonishes me, why do you favour her above the Madonna?' I asked in awe.

'She intrigues me, like you and my mother, she is portrayed as having red hair; without a shred of evidence, history has painted her as an undesirable woman. In my opinion, she is the exact opposite, to me she embodies everything a woman should aspire to be,' said Guido, watching me intently, gauging my reaction to his anti-feminist diatribe.

'Now I see why we are so unsuited, I would never enter into an unequal relationship with any man,' I replied vehemently, turning on my heels.

'Come, come, Inez, please be reasonable, let's not disagree, must there always be a need to placate you, is this what I am to expect of our relationship?' he pleaded.

*There is no relationship.*

Returning to the anteroom, I spied an exquisite gold inlaid marquetry breakfast table, glowing mysteriously in the light from a glass lamp. The wood felt warm under my fingers.

'This table belonged to my mother, she took breakfast here every morning of her married life, my hope is that we will too,' said Guido speculatively.

'Guido, the mist has lifted. Open the window, let me see the view,' I said excitedly in an attempt to change the subject.

Leaning out into the darkness, I saw carnival-goers festooned in vainglorious costumes gathered in large groups, shouting and whooping as a parade of young men and women dressed as mermen and mermaids passed by.

'Guido, I want to go out, drink champagne with the revellers and be part of this amazing spectacle,' I demanded hotly.

'I love your childish enthusiasm but sadly we must remain here tonight, I have duties to perform tomorrow that will require a clear head. Next year, as my wife, I will take you to every event.'

*Wife... wife!!*

His words chilled my blood, there was a time when his beautiful face and courteous manner had beguiled me but no longer, the very thought of being alone with him frightened me.

Balancing on the edge of a chair seat, I leaned further out to gain a better view of the procession, lantern-lit gondolas decked with flowers and figurines made their stately progress along the Grand Canal and how I longed to be with them.

'Come away from the window; a fall would prove fatal from this height,' said Guido grabbing my arm.

'I don't want any accidents, well not at least until we are married, and our diamonds are safe in my hands.'

Hurt and angry, I rounded on him.

'How dare you speak to me of marriage, when we both know your only interest is the diamonds, you are a liar and a crook just like Henry.' He stepped back in recoil.

My harsh words like shards of splintered glass left him momentarily stunned, then a hateful smile creased his features.

'No, Inez, you are wrong, I want both you and the diamonds, furthermore until you agree to my terms, you will remain here and speak to no one beyond the watergate.'

My staff are old family retainers, paid well for their loyalty and discretion, your phones and that pretty little gun have been confiscated for your own safety. The gun was a museum piece, the barrel was not aligned; inevitably, it would have backfired and maimed or killed you, so you see, my love, I have already saved your life,' said Guido confidently.

'How dare you keep me captive. Gaston will hear of this,' fear sat in the pit of my stomach like an undigested feast.

Guido sank into a sofa and crossed his legs, A look of supreme confidence on his face.

'Forget Gaston, he is in no position to help you,' advised Guido with conviction.

A long and tense silence hung in the air as we gathered our verbal weaponry for the revelations yet to come.

'Inez, my love, you are everything to me, describing yourself as my captive is cruelly inaccurate. However, since you have made your feelings for me crystal clear, it would appear the description fits you admirably. Now you can either enjoy your captivity and graciously consent to become my wife, or continue to struggle against my will, but I must tell you that whatever happens you and your family will never succeed. My patience is infinite, so I urge you to accept my feelings for you are genuine and will never change, however much they are tested.'

'So, I am to be your prisoner,' I screamed, as perspiration began to form on my brow.

'No, my love, tomorrow you will become my wife, we will be married in secret after the guests have departed Allesio and Simone's celebrations. The priest will linger until late evening, he will officiate, and we will be joined in holy matrimony for life.'

A red mist clouded my vision as the room began to spin; struggling for breath, I ran to the door, but he was faster and stronger, he held my arms behind my back his hot breath stinging my face.

'Understand this, Inez, in the past there have been numerous occasions where your strength of will has prevailed, but trust me, in the future it will not,' said Guido breathlessly.

Speechless with horror, I shook my head in denial then vomited right there on the carpet. Wiping my face with a napkin, I doused the offending vomit with soda water, then poured a double cognac and drank it straight down to extinguish my foul breath and calm my fears of a forced marriage.

Guido sat down and patted the seat beside him as if nothing was amiss.

'Come sit with me stop this nonsense, in time you will learn to love me.' He sounded completely unperturbed at my reaction to his demands.

'Guido, this is madness you cannot keep me captive forever, Gaston will inform the authorities, they will search for me; everyone is aware of my visit to Venice. You will be charged with abduction, and I will inform the authorities of your lesser-known business activities,' I retorted hotly.

'Who will believe a wife? Not our Carabinieri, not my own countrymen,' he sneered.

He sat staring at me like a predator toying with its prey, a bemused expression curling his beautiful mouth.

*I will play this man; he shall not prevail.*

'Guido, listen to me, you will rot in prison for your crimes, I will testify against you and let me warn *you*, if Allesio causes harm to my family again, I will take great pleasure in killing him myself.'

'Now it is you who exaggerates,' Guido replied wearily. 'My love, you will take no pleasure in seeing me rot in hell or anywhere else when every member of your family is dead. My assassin is in Menton this very minute drinking an aperitif at Café Villande awaiting my instructions, your failure to comply with my wishes will sign their death warrants, the choice is yours.' He stated his intentions without guile or menace, my time had come.

'Then you leave me no alternative but to agree to your demands, but hear this, you will never be welcomed into my bed, and the location of the diamonds will remain my secret.'

Guido stretched out his legs and placed his arms behind his head in a gesture of self-satisfied relaxation.

'You clearly don't remember, do you?' he said a knowing smile curving his lips.

'Your precious secret, the secret you shared with me after tasting spikenard on your tongue and the intensely pleasurable feeling of satiation you derived from my perfumed silks, you loved it, couldn't have enough of it, well there will be more, much more, after we are married. We are both good Catholics and our shared faith dictates that my conjugal rights must not be denied,' said Guido confidently.

The stark realisation of my entrapment made my head swim. Here am I, trapped by one man's obsessional greed and my own stupidity. Alex had warned me over again to leave the past undisturbed, how could he a childless man understand a mother's grief at the loss of a daughter, who was murdered so that her half-sister could steal her inheritance. For 10 long years the mystery surrounding Honoré's accident had haunted my days and consumed my life, a pain undiminished, a violent silence tinged with my steaming hatred of Simone, of her life and good fortune while my daughter is dead.

# Chapter Eighteen

I am locked in my room, escorted here by a heartless charlatan falsely professing love and offering marriage, when in reality his only interest is my wealth. Like a caged bird, I try every window lock and find one small casement in the bathroom broken, so I push it open to breathe the air and see what little view there is to be had, then quickly close it as the air rising from the canal smells stale and fetid.

My gun, credit cards, passport and two mobile phones have been confiscated, all communication with the outside world is forbidden by Guido Faconi, the man I must marry to save my family from destruction.

We are in the month of February in the year of 2016, a technological age where almost anything is possible, yet I am a captive listening to the sounds of joyous carnival-goers calling to each other, their laughter filling the air with a gaiety I am unable to see or share.

My attention is drawn to the tapping of high heels, as beautiful women walk along the side canal near the palazzo's locked watergate, living pampered lives of indulgence and freedom, while I am a prisoner without means of escape.

Where is my joy, my strength of purpose and infallible good humour? All gone, reduced to dust in the space of 24 hours. In my absence, a person unknown to me had unpacked the remaining few flimsy garments contained in my heavy leather overnight bag.

A meal consisting of three courses served in silver-covered dishes to retain heat had been left in my room, a bottle of cognac and my favourite Chablis with two glasses placed on a silver salver stood on the dressing table with a note in Guido's handwriting.

*My love*
*Enjoy your solitary meal tonight, for tomorrow your new life will begin.*
*Felicitations, Guido.*

I will not eat his offerings or drink his drugged cognac, by now I will be missed. Giselle will be concerned for my safety as we usually ring each other daily, she will know something is wrong, she must not have cause to worry in her condition.

Eventually a fitful sleep claimed me until dawn, my room felt cold and damp. Leaping from the bed, I opened the window shutters to see the view and watch as flimsy grey clouds floated away over the lagoon, a clock in some high tower chimed five o clock. The city of my dreams lay silent, revellers had returned to their hotels happily drunk and in need of sleep. Gondolas swayed gently at their mooring while gondoliers snored softly under canvas or nursed fearful hangovers with an espresso in each hand.

Lifting the crystal orb from the bottle of cognac, I poured a generous measure then climbed back into bed, dived under the soft velvet cover and waited for the amber liquid to circulate around my body. As I lay drowsing, my imagination took me to home to Villefranche, my safe haven and to the sound of waves lapping the harbour walls outside my bedroom window, how I longed to be there and wake up in my own bed.

Sometime later, I was woken by a faint knock on the door.

'Come in,' I called, stretching my aching limbs.

No answer, putting my ear to the lock I heard steady breathing.

'Who are you, what do you want?' I called out, still no reply just the sound of steady breathing.

A feeling of terror stole over me as I listened in the clear morning light, paralysed in fear, there it came again; someone was standing outside the door in a deliberate attempt to frighten me.

'Who is there, what do you want?' I screamed out.

'Quiet, Inez,' someone will hear you,' hissed a familiar female voice.

'Simone, is that you? Let me out,' I called through the door.

Something touched my bare foot, a note which read:

*Inez*

*Do as we ask or risk the lives of your loved ones, there will be no second chance. Simone.*

'You are a murderer; how dare you dictate to me,' I shouted through the keyhole.

Simone stood close to the other side of the door, just inches from my face. I could hear her panting like a wolf, taunting me with her power.

'Inez, accept your fate the diamonds are cursed, they belong with me,' Simone whispered through the keyhole.

'Go to hell where you belong,' I called out.

I was beyond livid; Simone's threatening note had raised the temperature of my blood to boiling point. Pacing the room my thoughts returned to the many acts of kindness

I had shown her in the past, and now *she* has the temerity this illegitimate daughter of my late husband, begotten with a woman capable of unspeakable evil, here, tapping on my door feigning friendship, well I will show her and these Faconis who will be intimidated and who will not.

# Chapter Nineteen

The bedside clock read 11.30, I had slept for hours and woke feeling in need of a hot shower after spending the night in a strange bed. Somewhere in the distance I heard voices, people laughing, and strains of harmonious violins being played in the rooms below.

Grabbing my wrap, I headed for the shower and luxuriated in Guido's favourite spikenard scented toiletries, the bathroom became warm and steamy, even the old antique bed looked inviting. While sitting on the bed drying my hair, I heard the sound of a key turning in the lock.

'Buongiorno, signora,' said Guido's odious cousin as he entered the room without first knocking. He was followed by an old woman carrying a breakfast tray, her lined face the colour of a walnut, she gave me a pitiful smile and peered at me over her spectacles while the odious cousin surveyed me like a prize animal being sold for slaughter. Flushing hotly under the weight of his insolent stare, I grabbed the bedcover and pulled it up to my neck; seeing my embarrassment he continued to stare, brazenly appraising my appearance.

'Cousin Guido has sent instructions for you to be ready to attend the wedding of his brother by one thirty,' he said, still smirking.

The woman turned to me, her dark eyes full of concern.

'Signora, mangiare,' she said, pointing to a tray of coffee and rolls.

'She wants you to eat,' said the odious cousin impatiently rattling the door keys.

After they had gone, taking care to lock the door behind them, I fell ravenously on the warm rolls and black coffee, so hot and bitter it stung the back my throat.

At one thirty there was a knock on my door and the sound of a key scraping in the lock. Guido entered closely followed by his cousin, who I now regarded as my jailer, wearing identical costumes of black and gold.

'Ah, twins,' I murmured cheekily.

'The men in our family will wear identical costumes for the purposes of identification,' said Guido disdainfully.

'Why the subterfuge?' I pressed.

'There is no subterfuge, we dress alike to represent family unity,' he replied testily.

Guido took a deep breath then turned to me, his eyes blazing in their sockets.

'Inez, please don't try my patience any further, I have neither the time nor interest in your childish repartee. Now please allow me to tell you how alluringly beautiful you look in your pale green costume, very soon you will be my treasured wife.'

'Why not have your share of the treasure and let me go home, you have been a bachelor all of your life, you have no need of a wife now at your age.' He flinched at my barbed comment and gave his cousin a glance of discomfort.

'Age is no barrier or consequence to me, please accept my need is for you, and you alone,' said Guido patiently.

'I don't accept or believe you, if you really loved me you would allow me to leave,' I argued.

'Never fear, you are safe with me, in time you will love me. Now, Inez,' he said gently holding my jaw in his fist, 'you must give me your word that you will not spoil the ceremony with public protestations of kidnap or attempt to escape, any deviation from my orders will result in Gaston's death. Do you understand me?' said Guido, menace glinting in his eyes.

'Yes, Guido, I promise, just leave my family out of this mess,' I said through gritted teeth.

'Very well, my love, at last you have seen sense,' he replied kissing my cheek before placing an emerald green velvet mask elaborately decorated with red feathers over my eyes, and a heavy cloak around my shoulders of a similar hue, its heavy silver clasp was fastened at my throat securing my armour, for it felt like armour in a war that was already lost.

He placed an emerald and diamond ring on the third finger of my left hand, tied my long auburn hair in a knot at the nape of my neck, leaving tendrils to frame my face, then stepped back with a look of satisfaction to admire the effect.

'My love, you are exquisitely beautiful, more ravishing than any women I have ever encountered, your skin has retained the luminous quality of a young girl so rarely seen in women approaching your years,' he said stroking my cheek.

Caught in a moment of uncertainty, a decision was made, today I will submit to his will, become his creature while planning my escape.

'Then kiss me to seal our truce,' I said impulsively.

Sliding his hands into my cloak, he took me into his arms, whispering I love you over and over, then came a fleeting kiss of such intensity, such uncontrolled passion that left me in no doubt of his depth of feeling.

'We must leave, time is pressing,' he said, gently pushing me away and checking his watch.

'Where is the ceremony to take place?' I asked, hopeful of fresh air and the possibility of escape.

'The Santa Maria della Salute just a short journey by boat from here, we have been granted permission to hold the ceremony in the sacristy, you will be seated on my right, giving you an uninterrupted view of the masterpieces painted by Tintoretto and Bellini.'

'Guido, how will you recognise your guests if everyone in the crowd is wearing costumes and masks?'

He waved his hand effusively. 'My people will check their invitations, there will be no problem, many weddings are held at carnival time, we all wear traditional costumes paying homage to our illustrious past, marred only by plague or war. This will be your new world, a world where the urbane realities of life are excluded, you are an accomplished artist your place is here with me, not teaching infantile amateurs with pencils,' he remarked drily.

Taking my hand, he drew me along a labyrinth of passages leading down a flight of stone steps covered in verdigris and stinking of foul water, then on through a rusted steel door which opened onto the side of the private watergate, where a large black motorboat with matching canopy swayed at its mooring.

'This craft is dressed for a funeral not a wedding,' I exclaimed.

Guido ignored my comment and leapt into the boat in order to offer me assistance, thereby preventing me from dampening my cloak. In the driving seat sat the odious cousin smoking a cigarette, his pointed mask more demonic in style than any I had ever seen.

'Inez, you have already met my cousin?' remarked Guido by way of introduction.

'Yes, unfortunately,' I replied tersely. Guido ignored my retort and turned to his cousin, who threw his cigarette into the water and started the engine.

'Let's go, pronto,' said Guido loudly.

Relieved to be released from the palazzo, even for a short period was heaven to me after the torture of having been locked in and treated as a child. As we moved away from the mooring, my spirits began to rise, familiar sights took me back to my childhood. My parents always referred to this city as the 'Serenissima', we would travel here every autumn after the tourist season had ended and the Venetian citizens had once more reclaimed the city as their own. How strange and alien the city feels now sitting beside a man who insists he loves me when I know he is a fake in every sense of the word. A man who would murder and steal in order to indulge his lavish tastes and preserve the good name of his dwindling family while threatening mine.

We set off at a sedate pace towards the Grand Canal in our sombrely decked boat, minding our wash to avoid splashing the sumptuously dressed carnival-goers cheering and waving on the edge of walkways and bridges on route, as they craned their necks to gain a clearer view of the procession. We carefully navigated around several flotillas of gondolas vying for the best position.

Damp air clawed at my lungs, leaving droplets of moisture on my hood and emerald silk shoes. I willed myself to remain focused and not wallow in regret at having agreed to consort with a demon named Guido Faconi.

Guido's impatience grew as our progress was delayed by several other boats travelling in our direction, he signalled to his cousin to make haste, then changed his mind by taking the wheel himself in an effort to alleviate his anger.

'I am Simone's sponsor, we must arrive before her, she will arrive shortly in her own gondola. Allesio has gone ahead to greet her, this is the first marriage in our family in 30 years, two on the same day is unprecedented,' said

Guido anxiously. He waited for my acid reply with raised eyebrows, but my voice had gone, lost somewhere inside my body, hiding lest it express more bitter words of unaccustomed self-pity.

My eyes were everywhere seeking avenues of escape, Guido no doubt assumed my rapt attention amounted to nothing more than sightseeing, when in fact I had enjoyed everything this enchanted city had to offer many times over the years with my students. We had visited every art gallery, basilica and museum, even the dark and shaded backwaters, so dull and uniform in their similarity.

Suddenly a feeble sun broke through the clouds sending shafts of light over the palazzos and illuminating the side canals with its glimmering rays, the cheering crowds chanted 'Long live the sun' at the top of their joyous voices.

'Look,' said Guido pointing to the baroque dome of the basilica glittering in the sun. 'Only in heaven would you find a building of such beauty. Simone has converted to our faith in order to be married here.' His voice wavered as proud tears clouded his eyes. 'We will remember this day for the rest of our lives, a day when everything I have ever yearned for will be mine,' he said, wiping tears from his eyes.

Just then a loud voice called out from behind, interrupting Guido's speech of self-satisfaction. 'Guido, my friend, pronto, pronto,' shouted the boatman behind us, waving his arms from side to side.

Turning our heads, we saw a gondola festooned in fluttering white satin ribbons interwoven with flowers, the gondolier his face red with frustration shouted to us to accelerate or move over. Guido revved the engine and sped forward at pace in order to reach the moorings reserved for the immediate family, leaving the magnificent front entrance clear for Simone's bridal procession.

'Forgive me, my love,' said Guido, jumping out of the boat.

'I have duties to perform and must leave, my cousin will escort you to your seat.'

Feeling crestfallen at being abandoned to this most detestable of men filled me with unease. After securing the boat to the mooring, he offered me a steadying arm, in order to alight safely in my long heavy cloak.

'Take my arm, signora,' he commanded, smirking offensively.

'I would rather fall in the canal than touch you. Out of my way.' His expression changed to one of ill-concealed dislike. I had made the worst kind of enemy but what did I care, they could all go to hell and take Guido with them.

'Get out and hold the boat still,' I ordered him.

He jumped out of the boat, scowling and cursing as crowds gathered around us, pushing and jostling for a clearer view of the bride. I watched as Guido stood at the bottom of the steps to the basilica, nervously pulling his shirt cuffs and checking his watch while waiting for the gondola carrying Simone to arrive.

For a moment I lost sight of the odious cousin, the women surrounding me closed in, calling for Simone to stand and display her dress. My heart fluttered uncontrollably in my breast, is this my chance to escape, find a Carabiniere and warn Gaston?

The gondola carrying Simone glided gracefully into a mooring below the entrance steps to the basilica. Simone was seated like a pageant queen on red velvet cushions with her two pages in attendance. From that point, the wedding planner choreographed her every movement by allowing photographers to capture her image in the rays of the sun. All attention was now focused on the bride and on her close-fitting dress of white satin overlaid with Venetian lace. Gasps of admiration could be heard as she stepped from her gondola into Guido's safe hands.

This is my chance; the crowd began jostling and pushing forward to applaud the bride. Stepping back, I drew my hood further down to my eyes and slowly melted into the throng of exuberant masked carnival revellers. A few more steps would enable me to turn and run, then suddenly to my utter dismay, the odious cousin emerged stern-faced from the crowd and stood, arms folded, in my path.

'This way, signora,' he said, pushing me forward.

'Take your hands off me.' My voice was lost in the sound of cheering for Simone.

He held my arm firmly, an implacable air of command on his swarthy features, He led me through a side entrance and into the basilica near the sacristy chapel where the ceremony was to take place, with his hand firmly gripping my arm, he showed me to a seat near the altar, then sat in the pew immediately behind me.

I looked around enthralled at the incredible beauty of the basilica, trying not to let my confidence ebb. The odious cousin would inform Guido of my attempted escape, now the very real fear of his reaction to the news that I had broken my promise crept over me. I dreaded facing him knowing that Gaston's life was in my hands. The odious cousin tapped on my shoulder from behind, I turned and saw the entire masked congregation staring in my direction, a rising panic tore through me.

'Who are these people, why do they wish to intimidate me, I am nothing to them?' I asked in hushed tones.

'They are our family and associates, naturally they are interested in Guido's intended bride, now face the altar you will meet them later if you behave,' he replied tersely.

Sitting alone, eyes fixed on the altar, my hand resting in the vacant space beside me, soon to be occupied by the man who held my life in his hands.

A novice priest walked the aisles swinging a censer clouding the air with incense, tension mounted as we waited for Simone to appear in her wedding finery. I attempted to meditate on the pictures before me, painted so long ago by Tintoretto and Bellini, pictures so exquisite in their composition, so vivid and so lifelike in their execution, immersing myself in their world of political intrigue, a time when Venice was the trade centre of the whole world.

Then a hush descended on this great basilica, and now from the principal entrance, a soprano with her violinist entered the basilica singing 'Ava Maria' announcing the arrival of the bride. Behind them stood Simone on Guido's arm, her two male attendants standing sentinel behind them, dressed in costumes similar to those worn by Vatican guards.

Simone paused in the doorway to allow the assembled company time to absorb the sight of her as a tableaux of pure theatre, golden sun rays shimmered through her long lace train, illuminating her veil and tiara like the halo of an angel. All eyes turned to Simone as she processed slowly down the aisle on Guido's arm towards Allesio, whose eyes filled with tears at the sight of his bride.

This is her moment of glory, never again would she be a powerless love child, this day she will become a scheming Faconi wife. Some six months had passed since our last meeting, during that time Simone had emerged from her chrysalis as an extraordinarily beautiful young woman.

Reaching the altar, she turned her piercing blue eyes on me, her mother's eyes, the light of insanity burning low in their depths, a sly triumphant smile passed her lips like an ice queen freezing my blood with a glance. She is telling me she had won and now it was my turn to be trapped, a captive of my own stupidity.

As the ceremony began, Guido slipped into the pew beside me; taking my hand, he kept it firmly encased in his own.

'I hear you bear watching, my love,' he whispered softly in my ear while pressing his nails into my palm. He knows, his odious cousin has told him of my attempted escape.

'You are mistaken,' I lied nervously.

Ignoring him, I turned my attention to the ceremony and upwards to the heavenly frescoes adorning the great dome of the basilica. My palms became clammy and swollen, red marks like stigmata appeared where Guido's nails had almost pierced my skin; his words had held undertones of menace, filling me with mortal dread, surely he would not resort to violence if I refused to submit to his demands?

When vows and rings had been exchanged, there came a fanfare from a single trumpet, heralding an invitation for the bride and groom to kiss for the first time as man and wife. Guido shed a tear as Simone and Allesio went on to take the holy sacrament of bread and wine, caught in a moment of raw emotion at witnessing the sincere gestures of love shared in equal measure by the newlyweds. I too shed tears, tears of anger and self-pity.

As the service progressed to the dismissal, the atmosphere inside the sacristy became increasingly oppressive, candles and incense burned low releasing a smoky vapour into the air, leaving me lightheaded and longing for fresh air.

'When will this interminable service end?' I whispered to Guido.

'Patience, my love,' he said as he kissed my burning palms. I tried to extricate myself several times, but his grip tightened.

As the service ended, we watched as Simone and Allesio turned to face the congregation, their faces wreathed in smiles. At that moment, a spear of jealousy ripped through me. Why was I denied true love when all around couples young and old enjoyed the loving security of a long and happy marriage.

'I envy them their true love,' I said wistfully.

'You will feel it, I will make you feel it,' said Guido passionately.

'My wealth is all that interests you.' My voice sounded sharp, my expression sour.

'Not so,' he said smoothly, adjusting my hood as we walked out of the Basilica into the freezing winter air.

Outside the crowds had grown larger, all waiting tightly packed together, craning their necks to gain a better view of Simone and Allesio posing for photographs on the steps of this, the most romantic of all basilicas.

The sun had been replaced by an eerie mist, a fine veil of moisture fell over the city, obscuring my view of the side canals as we travelled back to Palazzo Faconi.

Guido took the wheel. While driving, he and his odious cousin held a conversation in a rapid dialect that was completely beyond my understanding, their furtive looks and gestures in my direction clearly indicated that I was their topic of conversation. Behind us a large flotilla of gondolas had set off at a staccato pace carrying guests to the wedding breakfast. Guido opened the throttle and sped along, creating a turbulent wash.

'Hey, Guido, why the hurry?' called the gondoliers coming towards us, waving their fists in mock anger.

Looking into Guido's face as he helped me alight from the boat, I saw his eyes were still reddened and puffy from the silent tears he had shed in the sacristy, my heart was moved to sorrow for this gifted artist whose life had been so bereft of personal joy. A man who on this occasion had been unafraid to show his tender heart and most private emotions.

The moment had come for me to play him false, to make him believe that my will mirrored his own. I went over and stood close to Guido, turning my back on the odious cousin.

'Guido,' I said, gently stroking his face with my velvet sleeve.

'This is your day too, you told me of your dearest wish to celebrate two weddings in your family.' He gave me a doubtful look.

'Why the sudden change of heart? I am not a fool, Inez, god knows you have made a fool of me under my own roof, why should I believe you now?' Our brief moment of intimacy had dissolved into the mist.

'Guido, sometimes you frighten me, please be patient,' I wheedled.

His face softened. Stepping closer, I kissed him on the mouth in full view of Simone and Allesio, who had overtaken us and arrived at the watergate with their guests whistling and clapping at the scene before them.

'Hey, Guido, you next, you old fox,' called a handsome gondolier.

'Fox and a snake,' I murmured under my breath, looking up at the stone grotesques over the grand entrance.

The odious cousin took up his position inside the entrance door, checking invitations as masked guests filed in resplendent in their festival robes, parading around the banqueting table in a never-ending kaleidoscope of shapes and colours, talking and laughing together as old friends and relatives do on such occasions.

Feeling out of my depth and utterly famished, I decided to put aside my woes and join in. What is there to be gained by sulking in a corner like a coward? For now, I am in no position to argue, however I am in a position to enjoy myself for a few hours at least, and if Guido is still determined to marry me, he will soon discover he has seriously underestimated my guile and tenacity of spirit.

The speeches were dull and thankfully brief, as everyone was more interested in the ostentatious display of rather mediocre looking food. The champagne was of an inferior vintage served slightly warm, after the first sip, I placed my glass on the table and beckoned the odious cousin.

'This disgusting brew is not champagne, fetch me French champagne.' A bemused expression relaxed his swarthy features, he answered me in his local dialect.

'Speak English, man, I insist you speak to me in English,' I demanded imperiously.

He looked across the room at Guido, who nodded and sent a text message. Minutes later, Arno appeared with an ice bucket containing my favourite vintage champagne.

'Signora, we were saving this fine champagne to toast your own nuptials later this evening, but there is more in our cellar should you wish, please follow me, I will show you to your place.' The old man limped away, almost stumbling under the weight of the ice bucket.

'Here, allow me,' I said, taking the bucket from his bony hands; he looked up in surprise, his eyes full of gratitude.

He led me to a seat at the head of the table, the odious cousin followed at a distance taking up his position behind my chair and fixing his eyes firmly on Guido, who sat brooding at the far end of the table.

The bride and groom occupied central positions opposite each other, in order to talk to their guests seated up and down the table. The initial celebratory joy was soon replaced by heads lowered behind fans held in gloved hands, enabling the guests to exchange gossip in secret whispers, furtive glances like darts of fire were fired in all directions.

The man seated on my right introduced himself in fluent French. 'Madame Inez, I hear you and my nephew are soon to be married, our family had no knowledge of Guido's serious attachment to you, a French heiress,' he said, holding his champagne glass aloft.

'Sir, you have been misinformed, I am neither French nor an heiress and your nephew is merely an acquaintance.' Sadly, I have become an accomplished liar.

I changed the subject to cover his embarrassment, we conversed throughout the meal on all manner of subjects, much to the annoyance of the odious cousin who stood behind my chair and texted throughout our conversation.

As the meal progressed, my fellow diner's alcohol consumption increased to such a level that he experienced some difficulty in maintaining our conversation. After the second course had been served, he excused himself to answer nature's call, and as he rose, his phone fell into his lap. Without hesitation, I fluttered my napkin and retrieved the phone, quickly slipping it into the pocket of my cloak.

As I stood up and turned to leave, the odious cousin gestured in Guido's direction, then stepped in my path.

'I require the bathroom, are you going to follow me in there too?' I said defiantly.

'No, but please allow me to escort you, this is a large palazzo you will lose your way.' He pulled my chair away, gesturing towards a door.

No sooner had the toilet door closed than I punched Gaston's number into the phone, no answer, again and again I tried, after three failed attempts, my frustration and panic vented itself in an unladylike expletive just as the powder room door opened.

'Scusi, signora, is anything wrong?' enquired the odious cousin.

Yes, I wanted to scream, go away, everything is very wrong.

Suddenly and to my horror the phone rang, Gaston's number was there in front of me on the screen.

'Signora, step out of the cubicle and give me the phone,' said the odious cousin menacingly.

With reluctance, I gathered my dignity, exited the cubicle just as the phone rang again, hearing Gaston's voice I screamed out, 'Guido is going to kill you, kill us all.'

The odious cousin snatched the phone from my hand, threw it to the floor, grinding it under his heel.

'Return to your seat and say nothing of this, if your friend comes looking for you his death will be on your conscience, now move,' he said violently grabbing my wrist.

I rounded on him, slapping his face so hard my hand stung.

'Don't dare touch me again, you filthy beast, or I will tell Guido you attacked me.'

His sneering laugh sent a chill down my spine, stepping closer, he raised his fist to me, his foul tobacco breath heaving in his chest. I waited, eyes blazing in defiance for the blow, clenching his jaw, he let his arm fall, turned then kicked the door in temper.

'He cares nothing for you.' He spat the words in my face. 'Why would he want an old woman like you when he can have young flesh, his models do everything to please him, he just wants your money, we all want your money, then you will be of no use to us,' he sneered.

So it was true; Guido's protestations of love were false, a sickening dread came over me on hearing the cruel and unvarnished truth, my suspicions of Guido's motives had proved correct, there was no doubt now, no play acting and no pretence, once again my only attribute in life is my wealth.

'I refuse to return to the table,' I said scathingly, determined not to show my fear.

'If you insist there will be an almighty scene, the choice is yours,' I retorted, standing my ground.

His eyes glinted with menace, he would enjoy striking me; I could see it in his face, hear it in his voice, if he had a wife, she must hate him too.

'Show me to my room,' I insisted, glaring at him.

He made a call presumably to Guido, which ended in him answering.

'Leave her to me,' he replied, giving me a devilish grin.

'Very well, signora, as you wish; and don't try to escape, every exit in this palazzo is locked and guarded including the windows.' He grabbed my arm and pulled me along, any resistance on my part would have been futile in the circumstances.

I had allowed my hot temper to ruin any hope of escape from this house of serpents and now I had endangered Gaston's life. I would never forgive myself if he were harmed or worse due to my ill-considered actions.

'This way,' said the odious cousin, grinning as he led me away from the celebrations, down two flights of stairs and through a locked door, which opened into a domestic storage area.

He unlocked the door of a cramped, airless room the size of a scullery.

'What is this?' I said, throwing my hands in the air with all the hauteur I could muster.

'A room without taps, signora, your family seem to have a liking for them, perhaps you will be more compliant after spending a few hours in the company of rats.'

'Do you seriously expect me to enter this rat-infested hole?'

'Signora, you will only be spending two hours here, now either you walk in or I will throw you in.' He laughed contemptuously.

This is his moment of power, his place in the sun before the inevitable storm clouds gather and break over his head as Guido hears of his inhuman treatment of me. He gave me a push that sent me sprawling into the cupboard.

'You French women are full of self-obsessed artifice, devoid of any genuine passion,' he jeered scornfully.

'I am Spanish not French, and you will be made to regret your insolence,' I shouted back vehemently.

'Ciao, Spanish lady,' he called, closing the door and turning the key.

Listening until the tapping of his heeled boots on the stone steps had faded into the distance, I looked around. A pile of half-chewed hessian sacks had been piled in one corner, rusty buckets and an old tin bath hung from a ceiling laced with cobwebs. Looking up, I saw a small arched window thick with grime, one of the panes was missing letting in foul damp air from the canal. I could hear fireworks exploding in the distance, no doubt illuminating the crowds of cheering carnival-goers and leaving plumes of smoke hanging in the night air.

Thankfully, I had taken my cloak to the bathroom, otherwise I would be standing here in a flimsy dress, with only dusty mildewed sacks for warmth. Wrapping my cloak around me, I sat on the floor and waited. I kept reminding myself that my imprisonment would be short, soon the wedding guests will leave, filter out into the early evening light, unaware that the lady of the house is imprisoned below stairs in a rat hole. Soon it would be my turn, but unlike

Simone, I would be a reluctant bride, but a bride still holding the winning hand. As darkness shrouded my eyes, the terror of rats grew, every sound set me on edge, even the drunken jollity of the carnival-goers failed to raise my spirits. Shivering with cold and fright, I began attacking the door with my hands and feet kicking, beating it with my fists until my knuckles bled.

'Guido, you evil devil, we could have shared the diamonds and now because of this you will have none, I will see you dead first,' I screamed into the darkness.

My tirade went unheard by the party going on somewhere above my head, my words of anger simply melted into the night. Agitation driven by fear for the safety of my family grew more urgent as the dark night hours wore on, how foolish of me to ring Gaston, as my thoughtless phone call might now endanger his life.

Huddling under my cloak, shivering with cold and faint from hunger, I waited seemingly for hours until the faint sound of footsteps could be heard coming in my direction. As the footsteps became louder, I stood cramped and numb with cold listening intently, desperate to be released.

'Guido, please, let me out,' I called, hearing a key turning in the lock.

As the door opened, a torchlight pierced my eyes, blinding me.

'Who are you, where is Guido?' I said, stepping back in terror.

'Come quietly, it's time,' said the odious cousin sharply.

He shone his torch up the stone steps leading through the kitchen quarters and up to the dining hall where a masked priest wearing cardinal's robes stood behind a makeshift altar, head bent, listening intently to what Guido had to say.

They both turned and scrutinised me as I entered the room. Allesio and Simone's guests had gone; all evidence of a wedding banquet had been removed.

Guido came forward, his eyes masked in black velvet to match his swirling floor-length cloak lined in magenta silk.

'I trust your temporary accommodation was not too uncomfortable, my love,' he said lightly as if I had been housed in luxury instead of a stinking rat hole.

'Any accommodation in this palazzo is unacceptable, including my unlawful detention,' I retorted hotly.

'Inez, please calm yourself, we have business here, don't make this any harder than necessary.'

'We have no business now or ever; you are as much a fake as your paintings.' A surge of anger rippled through me as strong as any incoming tide.

'Have a care, Inez, like the moon my patience is waning, if you value the lives of your family you will obey me or suffer the consequences. When this good priest has performed the marriage ceremony, we will like all newlyweds enjoy a feast before bed, for tomorrow we leave for Villefranche,' he replied with exaggerated patience.

'You can have your share of the wretched diamonds, but you're not having me,' I said firmly, regaining some measure of composure.

'A generous offer, my love, but one that is quite unacceptable, as I have told you many times, I want you and everything you own.' He spoke with an infuriating air of certainty.

'Alex will support me.' I spat the words in his face. 'He will never allow you to succeed, he warned me against coming here.'

'Alex has locked up and gone, so don't expect any help from that quarter.'

A condescending smile lit Guido's face, revolting every fibre of my being. Trapped and bereft of power, a cruel dawn of realisation washed over me in waves of despairing horror; he had left me no choice, he had won.

'Your odious cousin foretold my death, he said when you have all that is mine you will have me killed.' My knowing sly voice left him unperturbed.

Ignoring my accusation, he turned to Arno.

'Call the witnesses,' he said curtly.

Arno spoke briefly on his mobile phone, after a few minutes Simone and Allesio stumbled into the room still dressed in their wedding finery, more than a little drunk, their faces alight with mischief.

'Well, Inez, I hear congratulations are in order. How extraordinary to have my father's absent wife become my sister-in-law,' she continued, swaying drunkenly, her satin wedding dress and shoes stained in red wine.

'Look,' she said, holding her hand out to me. 'Look at my beautiful ring, Allesio had it made to his own design,' she crowed with self-satisfaction.

She came closer, circling around me, examining my appearance and flicking her nails at my sleeve. She had her mother's face, the face in my memory of a woman denied marriage to the man she loved because he was already married to me.

Suddenly her face, distorted by alcohol and greed, became wolfish and sly, her eyes narrowed like the arrow slits at Roxberg Gate.

'My mother should have poisoned you, I kept telling her, but she said Father would shoot her dead if she laid one finger on you. But now, we are going take what is rightfully mine, then I will kill you myself.' She ceased circling me and stood so close I could smell her breath and feel her spittle on my face as she unleashed torrents of bitter jealousy, her vile words washing over me in never-ending waves of terror.

'Enough of this,' barked Guido, taking my hand.

Recoiling, I rounded on them all. 'I will agree to your bogus ceremony, but first I want to know the truth of how Honoré met her death.' The room fell silent, Simone darted a look at Allesio; for the first time I saw fear in her face.

The priest tried to intervene with placatory words hidden beneath nervous smiles, saying this was neither the time nor place for such morbid and inflammatory talk.

'Come, come, we have cause to be happy, this talk of death is unsuited to the occasion,' he said, holding his arms aloft in gestures of all-encompassing harmony. I told him to save his meaningless words and turned to Simone.

'Tell me the truth, Simone, did you push Honoré down that mountainside?' I persisted, moving closer until our faces were inches from each other.

'Tell me, confess, did you kill my Honoré?' I screamed in her face.

Simone's face flamed with colour as Allesio put a restraining hand on her arm.

'Get off me,' she screamed, struggling in his grasp, then turned on him like a vixen. 'It was all your idea, you said no one would ever find out,' she raged and screamed accusingly. 'You said we would be safe and that the avalanche would cover our tracks, we killed my sister because you wanted her inheritance.' She sank to the floor in floods of tears.

A stillness came over the room as we stood immobile, like figures suspended in time, attempting to assimilate Simone's damming revelations. All the years of heartbreak and suspicion fell from me in an instant, the room spun as my chest contracted in painful sobs of unspent grief.

The red mist clouding my eyes returned as I flew at Allesio with a force so great he fell to the floor. I clawed at his face, my sharp nails leaving grooves oozing with blood. Guido grabbed my blood-soaked hands and dragged me off his brother, then turned to Simone his face white with anger.

'You little fool see what you have done, I told you to keep quiet until after the ceremony,' said Guido through gritted teeth.

'Honoré deserved everything she got and more,' retaliated Simone angrily.

'She made my miserable childhood unbearable, always taking my possessions as if it were her right as daughter of the house, she even tried to take Allesio. She was conceited and spoilt like Giselle and like you, Inez. My mother should have poisoned all of you and now, my dear sister-in-law, you are going to compensate me for a lifetime of prejudice that was not my fault; we will see if you like being treated as second class in your own home.'

She had confessed. Now I must stay alive long enough to see them both convicted of Honoré's murder. Suddenly the red mist before my eyes took hold as I fell to the floor.

'Cognac, pronto,' said Guido frantically gesturing to Arno. 'Come along, man, move and keep the other servants out.'

Guido dabbed my face with a linen cloth soaked in water from an ice bucket.

'Allesio,' he said, turning to his brother, 'give me the ring then take your bride to bed and keep her out of my sight,' he warned.

Guido roused me with sips of cognac forced between my lips, he rocked me back and forth while stroking and kissing my head.

'My love, I should never have allowed Simone's tirade to continue, forgive me,' he said, offering morsels of chilled food left over from the wedding banquet, food that made me want to retch.

'Inez, my love, sustain yourself, forget these lies, we will enjoy our wedding banquet in the privacy of my room after the ceremony,' he whispered, caressing my cheek.

Guido's silken voice like golden rays at sunset soothed my anguished mind, his lips parted in pleasure as I opened my mouth to eat the unpalatable food. Holding my head, he put a crystal goblet to my lips containing the golden liquid that would render me half senseless, but what did I care? Oblivion would be preferable to the stark realities facing me on this my wedding night. Leaning forward, I took the glass from his hand and tipped the remaining cognac down my eager throat. A tranquil peace seeped over me like a soft breeze whispering over a lily pool, leaving the air still and expectant like the lull before a storm.

'Come, my love,' said Guido tenderly. 'Let me help you, the priest is waiting,' he said quietly, his eyes searching my face for signs of dissent.

Guido attempted to give me a supporting arm in order to rise from the couch, but I waved him away.

'Fetch me a chair then get it over with.' I said savagely.

Candles and incense burned on the hastily arranged altar where a bottle of spikenard oil rested uncorked in readiness to anoint and seal our union. The priest looked at Guido expectantly, seeking his permission to begin.

Guido nodded in assent, nervously removing his mask and straightening his crumpled costume.

'Please, let us begin we have wasted too much time with pointless arguments,' he said firmly.

The priest cast his eyes upwards to the ceiling painted with frescoes of beautiful maidens carrying platters of grapes and pitchers of wine, surrounded by plump cherubs. Surveying the scene, I thought how ludicrous this farce would appear to an unsuspecting onlooker; me a dishevelled middle-aged bride, whispering curses in my native tongue to an assembled company, who no doubt assumed that I was praying for my deliverance.

The priest made the sign of the cross then began reciting in Latin. after a few minutes, he spoke to Guido, whose responses were unintelligible to me as my knowledge of Latin was similar to that of his Venetian dialect.

Then turning to me a gracious smile lifting his lips, his eyes creased in sympathy for me, a bride forced to marry a demon to save her family. I wondered how much he had been paid to perform this secret ceremony and for his silence. Perhaps I have been duped, perhaps he is an actor playing his part and the marriage will be nothing more than a nonsense designed to fool me into accepting that I am a married woman, who will be forced into obedience by her grasping husband.

The priest glanced to heaven then began chanting in Latin as before. When the time came for me to respond, I merely nodded my head.

'Signora, you must answer,' he commanded sternly.

Once again, curses in my native tongue, whispered low to avoid detection, left my lips with such venom that the priest stepped back and crossed himself as if he were in the presence of a she-witch.

'Yes, si, ciao, oui; however you prefer to hear it,' I screamed into his self-righteous face.

The priest's face turned white at my outburst, hastily and without grace or deference, he placed the two gold bands fashioned into twisted ropes on a red velvet pillow, offered up a blessing then asked Guido to place the smaller of the two rings on my finger beside the diamond and emerald ring he had given me earlier.

Tears stung my eyes and were mistaken for belated feelings of affection for my new husband. Nothing could have been further from the truth as they soon realised when I flatly refused to reciprocate. Guido took his ring and placed it on his own hand, then looked into my tear-stained face.

'I have waited all my life for this moment.' His voice wavered with emotion. 'I can see and feel your disbelief, but it's true and in time you will come to know what you mean to me.'

*Money, my money; that is all I mean to you.*

# Chapter Twenty

The spring equinox of 2017 is approaching, an age where almost all things are possible, freedom of choice to live our lives as we please within the law is our right. But I had been denied that right and had been forcibly married to a man in a language I did not understand, whose brother had pushed my eldest daughter to her death and had threatened kill my son-in-law if I fail to agree to his demands.

Guido turned to Arno standing in a dark corner mute as a statue, he had borne witness to my forced marriage and also to Simone's accusatory revelations regarding Honoré's death. Somewhere in his old bones there may be fragments of compassion and outrage for the crimes committed against me and my family. At some point in the future, I will test his loyalty with exorbitant bribery, as he will prove a valuable witness when I report my new husband to the authorities.

'Arno, we will dine in my room, leave the food on hotplates, the cook has been instructed, now leave us,' ordered Guido imperiously.

'Si, signore.' He bowed then left the room, quietly closing the door behind him, leaving us alone, tense and silent. I waited for Guido to speak, I waited for him to apologise and tell me it was a joke well played.

'Tell me this is a nightmare and that I will wake at any moment, and you were just a figment of my imagination.'

A triumphant smile spread across his beautiful features. 'Inez, my love, this is real, I am your husband, we are legally married, and here in Venice there are local customs to be observed that are beyond the understanding of people living beyond the lagoon, but more of that later.'

'You would force me, knowing that I hate you.'

'Hate and love are close bedfellows; come, Inez, please accept me, be assured you will not regret this marriage,' he said with an air of absolute certainty.

'The opening of La Maison des Artistes would be a terrible waste of your talents, I have a much better use for them,' he said, lifting his chin arrogantly.

'So I will be allowed to live? Your odious cousin said you will kill me, he said I am too old and that you prefer your young models.' My taunts were brushed aside.

Guido laughed out loud. 'He was merely trying to frighten you; he has no success with women and resents any man that has. Now let us stop this ridiculous talk and concentrate on this evening, on us, on our new life together,' he said silkily.

My new husband held out his hand in a gesture of reconciliation, his eyes searched my face for signs of my secret loathing of him, a loathing he must dispel in order to consummate our union.

'Inez, my love, you are no longer Henry's widow; had I known your estrangement from Henry was of a more serious nature, I would have contacted you years ago.

You are rather belatedly my wife, a Faconi wife, you will carry the name of my ancient family, you must understand that I will never allow you to leave me as did Henry. This is our wedding night, let us be happy and look forward to our future together.'

'You stifle me, I cannot tolerate suppression of any kind, I want to speak to Giselle, she will be concerned she has not yet heard from me.'

Oh, but she has heard from you, I have sent her reassuring texts twice a day from your phone on your behalf. She sends us her good wishes and envies your stay in our beautiful city,' he said as a reflective look clouded his eyes. 'Giselle should have been my daughter, her unborn son, my grandson, a grandson to carry on the Faconi name. Instead I must rely on Allesio to do his duty, and god only knows what kind of mother Simone will make with *her* tainted blood and volatile nature, she is wholly unsuited to motherhood,' he said despairingly.

'If Simone is tainted then so is my Giselle, you forget they share the same grandmother there is no escaping that fact,' I said tersely.

He spun round, taking my shoulders in his hands.

'We will play our part, keep their children close watch for signs, they must be protected at all costs,' he said earnestly.

'Gaston will not tolerate any interference, I know him well he will prevent us from seeing the child if we interfere in his plans, he is so looking forward to having a son. Henry, for all his faults, was a good father and would have relished the thought of being a grandfather,' I added loyally.

'No, Inez, Henry was a cold-hearted bastard,' retorted Guido nastily. 'He had associates in every corner of the globe, they were his eyes and ears, he used every one of them to sell my work then tried to pay me a pittance. He took your money then disregarded you.' Pausing momentarily for reflection, he began again.

'That mistress of his knew how to handle him; she played him like a fiddle. I will show you what it is to be loved and respected,' he said warmly, taking my hand.

'You will have to drug me first,' I replied contemptuously.

'Do you find me so physically repulsive?'

'What I find repulsive is your criminal activity and your keeping me here against my will,' I retorted hotly.

'Calm yourself, Inez. Tomorrow we leave for Villefranche, but tonight you must behave as a wife, now please I am hungry, and our dinner is spoiling while we continue with these senseless arguments, we need food and rest it has been a long day.'

Guido's persuasive tones had dropped several octaves in order to coax me into consummating our union, I wondered how many women had fallen for his superficial charm. Placing a forefinger under my chin, he turned my face to his and looked into my eyes.

'Inez, I say again that I have loved you all my life, ever since that first meeting at a friend's wedding, the wedding where you met Henry. I think we both fell in love with you that day and he, being more decisive than I, claimed you as his prize.'

'You will still have to drug me into submission.' My hollow laugh echoed around the room.

'As you wish, my love,' replied Guido with consummate ease.

My thoughts returned again to the memory of our first night together, the slips of perfumed silk, the caresses, the waves of pleasure that had engulfed me.

*This, my husband, will be your one night of happiness, for tomorrow or the next day or any day, I will take my revenge, and you will regret ever threatening me.*

# Chapter Twenty-One

Next morning I woke to find a light-emitting bracelet secured to my wrist, the signal would no doubt transmit my whereabouts to Guido, and a note explaining he had gone out early to say goodbye to Simone and Allesio, who were returning to Roxberg Gate sooner than originally planned. He went on to say he would join me for breakfast, then give me a tour of the palazzo before leaving for Villefranche.

Feeling violated and numb, I stumbled into the bathroom to shower and dress in readiness for the journey to my home and the life I had left just a few days earlier.

I will not eat his breakfast or look around his palazzo as though nothing has happened until my phone has been restored to me. I wondered how he would contrive to keep me within his jurisdiction when out in the world leading a comparatively normal life, as there was no possibility of me tolerating his odious cousin.

*Perhaps none of this matters if they have already planned my death.*

At 10 o'clock, I entered the dining hall expecting to find Guido having breakfast, my luggage had been packed and labelled in readiness for the journey but there was no sign of Guido.

Just then Arno appeared with a breakfast tray consisting of an espresso and a plate of almond biscuits. Looking up into his weathered face, I saw compassion in his eyes.

'Come back to us with love in your heart, signora.' His eyes shone with emotion. When Guido returned, he seemed troubled at finding me waiting ready to leave.

'My wife, my dearest love, why are you waiting here in this draughty hall, let us have breakfast together, this is our honeymoon.'

'This may be your honeymoon, but it definitely is not mine,' I replied testily.

'Come, Inez, content yourself, each day you will learn to love me a little more, I have no wish to restrict you more than necessary.'

'Well, in that case, Guido, you can start by returning my phone.'

'No, my love, that is not possible as your old phone is floating somewhere in the canal network, a new phone will be yours when we land at Nice airport,' he informed me brightly.

'Guido, my whole life was in that phone,' I said angrily. 'It contained irreplaceable images, not to mention the details of almost everyone I have ever known.'

'You have a new life now, you have no need of others, you are mine, and I will not share you with anyone,' he said firmly. I suppressed an urge to slap his face and resignedly called on every ounce of patience left in my body to keep my lips sealed.

Guido ordered a light continental breakfast to be served in the dining hall, where I had been sitting for the past hour listening to the jocular calls of residents and tourists alike, going about their daily lives in freedom while I remained my husband's prisoner.

Guido ate quickly and in silence, then disappeared upstairs to freshen up. Eventually he appeared, having changed into a dark blue suit with matching overcoat, carrying an enormous case.

'I see you are planning a lengthy stay,' I said dismally, looking at the size of his luggage.

'A lifetime, my love, a lifetime. The winter season here in Venice can be cruelly damp, in contrast to Villefranche where the light-filled sea air will warm and invigorate us.'

Hearing the sound of an outboard engine, I ran to the window and saw the odious cousin had arrived to take us to the mainland.

'After today I don't want to see that man ever again,' I said angrily, pointing to the boat.

'Very well if you insist,' said Guido pleasantly.

Arno entered the room to collect the breakfast trays and stood waiting to say goodbye. Guido ignored his outstretched hand; the old servant recoiled in shame of overestimating his master's affection for him. Seeing such callous disregard was almost too much for me to bear.

'Thank you, Arno, and please thank your staff for welcoming me into your home,' I said warmly, stepping forward and squeezing his hand.

I glared at Guido; how dare he treat Arno as a mere servant when previous generations of his family had served the Faconi's with such dignified loyalty and discretion. One day soon I will gain Arno's confidence, then perhaps I will hear what other iniquities have occurred behind the walls of Palazzo Faconi.

# Chapter Twenty-Two

As the door opened, Guido ordered me to stay until called, then went out to speak to the odious cousin.

'Arno, please tell me what they are saying,' I implored.

He hesitated before speaking, fearful of being overheard. 'There has been a man hanging around our private watergate, signora, over the years the master has learned to be watchful, he has many enemies,' said Arno quietly.

When Guido returned, he was smiling; he collected my belongings and held out his hand.

'Come, Inez, it's time to leave.' As we walked away, he looked back at Arno and made the sign of a cutthroat.

My heart stopped, he saw my expression and laughed.

'Not you, my love, I would never harm you,' he drawled.

I was speechless with concern for Gaston. Guido had done something, I could see it in his face, he had visibly relaxed and his body language had altered, he seemed relieved to be leaving his beloved Venice.

Taking my arm, he led me to the boat, a cold breeze brushed my face and whipped my hair, panic blurred my vision and set my heart racing. I gazed around, expecting to feel the magnetic beauty of the city I had loved and revered all my life and vowed that I would never return.

*What has he done, who has he murdered?*

The odious cousin gave me a supercilious look as I climbed aboard the boat.

'I hear we are never to meet again, signora, a fact I had decided on after spending only one hour in your company, but the situation has changed. I am a proud man, a senior member of your new family, you have never asked my name and have treated me like a mangy dog. Look at this face and remember my name, Cousin Inez. I am Venerio Faconi. Until we meet again,' he said coldly then looked away.

'Ignore this beast of the lagoon, he will not insult you again,' said Guido, eying his cousin dangerously.

We travelled as amenable companions might, I hid my face in a book and drank endless cups of coffee while waiting for our travel connections. As we walked out of the airport at Nice, I caught several glimpses of a familiar face. My heart leapt into my mouth as I managed to distract Guido's attention away from the crowds of people waiting to meet relatives or friends emerging from the arrivals department.

Had I been mistaken? Did I just see Alex's profile in the crowds? Guido had told me that Alex had locked up and left the district in fear of his life, and I had believed him.

We fell gratefully into a waiting taxi ready for the long drive to Villefranche. I was in no mood to engage my new husband in pointless conversation, calculated to divert his attention from the retribution I hoped would soon follow. I settled down under a shawl and slept peacefully for the first time since leaving France just three days earlier.

Some tense hours later we arrived at my front door, slivers of light could be seen coming from under the door, in the hall a small arrangement of flowers with a note saying *Welcome home, Inez* lay on the hall table written in Alex's familiar handwriting.

Guido clenched his teeth, took the crystal vase then threw it through the open door into the street. I had never seen

Guido lose control of his temper, he began fumbling with his phone cursing and pacing the floor in agitation.

'There is no phone signal in this place, stay here, I need to make a call,' he barked furiously.

As the door closed behind him, my response was both swift and immediate. I locked and bolted the door behind him, then ran upstairs to the sitting room to find Giselle's number, the clock with a pearl face stood glinting in the lamplight.

'You are the cause of my troubles,' I shouted, kicking the base.

My fingers fumbled nervously with the pages of my old address book; some moments passed before she answered.

'Mother, where are you for goodness sake? Why didn't you answer my calls? Gaston has been missing for two nights and is not answering his phone, I am out of my mind with worry,' she said breathlessly, her voice breaking into a sob.

'Giselle, I cannot bring myself to explain the reason for my absence over the past few days, but I promise you, my darling, I will make everything right,' I said calmly.

'You can't until you find Gaston,' she shrieked tearfully.

'Giselle, listen to me, are you alone?'

'No, all the staff are here waiting for Gaston,' she wailed.

'Good, now tell me what happened, did he have an appointment?'

'Yes, a new client rang asking for a picture valuation on some yacht moored off Antibes, the police are exploring all avenues in their investigation and have alerted the coastguards. Mother, I can't bear it if he is dead, I won't want to live.'

Hearing the anguish in her voice cut through my heart like a dagger, knowing that I may have been the cause of Gaston's disappearance. How could any mother admit to her daughter that she had unknowingly ruined her life?

'Giselle, listen to me, you know how Gaston likes to sulk, he will come home when he imagines our nerves are sufficiently frayed enough to agree to any of his demands.' She agreed to eat a light meal and made me promise to go to her the following day.

In the hour that followed, I had expected to hear Guido breaking down the door or at the very least a vitriolic phone call ordering me to admit him. No word came, no hammering on the door. *Nothing!*

My home was silent except for the incessant ticking of the clock with a pearl face, Henry's evil legacy had brought every conceivable misery to me and our family. I poured myself a cognac and sought sanctuary on the window seat, my ears straining for the slightest sound of someone breaking into the house.

There I sat rigid with fright, waiting for the wrath of my new husband to cascade over my head like shooting stars. Looking out, my eyes searched the shadows, searched the pools of light from the restaurants on the harbour reflected in the dark waters beyond, my eyes grew dry and sore, but still I watched until the stranded rays of dawn light bathed my eyes in slumber.

I woke some hours later feeling cramped and numb, memories of my conversation with Giselle the previous evening came flooding back, the pit of my stomach felt heavy with dread.

*I must find him; I must find Gaston.*

Somewhere upstairs I heard a noise and footsteps coming down my staircase.

'Guido, I am so sorry for locking the door, it's just that...' my voice trailed to a whisper of fear. As the steps came closer, I pulled the blankets over my head to blot out the sight of Guido's inevitable rage.

# CHAPTER TWENTY-TWO

As the door opened, Alex came bounding into the room.

'No need to apologise, boss, I live here, remember? You look rough; fancy some breakfast?' he said in his usual cheery manner.

'Oh, thank goodness it's you and not...'

'Not Guido, well he won't be giving you any more aggro, a fisherman found him floating in the harbour this morning, must have fallen over the wall, they think he was electrocuted,' he said pleasantly.

For a moment I thought he was joking.

'Oh my god, Alex, did you push him?'

'Are you serious, do you really think me capable of premeditated murder, come on, Inez, don't insult me, well at least not before breakfast,' he said snorting with laughter. 'Although there were times when I would have liked to get my hands around his throat again, but no, of course I didn't push him, someone robbed me of that pleasure.' Alex hesitated before continuing.

'You would have thought a man whose home is surrounded by water would have learned to swim. I formally identified him so you won't have to, it was not a pretty sight, and I think you have had enough stress without adding more,' he said, frowning.

Whatever our differences, I would never have wished Guido dead, even so, his death had resolved some of my problems. Then a terrible thought came to me: Supposing the authorities question me and members of Guido's household, if they discover I have been the victim of a forced marriage, they may suspect me of Guido's murder – and the diamonds, what if they find out about the diamonds?'

'Alex, I must tell you that Guido and I were married yesterday, it's a long story and one that will shame me to admit to anyone, especially you,' I said sadly.

'What! You're telling me that you actually married that rogue, why did you do it?' he asked in amazement.

I stood motionless, stunned as the full implications of Guido's sudden death began seeping into my brain. If my marriage to Guido was proved legal, then I would stand to inherit his property in Venice instead of Allesio, who would no doubt contest my claim.

Arno had borne witness to Simone's outburst and her subsequent confession of how she and Allesio pushed Honoré to her death, perhaps he could be persuaded to testify against them if I granted him and his family an annuity and a lifetime of security from eviction.

Alex peered into my drawn face.

'You OK, Inez, all bit of a shock, eh?' said Alex, chipper as ever.

'Yes, yes, my whole life is in shock.' My mind was dazed and in shreds of confusion. 'Guido forced me to marry him.' I looked up, defiantly meeting his concerned gaze.

'He threatened to murder Gaston, and now I wonder if that was his intention from the beginning, there is so much bad blood between Gaston and Faconi brothers.'

'Were there any witnesses to this marriage and a certificate to prove it was legal?' said Alex, raising his eyebrows quizzically.

'Yes, Allesio, Simone and the priest... oh and Arno, a servant.'

'That's a pity, even so, it may have been a sham ceremony,' he said thoughtfully.

'You have heard about Gaston's disappearance; I hardly dare think what has happened to him. Giselle is terrified, we are all terrified that he may be dead.'

'Don't worry about Gaston, he's capable of looking after himself. OK, so here's what we do, eat, all this excitement is making me hungry,' said Alex urgently.

We went downstairs to the schoolhouse kitchen, where a breakfast of vegetable fritters topped with ham and poached eggs were quickly assembled. I had no appetite but ate to please him.

'Right, boss, tell me everything,' said Alex, pouring hot creamy coffee into large mugs, adding a little breakfast cognac for courage.

Alex's expression changed like a set of traffic lights, as I recounted every detailed event of my brief visit to Venice.

'I will never go back, not even for Guido's funeral,' I said with firm conviction.

'I absolutely agree, it would be far too dangerous under the circumstances. Venerio is known to the Carabinieri as a murdering thug; so far, he has managed to evade prosecution for his many crimes, but believe me, Inez, he will be looking to avenge his cousin. Unless the authorities manage to put him away, your life will remain under threat.'

He gave me a quizzical look as if expecting to hear more of my time in Venice.

'Inez, you haven't told me everything, and you know you should always tell a policeman the whole truth and nothing but the truth,' he remarked wryly.

My head shot up like a cannon ready and loaded to fire.

'A policeman! You a policeman! You are a chef, my chef.'

'Glad to hear it,' said Alex, smiling.

'Why did you deceive me?' I said, feeling disappointed in him.

'Just hoped you would come clean and tell me where you stashed the diamonds,' he said, making a sad face. 'I was deployed to keep you under surveillance from the day you moved here. And, yes, you did look great in your carnival costume, had I known Guido planned to marry you, we would have had the place raided and got you out of there.'

He looked deep into my eyes.

'Would you at some point in the future disclose the location of the diamonds?' he asked tentatively.

'No, they are mine,' I replied sharply.

'They are Henry's parting gift from a husband to his wife, and I shall keep them.'

'Even if they were not his to give?' Alex's words rang in my ears with undeniable conviction.

'So prove it,' I said, standing my ground. 'And one more thing, I want Allesio and Simone charged with Honoré's murder, the servant Arno was present in the room and clearly heard them arguing over who had pushed my daughter to her death.'

'My god, so your instincts were right from the start.' Now it was Alex's turn to be shocked.

'What an unholy mess,' he said, raking his fingers through his hair.

'Look, Alex, I have promised to go to Giselle, she is bereft and needs me more than ever until they find Gaston.'

I walked round the table and dropped a kiss on the top of his head.

'Are you really a policeman? I don't want to lose you when this is all over,' I said, tears welling in my eyes.

Don't worry, boss, you won't. I'm not leaving, now or ever.

# Chapter Twenty-Three

I found Giselle huddled forlornly in a cleft between rocks at the far end of the beach, staring out to sea, as she had done every day since Gaston's disappearance, rising at dawn and sitting till dusk, waiting, wishing and praying for his safe return.

Nothing I could say or do lifted her spirits, she is an inconsolable shell of misery and grief for a husband now lost to her, perhaps forever. As the days pass, her speech becomes more monosyllabic, she eats so little that I fretted for the health of her unborn son. Listening to the radio or television news had become a daily ordeal, we lived in terror of hearing a body had been washed up on the shore.

Unbeknown to her, I visited the local gendarmerie to give a full and true account of the unfortunate events which occurred during my trip to Venice.

As Guido's widow, I will inherit all of his property and possessions. His loyal servant Arno has provided a statement condemning Allesio for the murder of my beautiful daughter Honoré and named Simone as his accomplice in exchange for a lifetime undisturbed by financial burdens at Palazzo Faconi.

The clock with a pearl face was returned to Roxberg Gate, minus my fabulous diamonds; they will stay safe in a sealed bank vault, where their tainted origins can do no harm.

On hearing this news, Simone avoided arrest, went back to Roxberg Gate and threw herself off the north turret into the sea.

Some months later, at home in Villefranche with our school of art thriving, Alex and I make indulgent substitute parents, fussing over baby Luc Gaston Villande, who Giselle had abandoned at birth, saying she felt unable to look at her son as he bore such a striking resemblance to his missing father.

My dearest daughter Giselle continues to sit on the beach at every dawn and sunset until the waves lap her feet, her eyes searching the horizon for her missing husband, she waits and waits...

*To be continued in 'A Man Lost.'*

My home is situated in the medieval quarter at Stratford upon Avon; nestling peacefully in a quintessentially English garden behind the Guildhall, where William Shakespeare began his studies.

The Bards potent influence surrounds my daily life. I walk where he walked, see what he saw, hear what he heard and live where he learned.